Mourning Glory

Also by Zach Lamb

The Suicide Killer

Dark Water Sacrifice

Mourning Glory

The Suicide Killer
Book 2

Zach Lamb

Copyright © 2022 by Zach Lamb

Cover by Elderlemon Design

Author Photo by Darlin Images

ISBN 979-8-9871527-0-6

For those who asked for it. I hope you're prepared.

Chapter One

Somebody always has to die. It's the story of our lives. It's the fear of death that makes everybody feel alive. It's a wonder to think that people aren't feeling more alive now than at any other time in history with all the death in the news. There's no hiding from it. Instead, people absorb it and continue like nothing ever happened. The world lacks empathy. There are times when empathetic collective waves role across the country. But it's almost always with an immense tragedy, or worse, the death of a child. At what age does the reception of unconditional empathy turn to apathy for an unknown soul? Is it the loss of adolescence when everybody is tried as an adult in the court of public opinion? When the perceived innocence is lost and the threat of who they are becomes apparent.

The only true feeling everybody observes is that of loss. Somebody always has to die, and there will be someone left to mourn for them. Even the most wicked among us will be mourned, just as they will mourn somebody. It's the human condition to lament the loss of a loved one. Some of the lost will be missed more than others, and those few who hurt the most will be haunted for the rest of their days.

Bobby couldn't bring himself to go to Greg Burns' funeral. He hid from the news and refused to drive anywhere near the graveyard. Working helped to distract him and busy his mind, but making skinny mocha lattes for the women who congregated in Rusted Lakes Park only did so much. It'd been six months since Greg's death, and this was the first time Bobby had managed to drag himself to the cemetery and pay proper respects. Though there were many reasons he'd decided not to go to the funeral, the main motive was Greg's daughter, Hope. She was a sweet little girl, and Bobby didn't want to see her upset. She was also the only person who could identify Bobby, or Stephen, as she had met him in person. There was no way to know if Greg had told anybody that the guy who picked his daughter up from school was the killer. Surely, he had told his wife. Detective Burns had his secrets, but even he would have said something if he'd thought his family would be in danger. It was too big of a risk for Bobby to chance.

He stood at the foot of the dirt patch. A few sprigs of grass poked through random spots, fighting for their share of the sun. Though the winters had been mild the last few years, it would still be early spring before any grass would take root and begin the long process of healing the wounded ground.

There were no tears to fight back, but he felt like he should cry. Greg had become such an important part of his life, and the suddenness of their relationship ending didn't sit right with Bobby. Greg wasn't supposed to die that night. Sure, he would have eventually had to be dealt with, but not so soon. There was a lot of time left in their game. He still had plans for them. Greg had become the only friend he'd had in a long time. Bobby felt the same way as he did when his dad killed his mom and then himself, forcing Bobby to go live with his grandparents. He'd been playing outside with his friend, Drake, when they heard the gunshots coming from inside his family's trailer.

At seven-years-old, Bobby was the youngest to play goalie for the US World Cup Team in the championship game against their world nemesis in everything: Russia. Drake lined up the red team's penalty shot and ran toward the ball. The kick sailed high and to the left. Three shots rang out in succession, and the ball passed inches from Bobby's head. Nobody cheered the winning goal, and the ball came to rest against the trunk of a large magnolia tree. Both boys stopped and stared at each other like they weren't sure what they'd heard. Confusion followed by fear etched across both of their faces. After the moment of silence, a final shot rang out. The trailer made the muffled shot sound like a starter's pistol.

Bobby ran across the yard and stomped up the back steps. He pulled the door back, but the kinked chain only let it open a foot before pulling it shut again. Bobby eased the door from the jamb and swung it open and closed until the rusted chain clinked loosely against the dented aluminum. All the lights were off, and the blackout curtains made it hard to see inside the claustrophobic living room.

Dust floated in a beam of light that stretched across the room. Bobby walked to the light and snapped his fingers at the floating particles. Behind his hand, he saw the outline of someone lying on the floor under a blanket. The light flipped on, and Bobby snapped his head to the door.

Drake stood just inside with his hand on the light switch. All color drained from his face, and tears fell from his eyes. He pointed at Bobby's feet.

Bobby picked his right foot up, a tacky, red substance pulled at his shoe. He looked back at the person on the floor and saw a blooming red stain on the blanket that he hadn't noticed initially. As he edged closer to the blanket, Bobby reached out to slowly pull it away. Tangles of his mom's oily, unwashed blonde hair clung to the fabric as he yanked it free.

Linda Cotton's remaining eye stared up at her son. The right side of her face was missing, and she had another bullet wound in her left shoulder. Bobby looked back at the hole in the wall that created the beam of light. One of the shots had gone rogue. How close had he or Drake come to being hit by the stray bullet? He looked back at his mom. Drake's scream startled him from his momentary shock, and he jumped back from his mother's body.

Another scream had him moving to his parent's room. Drake had tried to flee the scene in the living room and run straight into another. He flew past Bobby, through the backdoor, and screamed the entire way back to his own trailer. Bobby traced the muffled screams along the wall and stopped when he saw his dad.

Ed Cotton slumped against the middle of the headboard on the queen-sized bed he shared with Linda. Blood splattered up the wall in a starburst of red and cascaded down from the stippled ceiling like grotesque miniature stalactites. Thick streams of blood ran down the black lines between the pieces of wood paneling.

Bobby walked carefully across the room, dodging piles of clean and dirty clothes like they were alarms set to warn his dad of an intruder. He stood next to the bed and leaned in close. Stale sweat and gunpowder emanated from his dad's body. Something rolled under the toe of his shoe. Bobby bent down to move the bed sheet that hung to the floor and picked up the 9mm bullet casing. The ejected brass was already cool to the touch, and he rolled it around in his hand. Bobby looked around the bedroom, searching for the presence he felt. Waiting to jump out from the shadows. He slid the bullet casing into his pocket and slipped on the bed sheet, causing his father to move.

Ed's body fell to the side, and he slammed his head on the edge of the nightstand. A small clot of red spit across the top of the table, and then the remaining contents of his skull fell to the floor with a sticky plop. Images of his father's corpse clawing and scratching to catch up with him filled his mind as he tripped over himself, trying to escape from the room.

He ran from the room, not sparing another look at his mother before he burst through the door and into the arms of a Scarsville Sheriff's Deputy.

His dad's parents were the only family willing to take him in. They were the only family he had ever known. His mom's parents disowned her when she married his dad. They wanted more for their daughter than to marry Scarsville trailer trash and never leave town, though they themselves were Scarsville trailer trash of the lowest stature.

Recently, Bobby had thought about visiting them. More as an experiment than a reconnection. He'd always heard fire could rip through one of those old trailers before the occupants even knew they'd knocked over a candle or space heater.

Bobby's phone pinged. He'd set up alerts to let him know if The Suicide Killer was mentioned anywhere online. The alert was for a news article on the local ABC affiliate, WRRL. Excitement coursed through Bobby's veins, and his muscles felt weak. There had been a few mentions by random people, but this was the first time in a while that the news had anything to say about him. Of course, he could have done something to get their attention, but he'd been mourning the loss of a friend, and besides, he wanted to test the longevity of his grip on the city. In truth, it had been severely isolated to the people in law enforcement intimate with the situation. And even they didn't know everything.

Danielle's disappearance made the local and state news. A pretty white woman missing usually does. Their biggest lead was finding her boyfriend, Stephen, but they could not locate him. No matter how much the family denied it, people generally thought they had left town together. However, it was strange that she hadn't used any of her credit cards and that she had left her beloved dog, Charlie, behind. If the police had found any blood left in the kitchen, they were keeping that to themselves. Bobby hadn't had the proper time to mourn Danielle. His life had changed so much since he first met her. He no longer walked home through the park after work for fear of walking past her grave and Emily's tree. An icy chill shuddered through his body at the thought of passing the downed tree and seeing the two women talking to each other. Having a good laugh at his expense, no doubt. Yet Emily would never allow it. She hadn't been happy with where he'd buried Danielle. She'd been giving him the silent treatment ever since, and he was grateful for the peace.

And Mike? Nobody gave a damn about that asshole. He only made the news once when they connected him to Danielle. Still, he became a footnote once Danielle's aunt started talking about the strange young man she'd met in Danielle's apartment. Bobby dodged a bullet with that one. Aunt Susan was more interested in her own reflection to pay too much attention to him. Bobby could have held the composite sketch up for her to compare, and she wouldn't have recognized either one.

Bobby placed his palms on the top of Greg's headstone and pushed himself up until he sat with both legs swinging freely. He pulled his phone from his pocket and typed the incorrect passcode three times before finally getting it right. He clicked on the alert, and it went to the WRRL main page.

Six Months Later: The Search for The Suicide Killer Continues, or
Does It?
by Jonathan Leonard

It's been six months since the senseless murders of two young women from Crystal Valley by the man calling himself The Suicide Killer. Six months since the selfish act of one of Crystal Valley's top detectives did nothing but cause the death of a suicide prevention hotline volunteer as well as the death of his long-time partner's wife. All the actions of Detective Gregory Burns led to the higher death toll. We don't know how long Detective Burns knew about the killer. For all we know, he started talking to him before he ever killed any of his victims.

Furthermore, all of these deaths could be on his hands. What we do know is that the bloodshed ended that night when Detective Burns was shot and killed by his partner, Detective Don Murphy. Not as an act of revenge, but as a final tableau set up by the elusive and apparently chatty Suicide Killer. Crystal Valley Police Officer Brian Wilkes also lost his life that night while pursuing the suspect. For those of you keeping score (I know one person out there who is), that is six confirmed deaths attributed to The Suicide Killer and not one decent lead for the Crystal Valley Police Department to follow up on. I say six confirmed deaths because I'm confident there are more that they aren't telling us about, or worse, don't know about. If I had to guess, I would probably assume the numbers are closer to a dozen.

All the critical information that could have been used to take this killer off the streets died with Detective Burns. There has been no word if he managed to do his job halfway and write down any of the details from the numerous calls he shared with the killer. The only living person known to have spoken with the killer is Morgan Cramer of the Crystal Valley Times, and she's not taking any calls for interviews at this time.

There has been a lot of incompetence surrounding this case, and assigning a rookie detective as the new lead is further proof that they don't care about solving these cases. They only hope they disappear. But I want everybody in the greater Crystal Valley area to know this reporter will not rest until the police department is held accountable for the insensible bloodshed and that they work to uphold the law and their oaths to serve and protect this city. If not, I will have to do a little detecting work myself. All further updates for this case can be found on my personal blog at bringSK2justice.com.

Bobby clicked on the link and the blog opened in a new tab. Before the website had a chance to load, he thumbed back to the original page. It would be better to read Leonard's blog posts later when he had a chance to sit back and relax while he read them. They would no doubt provide cheap entertainment for the night. How somebody thought they actually had a chance to catch Bobby was beyond him. It would never happen. At least it would never be somebody as incendiary as Jonathan Leonard. It's a wonder he was still allowed to write articles for any news agency not found in the grocery store checkout lane.

Though most of what he said was garbage, one statement did stand out. Apparently, they had assigned a new detective to the case, but Bobby hadn't seen anything in the news about whom that could be. He scanned the page of other News stories, but nothing stood out.

A strangled cry from a familiar voice floated across the breeze and hit Bobby as he tried to concentrate on the phone screen.

Bobby...

Bobby shook his head, trying to throw the invasive voice from his mind. Her cries entered his ears and fell like icicles in a warming cave. A cold chill ran up his spine and caused a reflexive spasm through his shoulders and down his right arm.

Bobby, please. Bobby ... I'm still here. I need help.

He put his hands to his ears to block her out. He thought she was gone. She had been gone for the last six months after he said goodbye to her. There had been no contact, and he didn't think of her most days. So why was she trying to contact him now? He didn't need the disruption in his life.

Bobby. Please come see me. I have to get out of here.

Bobby pushed his hands tighter to his head and rocked back and forth on top of the hard granite headstone. Why wouldn't she leave him alone? He couldn't let her get back into his mind. The last time he listened to her, he killed Danielle. There wasn't anybody he needed to protect from Emily in his life, but he didn't need to risk it.

Bobby rocked one more time and slid off the top of the smooth, polished stone. The firm, compacted ground jarred his hands from his ears, and her voice slipped in again.

Bobby. Come to me, my love.

He wrestled himself to his feet and pulled the hair about his temples, trying to cause enough pain to eradicate her voice.

"No. Never! I'll never come back to you! It's your fault she's dead," he screamed across the empty graveyard. A few birds in a nearby tree took flight and cawed their protests as they flew overhead.

Everything grew silent, and Bobby let go of his hair. He stood motionless, stunned by the sudden disappearance of all noise. He searched the area for his phone and found it between the Burns and Pechman family plots.

All feelings of loss and remorse had fled Bobby's system. It was time for him to go and pray that Emily could not follow him home.

He adjusted the blue flowers in the stone vase he'd picked climbing up a trellis in his backyard. His grandmother called them Heavenly Blue, but he wasn't so sure that would be the color of the afterlife. At least not for him.

He trotted up the hill to his waiting Bronco and gunned the engine as he slammed it into gear. As he raced to the front gates, the back tires slid off the winding road and kicked gravel from the shoulder in the air. As he came around a ridge, it dawned on him why he was only now hearing Emily. She was buried in the same cemetery as Greg.

Bobby lifted his foot from the accelerator, and the vehicle coasted around the sharp curve that led to Emily's grave. The Bronco rolled down the small hill and came to a stop where he comforted Emily's mom when she left her daughter's funeral.

Bobby stared straight ahead. He didn't want to look at her headstone for fear that her rotting corpse would be leaning back against the cold granite, beckoning him to join her. Sweat dripped into his eyes, and he squeezed them shut.

Bobby. I need your help.

He shook his head to rid his brain of her pleas, but her voice only grew louder. He jammed his foot on the accelerator, but the engine only revved. The needle climbed to the redline before he let off the gas. When did he put the truck in park? Or was it her? He shook his head again and dropped the transmission into drive.

A muffled pounding came from Emily's direction, like somebody continuously knocking on the door after you've rolled over and covered your head with a pillow. It was her. She was trying to get out. Bobby choked on his own spit and felt like he was swallowing cotton balls when he forced it down his throat.

I can't see anything. I'm scared. It's dark all the time, and I don't have anybody to talk to. Bobby, please help me get out of here.

"I've already told you. I'm done with you. We're finished. I can't help. You have to stay buried."

Please. It's so lonely and cold here. Nobody will talk to me. Don't you miss our talks?

Sharp fingernails scratched across smooth concrete. Had she broken through her casket? Bobby needed to get out of there before she clawed her way out of the hole and called shotgun. That's what he needed to do, and he knew it, but there was an overwhelming urge to argue, to let her know everything was her fault. The only person to blame for her being alone was herself.

"I do. But you ruined everything when you made me kill her."

I didn't make you kill anybody. That was your choice to make. I only told you what the bitch was doing and how you should take care of her.

"Don't you dare call her that. You have no right."

Bobby buried his face in his hands before slamming them violently into the steering wheel.

"Lies. Everything that comes from your mouth is lies."

He whispered these last words.

You're fighting with me, but you will get me out of here. You won't be able to help yourself. And then it will be just us two again. I'll let you go for now, but I'll only be patient for so long. I'll see you again, my love.

A rooster tail of dirt and rocks shot in the air behind the Bronco as it sped to the gate. Bobby didn't bother with the slight curves in the road anymore and floored it in a straight path across asphalt and grass until he reached the front gate.

Pine Grove Cemetery was tainted. There was no way he could ever go back there again. Emily would never leave him alone until he helped her escape, but he'd never be rid of her if he did that. The only thing Bobby could do was stay as far away as he could. It shouldn't be too hard because Pine Grove was on the other side of town, and he rarely drove this way. The most important thing he could do now is to ensure he didn't end up there when he died.

Emily was trying to worm her way back into his life, and he needed a distraction. Work usually provided a decent enough distraction from the mundane, but he doubted it would help with her. And besides, he was off for the next two days. There was only one thing he could think to do.

He needed to visit Morgan Cramer. It had been a while since he'd seen her, and maybe she would be able to provide some information on the rookie detective who took over his case. Bobby hoped the new guy was as charming as Greg had been.

Chapter Two

Coffee sloshed over the rim of the cup and splattered across the white granite countertop. Morgan sat the carton of milk down and swiped her hand across the lukewarm liquid. She ended up smearing it more than cleaning the counter, but she didn't care. It was too early to worry about such trivial things. The coffee would still be there, waiting to be swiped away after she'd had the proper amount of time to wake up. That time seemed longer these days than it had been in the past. It was hard to fall asleep and stay that way for the entire night, even with the sleeping pills the doctor begrudgingly prescribed her.

She hadn't felt safe at night since her run-in with The Suicide Killer. It didn't matter that he promised not to kill her. Knowing that he'd taken lives without remorse, the lives of people who had never done anything to him, was enough for her not to trust anything he promised her. The pills weren't working, and she was running out of options. The alarm system had worked for a while, but that illusion was shattered when it went off in the middle of the night and woke up half of her neighborhood. When the cops finally showed up thirty minutes later and found her curled up in the fetal position beside her claw-foot tub, she realized the alarm wasn't any good if she wasn't prepared to defend herself or if it was going to take half an hour for any help to arrive. She never figured out what made the alarm go off, but she continued to set it every time she walked in the door and didn't turn it off until she was ready to leave again.

Getting a dog had been the biggest mistake. Morgan thought she would feel safer if she had a big dog ready to protect her when the alarm went off. But it didn't take long for her to realize that she wasn't up for the responsibility of taking care of an animal that needed so much attention. It also reminded her why she had always been a cat person. Luckily, she didn't have to wait long, and a friend from work took the dog in. She didn't care for the animal, but she wasn't going to drop it off at the shelter, either. She wasn't heartless.

The alarm on her cellphone went off. Time to get up and start work. She had a deadline by the end of the day for her article on the delays of the Crystal Valley Shopping Complex being built on the site of the last mill to go out of business. The mill had been gone for at least fifteen years, maybe more. It was hard to remember, but the old, dilapidated building had always been there, and more than a few people weren't happy with its demolition. The latest delay came from the death of two construction workers who fell down a buried drainage pipe and drowned in the toxic dyes that had not yet seeped into the waterways. As much as people wanted to reminisce about the glory days of the mill that stretched out on two hundred acres on the north side of town, it created many environmental hazards and destroyed the surrounding ecosystem. The new shopping center wasn't going to do anything to help the environment, but the mill had tainted that land long ago.

Current events around the city weren't as thrilling or sexy as the crime beat, but Morgan had been in that game for a while and gotten too close to becoming a lead story. So she was fine with the break and the slower pace. The construction workers' deaths were the first fatalities she'd had to report on in months. It was different from the murders she used to cover, but the loss of life was the same. There were still grieving families that didn't understand why it had to happen to their loved ones. It was too close to comfort for her, but she still had a job to do. If she would sit down and finish the article, she wouldn't have to think about it anymore. She could move on to the postponement of The Valley Airshow because of misappropriated funds by the city manager or the mayor. There was a lot of finger-pointing going on with that one.

Morgan walked to the kitchen table and sat her coffee mug down on the light brown ring worn onto the surface of the cheap wood. Her laptop was missing from its regular spot. She walked into the living room and back to her bedroom, but it was nowhere to be found. The one place she knew it wouldn't be was in her old office. She still hadn't spent more than a few minutes at a time in that room since the break-in. Confusion turned to concern, and then ran straight to fear. After fighting the urge long enough, she walked to the door of her old office and flipped on the light. She didn't step inside the room, but remained firmly entrenched in the doorway. The computer was not there. A wave of fear and held breath escaped her mouth. She laid her head against the doorcase.

The car. That was where her laptop was. She'd hit a block with her article and decided to try a change of scenery. The park had been her first thought, but that was quickly dismissed at the idea of being alone and an easy target, so she opted for The Daily Grind Coffee Shoppe instead. She was feeling adventurous yesterday, not crazy. Everything had gone fine, even though the barista paid a little too much attention to her for comfort, and his voice sounded weird, like he was sick or something. After she finished writing for the day, she ran to the grocery store to pick up a few things, and when she got home, she forgot the laptop in favor of her dinner ingredients.

Morgan turned the alarm off, walked to the door, unlocked both deadbolts, and slid the chain from its base. The doorknob turned easily in her hand, and she swung the door open.

The first thing she saw was a glove-wrapped hand at eye level, preparing to knock. Everything moved in slow motion. She ducked, afraid the hand was reaching out for her. When she looked up, a familiar ski mask-covered face looked down at her, hand still suspended in the air. It was the eyes. His eyes had the same dark, shark-like stare they had the last time he broke into her house. She reached a shaking hand out and grabbed the door casement to steady herself. Tears filled the corners of her eyes, and a scream built up in her throat, but neither would release.

"What are you doing down there?"

His voice was calm like he'd just dropped by to see an old friend, it unnerved her, and she fell back on her ass. He invited himself in as Morgan slid back with her hand in the air to defend herself like a jujitsu fighter.

"Seriously, Morgan. What is your problem? I've told you that I wasn't going to kill you."

He looked around the small mudroom and stuck his head into the kitchen.

"Looks like you've installed a nice alarm system. I bet that makes you feel safe at night."

Morgan hadn't moved a muscle. She still sat with her back to the wall, her arm extended, ready to defend against attack. He turned back to her, and she flinched. A small squeal escaped her lips.

"Well, maybe not. Perhaps I can rectify that while I'm here. I promise I only want to talk."

She cursed herself for sounding weak. He walked into the kitchen, and she allowed herself to breathe again. This wasn't happening. How could she be so stupid? All these months, she'd been terrified even to leave the house, constantly checking to make sure no one was waiting in any shadows to jump out and grab her, only letting her guard down when she was in the comfort of a large group of people. Her life had made a complete one-eighty in that regard. But of all mornings for her to slip up and not check outside the windows and the peephole five times like she had a compulsive disorder, he's there waiting for her.

"I see you still work in the kitchen where you can see everything. I don't guess I blame you too much, there. One question, though."

Morgan stood on trembling legs and inched her way to the front door. She had to stop shaking if she was even going to think about making a run for it.

He quickly stuck his head into the mudroom. She hadn't heard him walk back, and she screamed again.

"Morgan? One question. Where is the bat? I see all of your knives are in their proper drawer, but I don't see the bat."

He stood waiting for her answer, but she couldn't summon the courage to speak. She was paralyzed. After a brief stare-down, he jumped at her and yelled.

"Where is the fucking baseball bat, Morgan?"

A primal scream she didn't know she was capable of forced its way from her lips.

"My room, my room. The bat's in my room."

Morgan covered her face and fell flat against the wall.

"That wasn't so hard, was it? I'm sorry I had to scare you like that, but it seemed to be the only way to get you to talk to me."

She put her hands down and looked at him. Maybe he wasn't going to hurt her? But what could he want now? It had been months since she'd written a crime article. There's no way they'd let her publish another article about him, especially after the last time. She'd almost gotten fired over that one.

"Look, I don't have time for all of this. You really must calm down. If I were going to hurt you, I would have done it already. I've had plenty of opportunities when you're going into the office, or that twenty-four-hour gym you think is safe because of the night security, or at that little Thai restaurant you love so much. They really do have the best spring rolls in town. Hell, I was about to knock on the door like a normal person before you opened it."

Morgan felt numb. She absentmindedly rubbed at the cold pin pricks radiating up her arms. The Suicide Killer had been gone for six months. Why was he showing back up now? Did he want to gloat because he had gotten away with it? She let her arms fall to her side without saying a word. She was done. He would never leave her alone.

"Just have a seat. You're wobbling all over the place. There's no reason for you to be scared. I forgive you."

Morgan's body radiated with an angry fire. Forgive her? What the hell did that mean? He's the one who broke into her house and threatened to kill her family if she didn't publish that stupid article about him. She stood up straight and fought to steel the rubber in her legs.

"What the hell are you talking about? You forgive me. Do I need to remind you what happened the last time you were here?"

"Oh, great. There's that fire I admire. Truthfully, I believe your work has been missing that fire lately. I hope you can keep it, and it crosses back over to your writing. But I forgive you for stabbing me. It left a hell of a scar."

He turned his back to her and looked over his shoulder like he was showing her where the scar was. She didn't need his help to remember where she stabbed him or the feeling of the blade sliding into his body. An arctic chill rippled through her body. She also remembered that if she had only stabbed him an inch or two over, he wouldn't be standing here and at least three people she knew of would still be alive, including Greg. That was the worst part. Knowing she could have saved lives if only she had been able to take one. There was no telling how many people he'd killed since he escaped from Greg's house.

The fire started to wane, and she walked backward so her back would not be to him. Her heel hit the kitchen wall, and she carefully sat down in her chair. She hadn't thought about Greg in a while. Tried not to think about him was closer to the truth. They weren't exactly friends, but he looked out for her and tossed her a few leads here and there. Not on anything major, but enough to keep her a step ahead of the local TV news. The media and cops didn't typically get along, but he was always nice to her. It wasn't because of his nature. It was guilt. Guilt that he had never been able to solve her sister's murder. Was that the same reason she mourned his death? Not because of a senseless death, but because the chances of solving her sister's case were even slimmer than before. Morgan wasn't even sure who the lead detective was anymore.

"I want to start by apologizing for Greg's death. I hadn't planned for it to go like that, but he wouldn't play by the rules, and it couldn't be avoided."

Morgan looked down at the table, and tears streamed down her face. She didn't wipe them away when she looked up at him, and they followed the contours of her face and rolled under her chin.

"Couldn't be avoided? All of this could have been avoided. You didn't have to kill anybody."

"Well, technically, I didn't kill Greg. That was Don."

"Yeah, and he'll have to live with that and the death of his wife," she said.

The anger fueled the fire, and Morgan started to stand again.

"Okay, let's not get testy. I'm not here to argue the philosophical differences between life and death."

Morgan looked down and then quickly realized her mistake and snapped her head up. She couldn't let him out of her sight. It didn't matter how many times he promised he wouldn't hurt her.

"Then why are you here?"

"I'm glad you asked," he said and gestured to the chair in front of him.

Morgan threw her hand in the air as if to say you're going to sit, whether I give you permission or not. The killer bowed his head, pulled the chair from under the table, and quietly sat down. It was unnerving to see how agile he was. No sound came from the chair or table. The clothes he wore didn't even rustle. No wonder he was able to get in and out of places so easily. He was like a ghost. Though he was a talker. Couldn't seem to keep his mouth shut.

He laid his hand on the table inches from her own, and she recoiled. The thought of touching him disgusted her.

"I need your help," he said.

"Never. I'm not doing anything for you again."

"You don't even know what it is yet," he said.

She knew he wouldn't take no for an answer, but she tried.

"I don't care."

A loud huff of air blew through the ski mask, blowing a stray strand of thread into the air. He was pouting. Morgan hoped he didn't start to whine.

"Come on, Mo."

Morgan jumped up from her seat.

"Don't call me that!" she screamed, and then more calmly added, "my sister was the only one who called me that."

The killer jumped back and threw his hands in the air like she was about to strike him. Maybe she should have. It would have caught him off guard. However, the last time she attacked him, she ended up with a severe concussion.

"Okay. Okay. Morgan it is. I didn't know you were so crabby. I'll even call you Ms. Cramer, if you'd prefer."

The killer leaned over the table again.

"I'm not here to ask you to write another article about me. The last one was great. It created a nice little buzz about me even though I didn't get to enjoy it fully. What with a crazy detective trying to kill me and all."

"Yeah, he was the crazy one," she said.

"Yes, he was. Among other things," the killer said and leaned closer to Morgan.

His voice had taken on a sinister quality that Morgan didn't like. Somehow it made everything he said worse, even if it was benign. She'd crossed the line and needed to jump back to the other side before he got mad. But at least now she knew where the line was.

He leaned in closer, staring at her with his cold blank eyes. The scent of Winterfresh gum wafted through the slit made for his mouth and assaulted her nose. She had hated the smell of Winterfresh ever since she drank from her dad's chewing tobacco spit cup as a child. She held her breath and fought to push the vomit creeping up her throat back down. The killer licked his lips, fighting with the rogue string. His losing battle distracted Morgan, and she didn't have time to react when he suddenly reached out and grabbed her hand. Her delayed scream echoed through the house.

"Guess you didn't know I could move that fast, did you?"

Morgan didn't say anything for fear of betraying how scared she was. She didn't want to give him any more power, but he would still find it in the rebellious tears that forced their way from her eyes and the tremble of her hand.

"Now, don't cry," he said and rubbed his gloved hand across the back of hers.

Morgan locked eyes with the killer, and he carefully removed one of his gloves so their skin would touch as he continued to caress her hand. Morgan tried to pull away, but he held fast. His grip did not crush her hand but held it still with no issues like a vise. His breath became heavy, and his voice softened.

"I wish we would have met under different circumstances. We could have had a very non-platonic relationship. Don't you think?"

"I don't think you'd be capable of having a non-psychotic relationship."

The words slipped from her mouth before she had time to think about what she was saying. For a split second, he had stopped sounding like a killer and started sounding like every other man she'd ever had the displeasure of encountering in any place that wasn't her home. Now, he'd ruined that, though he'd already ruined it months ago. Her body tensed as she awaited his response.

His eyes grew wide, and an obnoxious, over-the-top laugh erupted from his mouth. The killer released her hand and jumped up from the table. He took care not to touch anything as he put the glove back on. Morgan pushed herself back against her chair, bracing for impact, but he didn't hit her. Instead, he continued laughing and walked into her office. The office chair squeaked as he sat down and rocked back.

Morgan wasn't sure what to do. Did he mean for her to follow him? Or should she stay in the kitchen? She looked towards the entrance of the mudroom, but it was directly across from her office. There was no way she'd be able to get out the door before he got to her.

"I'm not going to lie. That was funny. Hurtful, but funny."

He hadn't given her any instruction but didn't seem to be in much of a hurry, either. Morgan slowly stood, trying not to make any sound that he might think was an attempt at escape. Finally, she crept to her office and peeked around the corner.

He sat in her chair, spinning around in slow circles. Then, when he noticed her, he motioned for her to come into the room.

"Come, come. There's nothing to be afraid of. I have more of a reason to fear you than you do me."

Morgan walked into the room and rested her back against the wall.

"How's that? You're the psycho killer."

He half laughed like he started and didn't mean to, so he cut it off.

"Qu'est-ce que c'est?"

He picked up a framed picture sitting on her desk.

"What?"

"Never mind. You're more dangerous to me because I would never hurt you, and I will always have to wear a mask around you. Also, there's the whole stabbing thing. Anyway, I don't want you to get bored with me, so I'll just get on with why I've asked you here today. I need to ask you something."

Morgan put her arms across her chest.

"I already told you I'm not helping you with anything."

He spun around in the chair again.

"But you still don't know what I'm going to ask."

"I don't care."

"You know I'm not going to leave until you hear me out, so you might as well listen."

There was no arguing with that. Defeated, she dropped her arms to her side.

"This is an interesting photo of you and this guy. Looks like you do know how to have fun," he said and showed the picture to her.

It was an old photo taken with a baseball player who Morgan dated for a short time.

"Yeah, that's Heath Clement. We dated a few years ago, but that isn't me in the picture. That's my sister, Amanda. We played a joke on him when we first met and switched to see if he could tell the difference."

That was the last picture Morgan had of her sister and the only reason she kept it. Four months later she would be dead.

"Hmm. Looks like she liked him, too."

"What? No. That's when he found out. She was having a good time. Anyway, I know you're not here to talk about my sister."

He set the frame back on the desk.

"I wasn't, but who knows where this will lead. I want to know who the new detective is on my case. I saw an article by that hack

Leonard, and he said there was somebody new. A rookie of all people, but no names were given, and I can't seem to find it anywhere."

Morgan's face dropped. He had come over here after all this time, scaring the hell out of her, just to find out a name.

"Leonard isn't a hack. He may be brash and obnoxious, but he is pretty good at his job. Why didn't you just call the police station and ask? You like talking to them, anyway."

He sighed.

"I'm not worried about that guy. I was going to call down there, but then I thought they might get suspicious. Believe it or not, I don't want to get caught. I just need you to find out a name, that's all. That's not so much to ask, is it?"

"I'm not giving you a name so you can kill another cop."

The killer stood up and walked around to the front of the desk.

"I promise I don't want to kill him. I only want to know who I'm up against."

"No. I can't do it. I'm not on the crime beat anymore."

He sat on the edge of the desk.

"Seriously? You expect me to believe that just because you don't write about crime anymore, you don't know anything about the crime that goes on in this city?"

Morgan pursed her lips and stared him down. There wasn't any reason she couldn't find out who was on the case. He would find out eventually, anyway. But she didn't want him to think she was helping him. And she didn't want to live with the guilt if he was lying and did kill the detective. Though she could always find out who it was and warn them that he wanted to know. They might be able to set a trap for him. A slight smile crossed Morgan's face, and she bit her bottom lip to stop it from fully forming. She couldn't just change her stance and sound eager, or he would know something was up. She continued to stare at him until he came up with another plan.

"Okay, I see you're going to play hardball. How about a little quid pro quo?"

"What do you mean?"

The killer leaned back across the desk and grabbed the picture of Heath and her sister.

"You get me that name and any other information you can on that detective, and I'll help you find your sister's killer."

Morgan fell back against the wall. That wasn't what she'd been expecting. She wasn't sure what she'd expected him to say, but that wasn't it. A large lump formed in her throat, and she fought it back down.

"I ... uh, I don't know what to say. I don't know why you'd be able to find her killer if the police couldn't."

"Just give me a chance. I'm not held back by jurisdictions and laws and shit like that."

Turning a madman on somebody was not something she could live with, but if he could find Amanda's killer, it might be easier to stomach.

"Don't worry. I won't kill them when I find out who it is."

He stepped back far enough for her to feel like she could think straight,

"Do we have a deal?" he asked.

The killer held out his hand. Morgan wasn't going to willingly put her hand in his and gave him a subtle nod.

"Great. We have a deal. And so you don't lose any sleep worrying about me randomly showing up, let's say when you find out the information, leave your porch light on. I'll knock on the door when I see it. Though it won't be until that night that I show up. Don't want to chance being seen during the day with this mask on again."

She nodded again, and he walked past her, through the kitchen, and into the mudroom. He opened the door and walked out, but before he closed the door, he stuck his head back in.

"One last question. Do you think you'd recognize me if we ever met on the street?"

He ducked back out and slammed the door before she had a chance to answer. But what would she have said, anyway? She ran to the door and locked both deadbolts. Her heart raced. Six months ago, he had ruined the safety she felt in her house. Now he'd destroyed the illusion of safety that she felt in the city.

Chapter Three

The Suicide Killer had lain dormant for too long. Bobby had allowed his emotions to cloud his judgment and confuse him into laziness. It was easier not to do anything. But the time out of the spotlight had caused people to forget about him. The city had seen twenty-one other murders since Greg died. The police had moved on and weren't worried about him anymore. And they put a no-name rookie on his case. Couldn't even be bothered to announce his name. They undoubtedly thought he'd been arrested for something else or moved on. They weren't taking him seriously anymore, and they would pay for it.

The urge to kill had been minimal for the last few months, but the news articles stoked the remaining embers. When Bobby walked into Morgan's house and allowed The Suicide Killer to come out and play, that fire caught the oxygen of the reporter's fear and became a raging spirit that could only be satiated one way. Death.

Bobby's knees bounced against the steering wheel from the rush of energy and adrenaline. Though he hadn't been in a state where resuming his game would have been a good idea, he'd still been hunting. He picked up the battered, spiral-bound notebook in his passenger seat. White crease lines crisscrossed the black cover, creating a lightning bolt effect surrounding the large white N rubbed on the front. Without looking, he flipped to a page containing seven names and addresses. The following pages were labeled for each girl and her daily routine for a three-week period. Bobby continued looking out the front windshield and only looked down at the paper after randomly placing his finger on a name.

Meadow Butler.

She would be the one to bring him out of hibernation. To strike fear into the heart of the city and make him a household name again. But he would have to wait. It was Thursday night, and she didn't get home from watching her brother and sister while her stepmom went to work until 11:00 p.m.

Bobby sat the notebook down and picked up the picture of Amanda Cramer and Heath Clement that he'd taken from Morgan's desk. A twinge of guilt for stealing from his friend hit him, but he ignored it. He needed the picture more than she did, and there was a good chance she would never know it was missing before he had a chance to put it back. It was 10:00 p.m., and he needed to get some information on the Cramer case so he could help out a friend.

The final light went out in the house across the street, and Bobby stepped from the car he'd stolen earlier in the day. The crisp autumn air added to his excitement as he pulled his mask over his face and crossed the street.

He pulled at his gloves like a surgeon preparing for surgery as he slowly climbed the stairs to the front porch. There hadn't been a squeaky board before, but things changed, and it was better to be on the safe side and not rush. Bobby eased to the doorknob and carefully tried to turn it. The door was locked. He sighed and looked under the doormat and only saw the outline of a key in the dirt and mold. At least she'd been smart enough to move the key. That would have been too easy for him, but as he looked around the porch, he spotted a terracotta pot full of dead mums two feet away from the mat. He slowly picked up the pot, revealing the spare key. She may have moved the key but hadn't gotten too creative with the new place. One day people would learn spare keys were in case you locked yourself out, not for those who wanted to get in but were too lazy to find their key.

The front door swung open, and Bobby stepped inside. A blue-red glow emanated from the living room. An old TV show played at low volume. Bobby couldn't remember the name, but he always hated the family togetherness and laugh tracks from 90s sitcoms. He walked to the back of the couch and peeked over the side.

Shelly Burns lay curled up under a threadbare crumb-covered

blanket. An empty double old-fashioned glass lay on its side on the coffee table beside an empty bottle of vodka. She snorted, and Bobby ducked back out of sight, but relaxed when he heard Shelly's soft snoring over the TV.

He crept out of the living room and went to Greg's office door. It was locked. Bobby ran his hand over the deadbolt, keeping him out. This wasn't going to be as simple as he'd hoped. The key had to be somewhere in the house. Greg had no doubt locked the door to keep young, prying eyes out. He was a good father, but his prudence was not a virtue to be celebrated at a time like this. Bobby walked into the kitchen. There was no key rack, and there wasn't one by the front door either. There was a good chance the keys were in the bedroom, which was the one place he didn't want to go.

He walked back to the foyer and sneaked up the stairs to the second floor. The door to Greg and Shelly's room was closed and had two boxes stacked in front of it. Bobby doubted that Shelly had slept a single night in there since Greg's death. Thankfully, the doors to both of the kids' rooms were closed. Bobby walked to the bedroom door and tried to slide the boxes out of the way, but the one on top threatened to fall over and spill its contents all over the floor. He picked up the top box, moved it out of the way, and then slid the bottom box to the side.

The door was stuck in the jamb, and he had to put his shoulder into it to get it to open. The popping sound of wood on wood pierced the quiet air, and he froze until he was sure he hadn't woken anybody. Bobby rolled his mask up on top of his head so he could see better before he stepped into the room and then eased the door closed enough so it wouldn't make a sound when he left. The air was stale and had a coppery, mildew smell. Bobby fished his phone from his pocket and turned on the flashlight.

He looked down and jumped back when he realized he was standing at the edge of where Greg had bled out on the floor. A faded red stain marked the area where his friend had fallen. It looked like whoever tried to clean up the mess gave a half-hearted effort and eventually gave up. Shelly should have let professionals take care of that. Replacing the flooring would be the only way to get rid of the blood now. Although, she probably didn't plan on coming back in here ever again. All of her clothes had been removed from the closet, and one of the vanity counters in the bathroom was empty. It would be better for her to move. It would never be the same for her again.

After a moment of silence, Bobby continued to the dresser in search of Greg's keys. He slid a glass ashtray closer and knocked a few pennies around. Squeaky door hinges creaked behind him, and he spun around, ready to defend himself.

The beam of his light flashed on a pale face with sleepy eyes. Hope Burns rubbed her face and squinted into the light. Bobby froze. He didn't know what to do. There was no way he could hurt a child and especially not Hope.

When he didn't speak, she did.

"Stephen? Is that you?"

Yes! Yes!, Bobby screamed in his head. Then realized he was still paralyzed from the fear and forced the words from his mouth.

"Yes, Hope, it's Stephen. I thought you were in bed?"

The little girl rubbed her eyes again.

"I was, but I had to go to the bathroom. Why are you in my mommy and daddy's room?"

Bobby couldn't think of what to say, but there was no use lying to the little girl. She would know. The only thing he had was the truth. Mostly the truth, anyway. He walked over to the little girl and kneeled down, so he was face to face with her.

"Well, Hope, I'm working on a special case, and your daddy has a case file that I need."

Tears formed in Hope's eyes.

"My daddy doesn't work on cases anymore. He's dead."

Tears flooded her eyes and ran down her face. Bobby put his arm around her and pulled her close.

"Oh, honey, please don't cry. I know he's gone, but he was working on another case, and now I have to solve it for him. But the door to his office is locked, and I didn't want to wake your mommy."

"I thought you were his friend?"

"I am his friend."

"Then why didn't you come to his funeral?"

That stung. Bobby had beaten himself up for six months for not going, and now Greg's daughter was working on him too. But she remembered Stephen, so it looked like it had been the right decision. Hope stood, waiting for his excuse.

"I wanted to be there, sweetie, but I couldn't because I've been working undercover. It would have been too dangerous if I had gone and somebody had seen me. I'm still undercover, and that's why I'm sneaking in here so late at night. I want to keep you safe from the bad guys."

Hope scrunched up her face and sized him up. She seemed to take in every word he said and think it over. In the end, the muscles in her face relaxed. Hope smiled and blinked away the tears still holding on.

"I knew you didn't forget," she said and wrapped her arms around Bobby's neck.

Bobby looked around the dark room. He was confused as to how he could have left such an impression on this child in the short amount of time they'd spent together. He hugged her back, and she whispered in his ear.

"I know where Daddy hides the key."

Bobby pulled away from her.

"What? You know where it is? Can you get it for me?"

Hope nodded like a bobblehead doll.

"Mmhmm. It's downstairs in the kitchen," she said and took off out the door toward the stairs.

Bobby jumped to his feet and chased Hope while trying not to knock everything down in his path. She stood in the kitchen beside the refrigerator when he caught up to her.

"It's behind here."

Hope pushed a stepstool against the metal side of the refrigerator. The clank echoed through the hall, and Shelly stirred in the living room. Bobby tiptoed toward the other room but didn't hear anything until Hope spoke up again.

"Don't worry. Nothing can wake her up."

Hope stood on the tips of her toes and reached behind the refrigerator. Her tongue poked out between her lips as she fought to make herself taller. Finally, she relaxed, pulled a magnetic hid-a-key from the back of the refrigerator, and handed it to Bobby. He stood there for a second in disbelief. The man used to put the spare key under the mat but went out of his way to hide the spare key to his office. What else was he hiding in there? Bobby looked at his watch. 10:30; he didn't have time to look around. He'd already spent way more time in the house than he wanted. He walked to the office, slid the key in the lock, and the door quietly opened. Hope stayed in the hallway when he turned to look for her to follow him.

"Daddy said I'm not allowed in there anymore. That's why the lock is on the door."

Bobby nodded and turned back to the room. The office was a mess. Papers were scattered all over the desk. Clothes lay across the backs of chairs. The scent of sweat and a fruity candle permeated the thick air. Two battered filing cabinets covered in bumper stickers slouched against the back wall. Bobby walked over to them and prayed they weren't locked. The first one slid open, and Bobby flipped to the Cs. There were no Cramers. He opened the second cabinet, but it started with the Ns.

It wasn't there. Bobby wasted all that time, and the damn file wasn't there. He gripped the handle and prepared to slam the drawer shut when the first file caught his attention. Natalie Hess. He looked at the file again. The first name in the Ns was Natalie. Who the hell alphabetizes by the first name? When he thought about it, he realized it shouldn't have surprised him. He returned to the other cabinet and flipped through a couple of names before finding Amanda Cramer in the A section. It wasn't as thick as he hoped it would be. But if it'd been really big, Greg would have been able to solve the case. Bobby closed the drawers, walked back into the hallway, and locked the door.

"I have to get going. Do you mind putting the key back for me?"

"You can keep it. Mommy doesn't know where it is, and you might need it again so you can help somebody else."

The little girl continued to surprise and touch Bobby. He must be getting soft from the lack of action.

"Thank you. I'll keep it safe," he said and patted her on the top of the head.

Bobby slowly opened the front door, and, before stepping out, turned in time to see Hope cover her mother up with the blanket she'd kicked off and kiss her on the forehead.

* * *

Bobby pulled up in front of an aging split-level home. He'd spent many nights in the upper room waiting for Meadow Butler to return home. Watching through cracked plastic mini-blinds as Meadow came and went through her daily routine. She never even glanced in the direction of the crumbling brick house across the street. The neighbors quickened their pace when they approached the house as they walked their dogs. Did they have a feeling that somebody was watching them? Or was this the neighborhood boogeyman's house? If dogs can truly sense evil, they didn't seem to mind as their leashes went slack at the sudden determination of their owners.

Fat raindrops splattered the windshield and rippled the light coming from Meadow's bedroom window. He should have already been inside the house before she'd gotten home, but he'd spent far too long at Greg's house. And if Hope hadn't woken up, he would still be there searching for the key. Hope had grown up a lot since the last time he'd seen her. Of course, she had to grow up fast. She now had to take care of her younger brother and apparently her mother, who couldn't even go into her bedroom anymore. The bloodstain didn't help, but they had people to clean that stuff up. If Greg had listened to Bobby, none of that would have happened. He'd still be alive with his family and still playing the game with Bobby. Now the game would never be the same. But he had to kill. The need to save Emily had been why he started killing; now, it felt like a compulsion. A desire. He hadn't killed anybody since the night Greg died, but he couldn't deny it anymore.

Bobby threw the Cramer file on the passenger seat with the picture of Amanda pretending to be Morgan. He'd planned on reading through it before his date with Meadow but had only stared out the windshield until he couldn't handle the craving.

A For Sale sign scrapped against the edge of the door as he kicked it open. The only sound in the neighborhood was the pounding rain beating on the pavement like tiny punches thrown at an unsuspecting stranger, contrasted with the distant metallic thumps against cars sitting in driveways because of garages turned to storage rooms.

Bobby plodded up the wooden steps and squeaked across the porch to the front door. The original plan was to hide and grab her when she wasn't looking and make sure it turned out better than Laura Cline. She'd almost gotten the better of him. The contingency plan was to wait until she'd gone to sleep and break-in, but it didn't look like Meadow was ready for bed, and Bobby was tired of waiting. He'd been waiting for six months, and that was six months too long. There was no time for the element of surprise.

He pulled the mask over his head and pulled a flashlight from his back pocket. Glass erupted into the foyer and slid down the hall across the wood floors. Bobby used the handle to clear any sharp pieces from the frame. He stuck his right arm through the opening and turned the switch to unlock the deadbolt. The button on the knob clicked, and Bobby turned it with his left hand. He calmly walked through the foyer, purposely making his shoes squeak on the floor and kicking shards of glass down the hall.

He stopped outside Meadow's room and looked into two terrified hazel eyes. He'd never been close enough to see them before, but now that he could, they were a beautiful swirl of brown and green he'd never seen before. Her lips trembled, and her arm moved to her mouth. She wasn't going to scream. She was too scared for that. But she did try to speak.

"T-t-take w-u-u-whatever you want."

The urge to talk to the woman he'd followed for weeks was strong. The opportunity for her to tell him what she was like and for him to tell her who she was could be an interesting conversation. She thought she was Daddy's Princess who wanted nothing more than to be away from her Evil Stepmother, but she was actually a scared little girl who had it pretty good at home and wouldn't come back and admit she was wrong. She was terrified now, in the face of something truly evil. Bobby wanted to tell her all these things and so much more, but there wasn't enough time. He had a thirst to satiate, and it wouldn't wait any longer. Maybe he'd have more time on the next occasion.

Her legs buckled, and she fell, but Bobby caught her before she ended up crying and balled up on the floor. Bobby picked her up and slammed her on the bed. Her legs flailed in the air, striking at a target she would never hit. He put his hand around her throat and started to choke her, and her arms instinctually went to his wrists to fight off the attack, but she couldn't get a good grip on his long sleeves.

Meadow's fight slowed down as he cut off her oxygen. She let go of his arms and began swinging wildly.

Bobby jumped back a few inches, just out of reach of her grasping fingers. She barely missed his crotch. He wasn't going to let that happen again. It'd almost gotten him killed the last time. Maybe he should start wearing a cup.

He pinned her arm back against the side of the bed and a strangled scream poured from her mouth. Bobby reached over her, grabbed one of the many pillows on her bed, and shoved it over her face.

Meadow's arm shot up again, grasped the bottom of Bobby's shirt, and snatched it toward her. He grabbed her arm, pulled it down again, and used his body weight to pin it to the side of the bed. She fought and pushed back against him and he let all of his weight fall on her arm.

A muffled scream exploded from under the pillow as Bobby crushed her arm and hyperextended her elbow, ripping tendon from bone and forcing the hinge joint in a direction it was never meant to go.

Bobby pinned her broken arm against the bed and held the pillow over her head with his shoulder until he felt the life drain from her body. He wished he could have seen the glaze form over her beautiful eyes. He stayed in that position a few minutes after her final spasm to ensure she was dead. Then, when he was certain she wouldn't attack him again, he slid to the floor.

Heavy breaths forced their way out of his mouth, and he pulled his mask off his face. He pulled his shirt to the top of his brow and wiped all the sweat off in one swipe.

Bobby felt great. Exhilarated. It had been too long since he'd felt this way. He shouldn't have waited so long, even though he was in a time of mourning. It might have helped him to stop feeling bad if he'd continued to live instead of letting Greg's death bring his life to a complete halt. It still would have been hard, but he needed to get moving again, not as a distraction but a way to celebrate their relationship.

The wood floor creaked as Bobby pushed himself up. A slight migraine slipped down his forehead and settled behind his eyes. The headache didn't bother him, but he hadn't had this much physical exertion in quite a while. He would be sore in the morning.

Bobby walked into the bathroom and flipped on the light. The single vanity bathroom was small for a master bath. The walls were bright white with five swatches of varying shades of pink, from neon to pastel on various parts. Good thing he'd killed her before she'd made that mistake. He looked in the mirror and couldn't help making faces at himself. Every time he came across a mirror, it was an impulse he couldn't fight.

As he attempted to stick the tip of his tongue into his left nostril, a whispery voice echoed through the house. The voice startled him, and he ran back into the bedroom and listened. He hadn't heard what they said, but somebody had said something. It couldn't have been one of her friends, and she wasn't dating anybody. It was Thursday night. She never had company over this late.

Bobby walked back into the hall.

"Hello? Is anybody there?"

No answer.

Bobby walked to the front door and looked out the broken window. The only car in the driveway was Meadow's. The car he'd stollen earlier was the only one parked on the street. He went into the kitchen, but all the lights were off. If somebody were in the house, they knew their way around in the dark. The soft voice called again.

The foyer was cold and drafty from the broken window. A cool breeze with a hint of the first freeze of the year blew through the broken window and swirled around Bobby. He shivered, and through his chattering teeth, he heard the voice again. Except it wasn't a voice. It was the sound of the wind blowing through the shards of glass, and down the wind tunnel of the hall he stood in.

He felt stupid. He was the one trying to strike fear in people, and here he was jumping at sounds made by the wind. How was he supposed to control an entire town's fear when noises made him jump? He wasn't afraid that somebody had caught him. Even if they had, he wouldn't have been afraid. He would have killed them too and been on his way. The last time Bobby could remember ever truly being afraid of something was his father. His death in the trailer hadn't scared him; it thrilled him to see the man who had caused so much pain and fear dead in a pool of blood of his own making. Losing his mom had sucked, but Ed's parents were a better option to live with. At least they were stable. He'd never figured out how two people as great as his grandparents could have raised somebody as horrible as Ed.

Bobby walked back into the bathroom and pulled open the vanity drawers. Various bottles rattled around in the wooden cubby. He picked up a bottle of generic ibuprofen, popped the cap, and shook two caplets into his gloved hand. He tossed them in his mouth and dry swallowed them as he searched through the prescription bottles.

He seized one of the amber pill bottles and laughed to himself as he walked into the bedroom with an entire bottle of Zoloft. It was hard to get the childproof top to twist while he was wearing gloves, but he wasn't about to take them off. Instead, he sat the bottle on the nightstand and used his weight to push the cap down while he twisted it loose with his palm. The cap fell to the floor and rolled under the bed.

Bobby forced Meadow's mouth open and used his hand like a funnel as he poured the medicine into her mouth. Pills filled her mouth. A few fell around her face when he moved his hand. He held the bottle in one hand and reached into his back pocket to get the note he would be leaving for his new friend when the voice returned. This time, he knew it wasn't the wind blowing through the broken window. It was a voice with a name, and she needed Bobby in order to survive.

Bobby. I've been trying to talk to you. Couldn't you hear me?

Bobby spun around to face the bedroom door and spilled the remaining Zoloft pills across the floor. They ticked and bounced around the room, but Bobby focused on the door. Emily spoke again, only this time her voice didn't come from the hallway. It came from behind him on the bed.

Why don't you lie down with me for a while, lover? You know she won't be missed for a few days at least.

The doorknob smashed a lock size hole in the sheetrock when Bobby quickly backed into it.

"No. You can't be here. You're supposed to be gone."

I was. But now I'm back since you killed for me. Why don't you come over here so I can thank you?

"I didn't ... I didn't do it for you. I didn't kill her for you. I did it for me."

Let's just say you did it for us. Does that make you feel better?

Bobby stumbled toward the bed and then pulled back with his arm across his face. What had he done? She was supposed to be gone. He left her in the graveyard alone. There was no way she could get out.

"I don't want you. We're done. You lied to me. You made me kill Danielle. I don't want you here."

I didn't make you do anything you didn't want to do. She came between us and had to be taken care of. I knew you wouldn't do it unless you had a reason, so I gave you one. I didn't lie. I helped you do the inevitable. Now let's forget about the past and start over. Come and join me.

Bobby backed away from Meadow. Her good arm slipped off of her stomach, and Bobby turned and ran out of the room before she could reach out for him.

He stopped at the door and thought he heard something moving around in the bedroom. He jammed his hand in his back pocket, grabbed his note, and threw the balled-up piece of paper at the door.

The scraping sound of scarred skin against bed sheets came from the bedroom, followed by a light thump like a cat jumping from its perch. Bobby stumbled as he ran toward the door. He fell against the wall and reached for the doorknob as Emily called out.

You can't get rid of me, my love. Every time The Suicide Killer takes a life, I will be there to fill the vessel you created for me. You can't run away from me.

Chapter Four

Ivy Chandler felt the weight. The weight of an entire career bearing down on her shoulders and pressing against her chest. She wasn't the first woman to make detective in the Crystal Valley Police Department. She wasn't even the youngest. The pressure came from within. Ivy wanted to be the best at everything she did. But she had a mediocre rise through the ranks. Not a horrible cop, but not the best on the force. There were no medals of bravery on her walls or letters of commendation in her file. She made detective by passing the test on her own. There was no mentor. No guidance. Nobody pushed her to do it. If she hadn't taken the initiative, she'd still be driving around in her blue and white patrol car on the Northeast side of town.

The Northeast side of town was considered the easiest beat. Most of the cops were screw-ups put there because there was less of a chance of them hurting somebody. The rest were lifelong patrol cops who were close to retiring. As a detective, she would go all over the city, depending on where she and her new partner, Don Murphy, were in the rotation. She always liked Don when she was a cop. He wasn't an asshole, but he knew what he needed and wasn't afraid to ask for it. Most people assumed he was the only reason Greg Burns had stayed around for as long as he did. Many higher ranking officials considered Greg a screw-up, but Ivy never saw anything alarming until the end. Greg wasn't the stereotypical depressed alcoholic detective one case away from swallowing a bullet.

Ivy hoped some of that mentality had come from working with

Don, but so far, he'd been on the verge of that stereotype. But who could blame him? A serial killer that his partner had access to, but kept a secret, had murdered his wife. She was dead because of Greg. Don had been on leave for four months. He came back two months ago when Ivy was promoted. For the most part, she'd been on the sidelines. The upper brass obviously weren't comfortable putting Don back on the streets, no matter what the department shrink had to say about it. The first month of her promotion was spent observing and riding along with other detectives. It basically meant she was the gopher and the one to do most of the paperwork and follow up on the leads they knew wouldn't go anywhere.

Ivy tried not to resent Don for her being held back. And when she finally decided to ask the lieutenant to assign her a new partner, they got a case. A husband went on a shooting spree at the Candle-light Lounge, killing two bouncers and a dancer, after discovering what his wife did on the side while he was working the graveyard shift. As far as cases go, it was a softball. Over thirty eyewitnesses, and a nice security system pointed to the same guy. Ivy wasn't sure, but she assumed it wasn't because of bad luck in the rotation. She believed the lieutenant was trying to ease Don back into the job. It made sense but added to Ivy's feelings of mediocrity. All of that changed today, though.

Today, she finally got the chance to work on a murder case that wouldn't be open and shut. And if she didn't find where she laid her cellphone, she would be late to the scene. She heard Don's biggest pet peeve was taking too long to get to a crime scene, but she hadn't seen that side of him so far. That pet peeve undoubtedly stemmed from working with Burns for so long. She walked back into the bath-room and searched all the vanity drawers, but it wasn't there. Her phone would end up being in some random place where she was standing when something else distracted her. She saw herself in the mirror, pulled her ponytail tight, and brushed the shorter strands behind her ears.

If it hadn't been a suspected Suicide Killer case, she and Don would have been overlooked again. Ivy had inherited all of Greg and Don's cases, including, to the dismay of many tenured detectives, The Suicide Killer case. It may have been the highest profile case the department had, but right now, it was one of the coldest active cases they had. Everything stopped six months ago when Greg died. Actu-ally, all the cases she inherited from Greg were cold. There hadn't been that many other cases, only five, but that was five families who didn't know what had happened to a loved one. Her cellphone rang. Ivy paused to make sure it wasn't in the same room as her before pulling on her navy-blue blazer.

It sounded like it came from the kitchen. She left her bedroom, hoping it wasn't Don wondering where the hell she was. The bright white and Caribbean blue kitchen lit up when she flipped the switch. It was by far the brightest room in her house. At first, she thought it'd been a mistake, but she'd grown to love it and spent most of her time in the equally bright breakfast nook. Ivy walked to the counter and held her breath as she flipped the open pizza box lid, expecting to find her phone lighting up with Don's name.

The name wasn't in her contact list, and she didn't recognize the number. Ivy grabbed a slice of cold pizza and hit the green button on her phone.

"This is Ivy," she said between bites as she made her way to the front door.

"Detective Chandler?"

"Speaking."

"Oh, good. Detective, my name is Morgan Cramer."

The caller paused, allowing Ivy a moment to recognize her name. When she didn't, the caller continued.

"Well, I was transferred around for a while yesterday and again this morning, trying to find out who the new detective is on my sister's case."

Ivy hesitated again, hoping Morgan would continue, but now it seemed like it was her turn to speak.

"Ms. Cramer, I'm sorry, but what is your sister's name? I've recently taken over a number of cases, and I'm a bit fuzzy on all the specifics."

There was a pause. An uncomfortable silence accusing Ivy of being like her predecessor and not doing her job.

"My sister is Amanda Cramer. She was murdered three years ago. They found her in Lake Oliver."

Lake Oliver, Cramer, of course, Ivy should have recognized the case from Morgan's name immediately. The Cramer case was the oldest active case that Greg hadn't solved. Ivy had looked through the case file. There wasn't much to go on, but Ivy had planned to look into it after she'd gone through the other cases. Morgan was the first family member to call her and ask any questions. Ivy also should have recognized Morgan's name because she was a reporter.

"Yes, of course, Amanda Cramer. I should have recognized your name, but yes, I am taking over your sister's case from Detective Burns. I'm sorry I haven't been in touch. As you can imagine, taking over a caseload is pretty hectic."

Ivy stopped in front of her door and stomped her foot. Damn it. She had to get better at handling the relatives. Morgan didn't care about her caseload. Amanda wasn't just another file to her. She was her sister. Twin sister, now that she remembered a few of the specifics.

"I'm sorry, Ms. Cramer. That sounded horrible."

"It's okay. I understand what you meant."

It wasn't okay, at least not with Ivy and probably not with Morgan, either. She'd been insensitive, and her apology hadn't been that much better.

"It's that I've only recently acquired all of Detective Burns' case files and haven't gone through everything yet."

"No worries. I understand. I only wanted to make sure somebody was still looking into her case, and she wasn't forgotten."

There it was. Morgan thought her sister's case would be forgotten and wanted to talk to somebody who would act like they cared, and Ivy had blown it.

"I assure you, your sister will not be forgotten."

"Good. I'm glad."

Another silence. Ivy couldn't tell if Morgan was waiting for an update or if she was holding something back. She felt like it was the latter but wasn't sure why a reporter would be so timid when speaking to a cop, or really, anybody. Hopefully, she wasn't using her sister's death as a way to try to get information on The Suicide Killer. Ivy grabbed her purse and gun and walked out the door.

"Good. I have your number now, so how about I call you back when I have a chance to go through the case file thoroughly? I hate to, but I really must go. It looks like The Suicide Killer has resurfaced, and I have to get to the scene. Shit, I uh..."

Ivy even stopped in her driveway and put her free hand to her forehead for effect, even though Morgan couldn't see her. It helped her play off that she had accidentally slipped up.

"Damn. I don't suppose ... I don't suppose I could convince you not to tell anybody yet, could I?"

Ivy had given her an open door. Time to see if she walked through or not. She wasn't giving her anything that everybody wouldn't know soon enough. If it was him, he'd be letting somebody know.

"No worries, detective. I don't work the crime beat anymore. Your secret is safe with me."

She really was only calling to find out about her sister's case. Ivy felt terrible about thinking the worst of her because of her job. Ivy had to deal with the same issues daily and was now projecting it onto other people. She opened the door to her unmarked car and threw her purse in the passenger's seat.

"I appreciate your discretion. I'll talk to you soon," Ivy said and hung up the phone.

She threw her car in reverse and backed out of the driveway. She may have told Morgan information she should have kept to herself, but she hadn't told her the most crucial part. The Suicide Killer may have resurfaced, and they had a potential witness.

Chapter Five

Morgan sat her phone on the kitchen table. Ivy wasn't who she'd expected. She sounded young on the phone. That didn't mean anything, but she had made a mistake and told Morgan about a potential new victim of a serial killer, and that could cause a panic if it were to get out too soon. That was a rookie mistake. Or had she done it on purpose to see what Morgan would say? That didn't make sense. Unless she thought Morgan knew more than she had already told the police. It wouldn't be surprising. Hell, Morgan wouldn't blame her if she did think she was hiding something. Morgan didn't believe herself most of the time.

All of that didn't matter, though. Morgan had plenty of other things to worry about now. She had spent a lot of time trying to find out who the new detective on her sister's case was, but why had she done it? Was it for her, or was it for someone unknown to her who liked to kill people? That asshole had promised he wouldn't kill anybody if she found out who was on his case. He lied. Morgan laughed and quickly sat up straight. The sudden break in silence as her laugh echoed through the house startled her. Of course he lied. He was a criminal. What else had she expected?

The worst part is he did it right after he'd left her house. He knew he was planning on killing somebody after they finished talking. If his bloodlust was as strong as he made it out to be, he could have saved himself a lot of trouble and killed her. Her hand shook as she picked up her coffee. She tried to steady it as she brought the cup to her lips.

She didn't know what to do. A car horn blew outside and startled her. Hot coffee sloshed over the edge of her cup and scorched her mouth and left hand.

"Shit," she yelled and grabbed a dishtowel.

She patted her swollen lip dry and then wrapped the towel around her burnt hand. Pressure from wringing the towel felt good and took her mind off the pain, which had taken her mind off her current situation. It had worked for a minute, but time was fleeting. The Suicide Killer had been to her house twice now. Both times he left without killing her, even though he almost had the first time, but that was her fault for attacking him. Now, she didn't think he would have hurt her that night. But why?

She had the information he wanted, and said she'd get it for him, but if she flipped on the porch light, she would be inviting him into her house this time. She'd knowingly allow a murderer into her home. He said he wouldn't kill her, and she believed him, but it was different for him to show up randomly. She couldn't be held liable if he showed up when he wanted to. She wasn't giving him any information that he wouldn't find out eventually, anyway. It wouldn't hurt if she told him. However, if she didn't tell him and he found out, he might change his mind about not hurting her. She might be his next victim. Plus, he said he would find out who killed her sister. It didn't look like the cops were in any hurry to find out who did it.

Morgan walked to the door and flipped the switch to the porch light.

Chapter Six

Ivy stood on Meadow Butler's front porch. She hadn't realized the victim had lived so close to her. It had only taken her ten minutes to arrive, and that was only because the light at Green Ridge took forever. Ivy turned her head to the left and then to the right to crack her neck. This was not her first time at a murder scene. She'd been to many of them over the years, but this was the first one she had been to with a high enough profile that people from outside the city knew about it. She took a deep breath and reached for the doorknob.

The door swung open before her hand could reach the knob. Mark Harper from the Crime Scene Unit stood holding the door open.

"What are you doing out here? Waiting for somebody to invite you inside?"

She had seen Mark at a number of scenes, but this was the first time he'd ever spoken to her. Everybody said he didn't speak to the uniformed cops because he believed they were beneath him. He had a contentious relationship with a number of the detectives because he thought he was smarter than all of them. And none of them were more contentious than his relationship with Greg Burns. Ivy was Greg's replacement, but she hadn't planned on being his substitute in a toxic game.

"Thank you," she said and quickly walked past Mark before he had a chance to say anything else to her.

A pleasant scent that Ivy couldn't place wafted into the foyer from the living room. Ivy pulled on latex gloves and stepped around several crime scene evidence markers. The scent grew as she walked closer to the bedroom. A recently extinguished candle sat on the coffee table. The label read: Eucalyptus and Tea. Ivy inhaled deeply.

"Hey, Detective, there will be plenty of time to check out the home and garden section when we're done," Mark said from the bedroom.

When had he walked past her? She needed to be careful around Mark. His creepy stalking butler routine would get old rather quickly. She straightened her blazer and stepped into the bedroom.

"Was that candle burning when you guys got here?" She asked.

The three men in the room looked at her like she was a crazy woman, worried about the wrong things instead of the dead body lying on the bed.

"Yes. Does that matter?" asked one of the men she hadn't met yet.

"Maybe. It's an aromatherapy candle to help with focus. Might not mean anything."

The man half smiled and let his shoulders drop.

"She might have lit it before she started studying. Her friend said she had a big anatomy test today that she'd been worried about. The friend came over when she didn't show up for the test. My name's Alex North, by the way."

"Ivy Chandler," she said, and didn't bother expounding on any other information.

Instead, Ivy turned her attention to the girl on the bed. She watched Alex gaze at her from the corner of her eye. They were all the same. There wasn't a day that went by when she was at the academy that one of her fellow cadets hadn't tried to hit on her. There was only one incident where he wouldn't take no for an answer. He'd put his hand on her shoulder when she tried to walk away. She moved faster than he had anticipated and used a hip toss to throw him on his back. In one swift move, she'd crushed his pride, and then with a stomp of her boot, she'd crushed his manhood. They left her alone after that. She'd effectively stopped all the stray bumps and grabs, but she couldn't stop the stares.

Meadow Butler stared straight up at the ceiling with unblinking, bloodshot eyes. Dried blood ran from her nose and mouth down the side of her neck and pooled on the mattress below her.

"Have you determined the cause of death and time yet?" she asked.

"None of this is official, but according to the witness, the time of death can be placed between 11:00 p.m. and 12:00 a.m. last night. Cause of death is most likely from being smothered," Mark said, holding up a bloodstained pillow. "Witness says she found it over her face. Her nose and right orbital sock are broken, and her jaw is dislocated. All of this is consistent with applied pressure to the face."

Pills filled her mouth and lay scattered across the floor. Small mounds of white powder showed the path of the foot traffic.

"What kind of pills are these? Were they scattered when you guys arrived?"

Mark picked up an evidence bag.

"The pills are Zoloft and were prescribed to the deceased. It's hard to tell. There didn't appear to be any signs of a struggle aside from what occurred on the bed. The woman who found her could have knocked the bottle over. She's still in shock and probably doesn't remember what she touched or knocked over. And don't worry, I didn't move or bag anything before Don got here. I've already taken photos as well."

Ivy stood up straight. Don had already been to the scene. Did he come and go? She hadn't seen his car outside.

"Don was here?"

Mark's face dropped, and Alex shuffled a few steps back toward the wall.

"Yeah. It's his first murder case back. He handled it a lot better than I expected. Especially given that it looks like The Suicide Killer did this."

Ivy paused. She could see the empathy in their eyes. At least they weren't completely desensitized to everything going on around them. She wondered if they would have the same compassion if she were in Don's place.

"What makes you so sure?"

"We found this balled up on the floor," Mark said and handed her an evidence bag containing a crumpled piece of paper.

Ivy took the bag and tried to spread it out well enough to read.

To Whom May Be Concerned,

Are we surprised that we are speaking in this manner? I tried to call out for help and made a friend, but at the end of the game I won, they left me, too.

N

Ivy handed the evidence bag back to Mark. It looked like another nonsense letter from the killer, but it did seem a little more personal, like he was reaching out.

"Don went through the scene but didn't speak with the witnesses. I think that is what got to him."

"Witnesses? I thought there was only the woman who found her?"

"Yeah, she's in the kitchen. The other one is in the backyard with a couple of uniforms."

"They're not really sure what to think about him," Alex said with a smirk.

Shit. This was not going the way Ivy had hoped. Her first high profile case and her partner walked the scene and went AWOL, and now she finds out there are multiple witnesses, or possibly a suspect. Ivy fled the room and quickly walked to the kitchen, dodging evidence markers and stray pills along the way.

All the lights were off in the kitchen. Ivy looked around the room, and the cop leaning against the cracked green formica counter pushed himself off and walked toward the door. The girl sitting with her head in her hands jumped at every hollow thump until the officer stepped outside. So much for being emotionally supportive. He looked like he had been impatiently waiting for somebody to come and take her away so he could get back to doing anything besides sitting with an emotional witness.

Ivy pulled a chair out from under the table, and the woman snapped her head up. She could see the tension leave the young woman's face when she saw an empathetic face.

"My name is Ivy Chandler. I'm a detective with the Crystal Valley Police Department. If you don't mind, I'd like to ask you a few questions."

The woman nodded, and Ivy sat down.

"Okay, Ms. ..."

The woman sat up straight and finished wiping the rest of her makeup off on the stretched-out sleeves of her mauve sweater.

"Torres. Cassie Torres," she said and wiped her face again.

Her face was puffy from crying, and her voice sounded dry and raspy.

"Would you like a glass of water, Ms. Torres?"

Cassie sat up straighter and cleared her throat.

"No, ma'am. I just want to tell you what I know, so I can leave. I feel like I'm trapped in here. I tried to talk to the other officers. They said I had to wait for you."

"I'm sorry. I'll be as quick as I can. What can you tell me about what happened?"

"Meadow and I are in the same anatomy class, and we had a big test today. We'd been studying for weeks, and she wasn't at school this morning. She never skipped class, and she would never have missed that test. We have to pass it to get into the nursing program."

Cassie took a deep breath and looked down at her clenched hands. Ivy nodded for her to continue.

"After the test, I um ... I came over, and there was a guy curled up against the wall. He wouldn't look at me. Just screamed, 'she's dead. She's dead and won't get out of my head.' So I ran through the house and found Meadow with a pillow over her face in the bedroom. I pulled it off and ... and ... she, I ..."

Tears welled in the corners of her eyes. Ivy jumped in to stop her train of thought before she started crying again and wouldn't be able to finish.

"Do you know the guy? Were he and Meadow dating?"

Cassie shook her head and pulled her hands into her sleeves. Ivy looked at her so she would continue without being prompted. It would be easier if she didn't have to pull all the information from her.

"I don't know if she was serious with anybody. Maybe. She didn't talk about anybody she was dating until it got serious. She didn't want to introduce somebody who might not be around next week."

"Does he seem like her type?"

"I don't know. Do you think maybe he killed her?"

Cassie's voice grew higher in pitch. She jumped up.

"Oh my God. He could have ... he could have ... I didn't even think. I could have been next," Cassie said. The fabric of her sweater muffled her voice.

Cassie's breathes quickened as she hyperventilated. She put her hand on her stomach and doubled over. Ivy remained seated. She needed to calm Cassie down. Ivy placed her hand flat on the table in front of her.

"Cassie. Hey, Cassie. Listen to me. It would help to calm down if you sat. Have a seat. You're safe now. Nobody is going to hurt you. They might have been dating. I'm sure you weren't in any danger."

"I didn't even think about it. He seemed more terrified than I was. I couldn't get anywhere near him, and I was concentrated on Meadow. I didn't think. I could have been killed too."

Ivy wasn't going to get anything else from Cassie. It would be better to let her leave and hope she remembered something helpful after she'd had a chance to calm down. Plus, the man in the house when Cassie arrived sounded like he may have more information. Or he might be a suspect.

Ivy stood and pulled a business card from the inside pocket of her blazer and placed it in Cassie's shaking hand.

"Thank you, Cassie. I don't have any further questions. You're free to go, but here's my card in case you think of something later."

Cassie accepted the card and pulled it into her sleeve.

"Thank you. Please catch whoever did this to my friend."

"I promise to do my best. Are you going to be okay to drive home? I can have one of the officers drive you."

She shook her head and headed toward the front door.

"No. I'll be fine. Everything will be fine," she whispered.

Ivy walked out the backdoor. The cop who had been holding up the counter in the kitchen stood with three other officers around a slumped figure sitting at the patio table. Apparently, they were treating him like a suspect instead of a witness. It didn't surprise her. Cassie made the 911 call, and he was already in the house, but he was clearly distressed. It could have been shock from seeing a dead body. Ivy still remembered her first. A teenager fell asleep at the wheel and ran off the road into a ravine. His truck hit a tree head on. They said he died instantly, but how do they know? Does anybody ever die instantly? Can life be turned off as quickly as a light switch? Unfortunately, it didn't work that way for Meadow Butler. Somebody held her down and slowly suffocated the life from her as she tried to fight them off.

"Can one of you guys make sure the other witness makes it home safely?"

The sound of her voice surprised the man sitting in the chair. He jumped and flipped over backward in his chair.

"Shit. No, no, you can't be here. It's not fair; you can't do this to me," the man yelled. The three officers waiting with him ran and tackled him to the ground before he could make any more movements toward Ivy.

Much to Ivy's surprise, the counter holder didn't jump at the man's actions. He walked around the side of the house without saying a word. She watched after him with the man still yelling behind her.

"He was the first officer on scene. He's been here dealing with this shit all morning," one of the officers informed her.

Ivy turned and watched the man futilely struggle against the cops. If this guy had been like this all morning, she didn't blame the cop for wanting to get out of here. Anything would be welcome from dealing with a possible psychiatric call on top of a murder.

The cops jerked the man back up and sat him in another chair. Ivy walked closer but didn't sit down and put herself at a disadvantage if he decided to freak out again. She also stayed clear of the table so he couldn't use it as a weapon.

"What's your name?"

The man didn't say anything. He covered his head and muttered to himself.

"His name's Bobby Cotton," one of the officers said.

"Okay, Bobby. I'm going to need you to answer some questions so we can figure out what happened here," Ivy said while staring down the cop who told her his name. He didn't hold eye contact.

His name, Bobby Cotton, sounded familiar, but she couldn't remember where she'd seen or heard it before. Or if she'd ever heard it at all. His first name was common enough that she could be remembering it from anywhere. She was pretty sure she'd arrested a few before.

Bobby stirred but didn't look up at her. She stepped closer and put her hand on his shoulder. His body stiffened, but he didn't move. He froze like an animal that doesn't want to be touched but is too terrified to run away. Two of the cops' hands slid to the butts of their pistols while the other reached for his cross draw taser. All CVPD cops wore their tasers cross draw as a failsafe so they would know what they were pulling on a suspect in a heated situation.

Ivy waved them off with her head, and they all took a step back but didn't move their hands. She didn't know if he was a witness or a suspect, but it was clear he was suffering from some sort of mental episode.

"Bobby?" she tried again. A wracking wave of emotion fluttered under her hand, and she had to hold the officers from moving in again.

"Do you need an ambulance? I need to talk to you, but if you are in distress and need help, I'll call somebody for you."

Ivy removed her hand, and Bobby raised his head but wouldn't look at her. Instead, he stared off in the opposite direction and slowly shook his head.

"No, ma'am. I don't need anything. I'll be fine."

His voice betrayed him. Ivy knew he wasn't telling the truth. He only told her what she wanted to hear so she wouldn't call the ambulance. Hopefully, his recounting of events wouldn't also be what he thought she wanted to hear.

"Okay, good. I know this has been a pretty traumatic day, but I need to ask you a few questions. Do you think you can do that for me?"

Bobby pushed back from the table and stared directly at her. It took everything in her not to jump back. It was apparent he'd been crying for a while, but his dark eyes looked like the black marble eyes of a discarded doll.

"I'm not a child. You don't have to handle me like I'm going to break."

The abrupt change in his demeanor caught her off guard, and if she was being honest with herself, it scared her a little. The hairs on the back of her neck and arms stood on end. The change in mood brought a shift in atmosphere as a cold breeze kicked up on an already cool morning. The cops felt it too. She'd never seen anybody ever make such a sudden about face. He wasn't acting the way she would expect somebody in his position to act, but a lot of people didn't react the way we expect they should.

"You're right. I'm sorry. I misunderstood your grief. It must be hard to lose somebody this way. Do you mind telling me what happened?"

Bobby licked his dry lips and looked her up and down. Ivy grabbed the opening of her blazer and pulled it closed. At this point in her life, it was pure instinct to cover herself from every leering man within proximity, even when they were across the room. But this was different. He'd completely changed. One minute he's terrified of her, the next he can't keep his eyes off her. It wasn't sexual. It was something different that she couldn't describe. Was it fascination? No matter what it was, she could still see the fear in his eyes and the slight tremble in his limbs. She needed to be careful with him.

"Yeah, I um ... Meadow and I were going to meet up this morning. When I got here, the door was wide open, so I walked in. I walked into her bedroom and ... and she was dead."

Another wave flowed through Bobby's body. Ivy hoped it was only a cold chill. She didn't think she could take another breakdown from this guy.

"Meadow's friend said she had an important test this morning. You were going to get breakfast?"

Bobby cut his eyes to the cops, then back to Ivy.

"Yeah, she did. She watches her brother and sister until eleven on Thursday nights. When she got home, she had planned to stay up all night cramming for it, so I was going to see if I could take her to Waffle House before class."

"Her family and friends don't know that you two were seeing each other?"

Bobby shifted.

"No. She had this weird rule that she didn't let anybody meet who she was dating. She didn't want her family to get attached to somebody that could be out of the picture soon."

"And how long had you two been seeing each other?"

"Two months."

That was a long time to go without anybody knowing who she was dating. After that amount of time, it'd seem like a chance encounter would have happened. But he did know about the rule, so he at least knew her well enough for her to tell him about her dating rule.

"I get not meeting the family, but it seems like a long time to go without being introduced to her friends."

"I guess she'd been burned in the past. She didn't want to talk to me about it either."

"What happened after you found Meadow?"

"I freaked out," Bobby said and sniffed as he rubbed new tears from his eyes. "I left my cellphone in my car, so I ran back through the house. When I got to the foyer, some guy came running out of nowhere and ran into me—"

"Wait. The killer was here when you arrived?"

Ivy's mouth went dry, and her hands broke out in a sweat. She was looking at Bobby like a possible suspect, but he might have been an eyewitness. She tried to hide her excitement from Bobby and the cops. It would be highly unprofessional to get excited while the witness was only worried about his dead loved one in the house. She looked over at the cops. They all had their hand on their guns, fighting back excitement as they rocked on their toes. The Suicide Killer had terrified the entire city, and with the help of Greg Burns, he had made the police department look like fools. High-ranking officers, many beloved within the department, had been forced into early retirement in the aftermath.

She hadn't anticipated getting anything good from Bobby today. With the way he was acting, she thought she'd have to track him down in a few days once he'd had time to calm down. Now, she steadied her hands as she reached into her blazer and pulled out a small notebook and pen.

"I know I look like a coward, but he scared the shit out of me. I thought he was going to kill me. I don't know why he didn't."

"I don't think you're a coward. On the contrary, you have every right to be terrified, being that close to a killer."

Bobby leaned back. The side of his face twitched. Was he trying to stifle a smile? She was still in control. There was no reason to let her nerves get to her and cause her to miss something. He looked her up and down again and stared at the metal patio table. Ivy shifted. Her legs were already closed, but she pressed them together harder until she was almost clenching. She was wearing pants, but Bobby made her feel vulnerable, like he was looking through the tiny diamond-shaped holes on the table, trying to see her from any angle he could.

"Thank you. I keep thinking if only I hadn't wussed out, I could have stopped Meadow's killer. I'd be a hero and talking to the news now instead of you."

The pitch and clarity of Bobby's voice rose as he spoke about being a hero. It was the first time she started to hear the full volume of his voice. Until now, it had remained slightly above a raspy whisper.

"There's no glory in being dead. He could have killed you, too."

"Life is nothing but a game of infamy."

This conversation was beginning to get away from her. If she didn't steer it back to the case, she'd end up listening to his entire philosophical diatribe.

"Did you get a good look at the guy who ran into you? Anything you can think of could be helpful. I know it was dark, and you were upset and not expecting to be blindsided by him."

Bobby looked over at the cops.

"He was about as tall as this guy," Bobby said, pointing at one of the cops, "though he was a lot skinnier, not as many doughnuts would be my guess."

The taller cop moved toward the table, and Ivy waved him off.

"Okay, so he was about six feet."

"6'2," the officer interrupted.

Ivy tried to ignore him.

"Okay, 6'2. Is there anything else you remember about him?"

Bobby smiled like Norman Bates in his jail cell. It was unnerving.

"He was dressed in all black and had a mask on."

Ivy took a deep breath and let it out. The height wasn't going to help much.

"Oh, yeah," Bobby said. He seemed to get a kick out of Ivy perking up. "When he got to the door, he stopped and laughed at me. When he did, I looked up and saw a long scar down his left arm. It went from the inside of his elbow down his arm and continued under his gloves."

A scar. That was great. It was a pretty distinct scar. If anybody else had ever seen it, they would likely remember something like that. Now that she thought about it, she remembered something about a similar scar, but she couldn't think of where it was from. She had never seen one like that but remembered reading about one somewhere.

"That's good. That will help a lot when we find a suspect. Is there anything else you can remember about him?"

Bobby adjusted himself in his seat and tried to speak but grabbed his throat before anything came out. Cassie said she'd found him screaming, and he was still screaming when the first cops showed up on the scene. It surprised Ivy that he'd been able to talk as much as he had.

"No. That's it. He was wearing all black, and it was dark in there," Bobby said in his original raspy whisper.

Until he'd mentioned the clothes, it hadn't crossed Ivy's mind that Bobby was also wearing all black. She didn't think he had anything to do with the murder, but it could be why the killer ran into him in the first place. She hoped he hadn't gotten as good of a look at Bobby as Bobby did at him. It could make him a target. It might be a good idea to put an unmarked car on him for a few days. Ivy stood and pulled a card from her pocket.

"Thank you for your time, Mr. Cotton. I'm sorry for your loss. Here's my card. Please don't hesitate to call me if anything comes to mind that might help us find out who killed Meadow."

Tears filled his eyes again as he stood and took the card from Ivy. She had to force herself not to react when he reached too far, and his cold, clammy hands grabbed hers. A shudder worked its way up her back, and she withdrew her hand before it made it down her arm.

As Bobby left, he didn't walk back through the house. He went around the side to the back gate. Before he crossed the street, he turned and took one last look. Ivy couldn't tell if he was looking at her or taking one last look at his girlfriend's house before leaving.

There was no doubt that Bobby Cotton was a strange and creepy man, but that didn't make him a murderer. Ivy didn't believe he killed Meadow Butler, but she would also make sure she was never alone with him if she had to speak to him again.

Ivy involuntarily shuddered again and pushed him from her mind. She had more important things to do, like notifying the next of kin and tracking down her partner.

Chapter Seven

Ivy walked onto the station floor, looking for Don Murphy. She'd tried to call him three times on her way to notify Meadow Butler's parents. It wasn't the first notification she'd been a part of, but it was the first one she'd done by herself. It went about as bad as she expected it to go. It was never easy seeing a family member hear the news that they wouldn't see their loved one again. It was even worse having to tell the parents of a young person or child. Tears wash the light from their eyes away, and it will never be rekindled.

Don didn't have any children, but Ivy could see the same dark look in his eyes from losing his wife. Ivy wished she'd known him before everything had happened. Don sat in his cubicle staring at the computer screen or the back wall. Ivy couldn't tell. She only saw his unblinking eyes glaring intently at something.

She walked around the side and grabbed the rolling chair from her own cubicle. One of the wheels stuck and screeched as it dug a trench in the freshly waxed floor. Don didn't react. Ivy clapped him on the back, rousing him from watching his blank screen.

"Sorry I missed you this morning. You okay?"

Don turned and looked at Ivy. It was obvious from his red-rimmed eyes that he'd been crying. He was beyond hiding it from the guys in the department. Ivy respected the vulnerability in a typically testosterone driven arena. She didn't want to rush him or ruin a potential reverie of a happier time with his wife, so she waited for him to respond and tried not to stare. When Don finally spoke, his voice was dry and cracked.

"I ... um ... I'm sorry. I had to get out of there. Sorry I wasn't around for the notification, but I don't think I would have made it through that. Were they able to tell you anything helpful?"

He was on the verge of breaking down again, so Ivy grabbed his lifeline question.

"No. There wasn't anything out of the ordinary when she left their house last night. They didn't know she was dating anybody, but according to people in her life, that sounds like SOP for Meadow when she starts dating somebody new. The boyfriend, who originally found her, ran into the perp in the hallway. We didn't get much. Height, size, and a description of a scar."

Don's eyes cleared. He sat up straight and sniffed. He was excited. Ivy put her hand up. He'd been through enough and didn't want to give him any false hope that they had a witness who could identify the killer.

"He was wearing a mask, so there's no facial description. He's a white guy, which we expected, so no real news there, either, but he did say the guy had a long scar going down the inside of his left arm. That sounds familiar, like I've read it somewhere, but I can't remember where it was. I looked through the files again but couldn't find any mention of it anywhere."

Don fell back in his seat like all the air had been sucked from his lungs.

"I'm not sure. None of that sounds familiar to me."

Ivy hadn't expected it to. Since working with Don, she'd tried not to bring up Greg's name, not knowing how he would react. All The Suicide Killer files were Greg's, and she'd assumed Don had been avoiding them.

"No worries. We'll catch him," Ivy said, trying to sound supportive and optimistic, but the words came out hollow and cliché.

"I pray you do, but I won't be involved."

Ivy's fake smile fell.

"Why?"

"Before this morning, all I wanted to do was find this fucker. I was fine at the scene until we found the balled up note, and I lost it. That's why I wasn't there when you arrived. I couldn't breathe and felt like I was having a heart attack. So I drove down the road and had to pull over in a parking lot until I calmed down."

"I wish you would have called me or at least seen the paramedics on scene."

"I was fine. It was only a panic attack. I came back here and asked Lieutenant York if she would keep you on the case but replace me. After I told her who it was, she said she wouldn't have kept me on no matter how much I'd fought her."

That made sense. Of course, Don couldn't work the case when his wife and previous partner were victims. A lot of people would have argued to stay on, but Don was beaten down and defeated.

"I'll get with her later and see what she says. Don't worry; I'll keep you in the loop with what's happening."

Don leaned back in his chair.

"I appreciate it, but I'd rather you didn't."

Don must have noticed the shock on Ivy's face because he continued before she had a chance to speak.

"I appreciate it, and I know it sounds crazy, but if you keep me updated, it will rip everything open every time there's a setback or a lead doesn't pan out. I don't think I can go through that. Just let me know when you find out who it is so I can be there when you arrest the bastard. Until then, I'll be working on all of our outstanding cases so you can focus on this one."

Ivy nodded and rolled her chair back to her desk. Don's reaction surprised her, but it was the right way to handle things. It was a hard decision to make, but it would be the easiest one for everybody. She'd read too many times where an officer, who was emotionally invested in a case, inserted themselves and made everything so much worse for everyone involved. Even helped a few guilty people's cases get thrown out of court. She pulled her notebook out of her pocket and prepared to type up her report when she heard Don's chair squeaking. She turned, and he had his head buried under his desk in a box of Greg's old case files. Greg wasn't the most organized detective she'd seen.

Don bumped his head on the desk as he popped up.

"Damn it," he said, rubbing the top of his head. "That hurt. I was thinking about that scar. It didn't sound familiar at first, but then I remembered a random note from another case we worked on."

Don flipped briskly through the thin pages.

"Here. Here it is. You didn't see it because it was in Greg's notes on a closed case. Some girl named Emily. Don't have a last name. Anyway, she killed herself in Rusted Lakes Park around the time all

The Suicide Killer stuff started. She was quickly ruled out as a victim. But Greg wrote this at the bottom of his notes. It didn't make sense to me at the time, but now—" he trailed off and handed the notebook to Ivy.

Ivy took the notebook. At the bottom, in quickly scratched writing, was the suspect's description: white, 6'2, black hair, hazel eyes, cleft chin, long scar on left arm from elbow to wrist. Ivy got excited by the potential break in the case, but what followed the description had her jumping out of her chair and making everybody stop and look at her like she was on fire. Flames of excitement ran through her arms and down her spine. In dark black ink like Greg had gone over the lines multiple times was Daily Grind Bobby Cotton.

Chapter Eight

Bobby sat outside Morgan's house. The porch light had burned bright for two days. He wasn't in a hurry to get back to her. Because of Emily, he not only found out who the new detective was on his case, but he'd met her face to face. Emily had almost driven him crazy. She wouldn't leave him alone and had cornered him against the wall. It was embarrassing that he'd been found cowering in a dark foyer. It sounded like multiple versions of her circling around and sweeping in closer to torment him. He could have left, but she would have followed. The last thing he'd needed was to be run off the road by somebody he couldn't prove was even there.

Everything changed when Ivy Chandler walked up to the table in Meadow's backyard. She looked exactly like Emily. She was professional and attempted to be a bit intimidating in her blue suit, but put her in a summer dress, and he bet she'd look just as sweet and innocent as Emily. She even wore her hair in the same high ponytail. It was light and flirty on Emily, but on Ivy, it was domineering. It was interesting how a style could affect the way somebody was perceived. At first, Ivy had scared Bobby because he thought Emily had physically manifested and wanted to hurt him. He hadn't seen her walk around since the first night he met her, when he was with Danielle. It didn't make sense that she'd been able to find him like that. The only thing he'd changed about his process was he hadn't waited for an unlocked door. He couldn't hold himself back and busted the window to get inside. It could have all been a coincidence, but everything started going to shit when he changed the way he played the game. He'd cheated, and Emily, ripped from the grave, was back in his life.

None of the cars sitting on the road were new to the street, and no vans were present. Bobby cautiously stepped from the car he borrowed from a neighbor he'd never met. There didn't seem to be any cops waiting to swarm him when he approached her door. He'd like to believe that Morgan hadn't told anybody about him showing up, but with the things that had been going on with him lately, he couldn't get too comfortable. Maybe he should have ordered takeout and waited to see what happened to the delivery driver before he knocked on the door. It was too late now.

He splashed in a puddle beside the curb and dragged his boots across the grass to dry them a bit. He didn't want to show up and track dirty water through her house. The hairs on the back of his neck stood on end. The feeling he was being watched flowed through his body, and he quickly ran up the stairs to Morgan's door. When he reached the top step, he turned and surveyed the dark neighborhood again. The street was silent, and all the windows of the surrounding houses were dark. Nothing moved or made a sound, but the feeling of being watched persisted. There was only one person who could sneak up on him like that. There was a time when it hadn't bothered him. He'd welcomed it. But now, for the first time, he was scared of her.

Bobby shook the webs of fear from his head and knocked on the solid wood hard. There was no time for "Shave and a Haircut." He bounced on his toes while waiting for Morgan to answer the door. He'd never been so anxious, like waiting for the door to open on your first date. It was a new feeling for him, and he hated it.

The door opened a crack, and a tired eye peered out at him. He saw the recognition when the eye opened further. There was still fear, but it was waning. Eventually, she'd realize he was telling the truth when he said he would never hurt her. Too bad he'd never be able to reciprocate. The ramifications were much too large for him to remove his mask around her. But, even if she didn't fear him, she still had her morals and wouldn't think twice about turning him in.

Morgan stepped back from the door and let it swing open. He stepped inside and wiped his feet on the mat as she backed herself to the kitchen table. Waning fear, but she still didn't trust him enough to show him her back. He didn't blame her for that. Empty chip bags and a TV dinner tray littered the table around her laptop. A crumpled blanket lay on the floor in front of the chair where she sat. She'd been camping out in the kitchen again. Waiting until he arrived. Anxiety that would never be confused for anxious longing tightened her shoulders. No doubt, a concealed weapon lay hidden somewhere within reach. She exhaled in a heavy huff as he sat down across from her and stared, waiting for her to speak as she waited for him. When he said nothing, she began.

"The light's been on for two days."

"Looks like it's been that long since you've been to sleep."

Morgan shifted stiffly in her chair.

"Or taken a shower, for that matter."

"Yeah, well, inviting a serial killer into your home will do that to a person. Especially if you don't know when he'll show up."

"I told you I'm not going to hurt you. I don't know how else to say it, so you'll believe me."

"You keep saying that, but there's no way I can believe you. I'm definitely not going to believe you after you promised me you wouldn't kill anybody and then you do it, anyway. You did it right after you left my house."

"You heard about that, huh?"

Bobby's facial features would have given her a look of hesitant self-reproach if she could have seen his face. But Bobby felt the movement under the knitted mask and realized she was the one person he didn't want to know what he was up to.

"Don't be coy with me. The detective on your case told me."

Bobby slid back from the table. The quick movement caused Morgan to jump, but she didn't make any sudden movements toward her weapon. Bobby started pacing in front of the table.

"So you found out who it is?"

"Against my better judgment, yes, I did."

"So, what's his name?"

He knew the answer but needed to play along with the game. Why would Ivy tell Morgan that The Suicide Killer had killed somebody else? That was a rookie mistake. Or a seasoned tactic. Maybe she tried to set her up since she was seemingly calling at random. Bobby pivoted and walked across the kitchen to the sink. There was no movement behind him. He couldn't let Morgan know he'd already met Ivy. If they talk again, Morgan might tell her, and Ivy might be able to put everything together. Everything was getting risky again. It was thrilling, but he had to calm himself. This wasn't like things were in the beginning, and he doubted Ivy was anything like Greg had been.

Morgan's lips trembled like she was fighting to keep the words in, but in the end, she lost the battle.

"Ivy Chandler."

Bobby looked up at the ceiling and laughed.

"Ivy? Like a girl? They have a girl on my case?"

"Yes, they have a *woman* on your case."

The truth was Bobby didn't really care if the detective was male or female. He assumed they didn't have a chance at ever catching him, no matter what sex they were. He had to have some reaction. Now he wished he hadn't gone the sexist route.

"And she sounded like she was on top of everything. She might be knocking on your front door sooner than you think."

She said it like she wanted to believe it was true, but the squirming in her seat gave her away. She didn't believe what she was saying, either.

"That's highly unlikely. It doesn't matter if they're a man or a *woman*," Bobby said and pushed off the counter.

"You sound off. What's wrong with you?"

"Aww. Be careful, or I'll start thinking you care about me."

Morgan's lip quivered, and an ugly sneer crossed her face.

"That will never happen. You're just not acting the way you usually do."

"Well, damn, you don't have to make that face. But how is it that you think I usually act?"

She didn't hesitate as Bobby slid back into the chair across from her.

"Like an obnoxious, pompous ass."

"Ouch. I bet that'd hurt if I cared what people thought about me. But you're right. I am feeling a bit off at the moment. Somebody I thought was gone has recently come back into my life, and I haven't been sleeping well."

"Why don't you kill them the way you do the innocent women you don't know?"

"Damn. Morgan has her claws out tonight. Although, I must say, I might be feeling off, but I do like this feisty side of you. I feel like I'm finally getting to know the real you."

"We're not friends, and I don't like you. Don't think for a second that if I knew who you really were that I wouldn't call Detective Chandler and tell her your name."

"No doubt. But that reminds me, I need to get Ivy's number from you."

Morgan stood up suddenly and stood with one foot in the living room and the other firmly planted in the kitchen.

"No way. I'm not giving you her number. You asked for her name, and I found that out, but only because you would eventually find out, anyway. I'm not giving you direct access to her so she can end up like Greg."

Bobby stood up but Morgan stood her ground. She wasn't going to waver on the number.

"Okay, that hurt. Greg was my best friend. I didn't get him killed because I wanted to. He gave me no other choice."

Bobby bent his head to the side, and his neck cracked four times. Morgan's face never changed, but he could see her cellphone lying next to her laptop. He backed up and leaned against the table in front of the computer.

"I'm glad we're not friends if that's how you treat them."

He reached behind his back and touched the edge of the phone. He slowed down before he pushed it too far away, and she realized what he was doing.

"I don't believe you won't hurt her, too. I couldn't live with myself if I gave you the key to get inside her head."

"I'd only enter if it was unlocked."

"What? That doesn't make sense."

Bobby wrapped his fingers around the phone and pulled it across the table until it rested against his butt.

"Doesn't it, though?"

He lifted the phone and slipped it into his back pocket.

"I don't have time for this. I'm exhausted and need to go to bed."

Bobby looked at his watch-free wrist.

"Yes, it's getting late. I should be going now. I have to work tomorrow."

A weird look that he didn't understand crossed Morgan's face.

"Oh. Not Suicide Killer work," Bobby laughed. "I have to go to my day job. If you need anything, just turn on your porch light again, and I'll come running like Batman to the Commissioner."

"Don't hold your breath. On second thought, do hold your breath," Morgan said, and a sadistic smile slid across her face.

He smiled beneath his mask. She was getting comfortable with him and building a rapport. Or she actually meant it. Either way, she turned her back to him and walked through the living room to the hallway that led to her bedroom.

Bobby turned to leave, and she poked her head back through the doorway. He froze at the sound of her voice. He'd been caught. She knew he had her phone, and now she wanted it back. He should have known she would miss it. Everybody always had their phone attached to them at all times.

"Umm ... I just realized I don't know what to call you."

"The Suicide Killer is a bit long, I suppose. Just call me Stephen. All my friends do."

Morgan gripped the doorway and looked at the ground.

"Okay. Stephen. Have you happened to have found anything out about my sister's case?"

He had her. She wasn't afraid of him, and she needed him. A new feeling of power flooded his body. He'd never felt this way before. Her tensed muscles fell when he didn't answer right away, and she sagged against the wall. He hated to let her down. He had some information but knew it wouldn't be enough to make her happy yet.

"I'm sorry, but I haven't found anything out yet."

She looked like she was about to cry.

"It was a long shot, anyway."

The last time he was here, she'd acted like she didn't want any help from him. Now that she'd had time to think about it, the thought of seeing the person who killed her sister brought to justice was stronger than the means by which the information was found.

"I did acquire the file for her case," he said and held up his hand. "Don't ask how I got it, but I haven't had a chance to read over it yet. I've been busy."

Her face lit up. The little things could make her happy. Then, as fast as it lit up, her face fell. She had to be thinking about how many laws he'd broken to get it, or maybe it had hit her why he'd been busy.

"Thank you."

He walked to the door and flipped off the porch light before quietly opening and shutting the door behind him. It was strange she hadn't begged to see her sister's file.

Chapter Nine

Ivy brushed a stray hair behind her ear and pulled her ponytail tight before stepping out of her car. It looked like she had arrived at The Daily Grind after the lunch rush. The small parking lot sat empty except for a few cars in front of Arkwright Construction. The sound of machinery moving large pieces of stone from the rubble of The Rusted Lakes sign was the only thing ruining an otherwise beautiful afternoon. Somebody rammed a stolen car into the sign two months ago, and the city was only now getting around to cleaning up the mess. There was no word on if they would be replacing it or not. They never caught the assailant, but it was a wonder they were even able to walk away from the wreck at all.

A small bell chimed as Ivy walked inside. The only person in the shop was the female barista behind the counter. Bobby wasn't there. However, there was a chance he was in the back.

"Good morning, welcome to The Daily Grind. What can I get started for you?"

Ivy hadn't planned on ordering, but she hadn't gotten much sleep last night, and some caffeine could help her make it through the rest of the day.

"Uh yeah, sure. Can I get a medium skinny mocha latte?"

"Sure thing. That'll be \$4.65."

Ivy fished a ten-dollar bill from her purse and handed it to the girl.

"I'll have that right out for you," the girl said, and handed Ivy her change.

Ivy put the change in the tip jar and walked around the counter so she could speak to the girl while she made her drink. Her tag said her name was Jody.

"So, Jody, is Bobby working today?"

Jody looked up with a shy smile. There was definitely some unrequited love in that look.

"It's not like that. My name is Ivy Chandler. I'm a detective with the Crystal Valley Police Department."

"Oh no. Is Bobby in trouble?"

Jody stopped making the drink. Her entire body looked ridged and tense.

"No, not at all. He might have seen something related to a case I'm working on, and I had a few questions to see if he could help me out."

The girl's body relaxed, and she continued making the drink. She seemed to buy that excuse.

"Oh, okay. He worked this morning and left about forty-five minutes ago. He'll be in again tomorrow morning."

"Do you happen to know if he was going home when he left here or if he was going somewhere else?"

Jody gave her an accusatory look. She was beginning not to trust Ivy.

"He doesn't really talk that much, but he was in a hurry to get out of here. I made a dumb joke, and he said he had something important to do, so I would guess he didn't go home."

Jody slid Ivy's drink across the counter.

"Thank you for your time."

Ivy stepped from the building and took a sip of her drink. After yesterday, she hadn't expected Bobby to show up for work today, but after the way he acted while she was questioning him, she preferred to talk to him where other people would be around. She didn't know why, but he got under her skin. It could have been because of what he'd just been through, but it was weird how quickly he changed on her. It was like he was two different people. Though, that could be said for most men. Her cellphone rang as she sat down in her car.

"This is Ivy."

"Hello, Detective."

"Yes. This is detective Chandler."

"Oh, I know. I'm the one who called you."

Ivy sat back in her seat. She hoped it wasn't Mark Harper. There shouldn't be anything that he needed to call her for, and she didn't feel like dealing with a smartass right now.

"Since you know who you're talking to, it'd be nice to know who I'm speaking with."

"I'm sure it would be."

Ivy sighed heavily into the speaker.

"Don't get so worked up. I called to introduce myself."

Ivy sat up straight against the wheel. It wasn't Mark.

"For reasons that I'm sure you'll understand, I can't give you my real name. However, everybody in town calls me The Suicide Killer."

All the breath left Ivy's chest. Pinpricks of fear ran up and down her arms. This couldn't be happening. Ivy was thrilled when she found out she'd be working the case but never stopped to think if she would be the new target for the killer, unless it was somebody playing a trick on her. One of the guys at the station could be screwing with her. Maybe they wanted to test her to ensure she wouldn't try to keep it a secret like Greg had. She cleared her throat.

"I understand why you wouldn't do that, but I don't understand why you'd be calling me."

It was his time to sigh into the phone.

"Because, Detective, how are we supposed to be friends if we don't know each other? I know that we can be the best of friends if you will allow it."

If she allowed it? Of course, she wouldn't allow it. She didn't care who was on the other side of the phone. As soon as she got off the line, she would call Lieutenant York.

"That's not going to happen."

"Detective Burns said the same thing in the beginning, but I think I grew on him."

"You killed him."

There was a long pause on the other end of the phone. Ivy pulled the phone from her ear, thinking he had hung up, when she heard him speak again.

"No. Technically, Don killed Greg."

Ivy leaned back in the seat again and chewed the end of her thumbnail.

"You set him up to be killed."

"I guess you could look at it that way, but if he'd laid on the ground, they would have figured out what was going on."

Ivy doubted that, unless they went to kick the gun away and saw that it was taped.

"I don't get that one."

"What don't you get? I didn't want Greg to die. As I've said, we were friends."

"Then why did you kill him?"

There was another long pause. For a serial killer, he was good at acting like he actually cared about detective Burns.

"I had to."

"You didn't have to kill anybody."

"That's easy for you to say."

"That doesn't make sense."

"It never will. But I had to kill Greg because I didn't expect him to be home so soon. He would never have let me leave that house. One of us was leaving in a bag, and it couldn't be me. That's when Greg decided we couldn't be friends anymore."

If he did care or thought he cared about Greg, she might be able to get him talking enough to trip him up so he'd give her something she could use to catch him.

"But every time you've killed somebody, you've made it look like a suicide. Doesn't that bother you?"

A booming laugh caused her to pull the phone from her ear. When she returned it, he was still laughing to himself.

"What makes you think those were my only kills? Just because you know about the ones I left my calling card on doesn't mean you know about all of them."

Ivy felt defeated again. Just when she thought she was getting somewhere, he was ready to pull the rug from under her. Plenty of killers inflated their numbers, but if the police had only chased cases with one MO, they might have overlooked related cases. There's no telling how many more murders were because of him.

"I don't believe you'd abandon your calling card."

"That's your mistake. However, Greg's death was suicide by cop. Given your profession, I would have thought you'd have figured that one out pretty easily."

Another rug.

"You didn't leave a note."

"Who says I didn't leave a note?"

Ivy sat up and gripped the steering wheel. They had been over every inch of that house, and nobody had ever found a note. Now he was screwing with her unless he'd hidden it. But why would he do that? He always wanted them found before.

"I don't belie—"

"Yes. Yes. That's nice. I really have enjoyed meeting with you and look forward to future conversations, but I really must be going now. I don't suppose you've reconsidered telling your superiors about this, have you?"

"Not a chance."

"Well, that wasn't the answer I'd hoped for. No worries. There's always time to turn this relationship around. As an act of goodwill, I'll save you some time from trying to trace my call. I'm in this little rural town that I've already forgotten the name of, but it's right outside of Scarsville. Isn't that a cool name for a town?" he waited for a response, but when Ivy didn't respond, he continued.

"Anyway, I was riding around thinking about us and ended up all the way out here, so I decided to drive some dirt roads. It has been forever since I've done that. I found this awesome road that has a creek running across it. I had so much fun driving back and forth through the water that I almost forgot to call you. I had to drive back to the beginning of the road just to get phone service to call you."

"Why don't you wait, and I'll be there as soon as I can."

More laughing erupted from the phone.

"You're as funny as he was. I'd wait, but I think you'd bring everybody else with you. I've got to go for now, Detective. It has been nice meeting you. We're going to have so much fun together."

The static-filled phone went silent before she had a chance to respond. She threw her phone in the passenger seat. Her hands hurt from gripping the steering wheel tightly. She hadn't noticed what she was doing while talking to him. She put the car in gear and headed to the office.

Chapter Ten

All the Crystal Valley B-squad was on the floor when Ivy burst through the doors. Not a single one of them turned in her direction. They were all caught up in their own cases and didn't have time to notice her. It always struck her as odd to walk into a room with huge news, and nobody knows or cares what's going on. She quickly walked across the floor to Lieutenant York's office, avoiding all eye contact for fear of being stopped.

Lieutenant Debra York stood behind her desk and waved Ivy in when she noticed her loitering outside the door. York didn't intimidate Ivy, but the woman was hard not to be in awe of for the way she ran her shift and kept everybody in line. Her one downfall was Greg Burns. At one time, he'd been her top detective with the highest clearance rate in the department, and she'd let him slide a little more than the rest of the shift. Nobody resented her for it, even when Greg started to slip. Everybody who worked for her loved her, and that was a hell of a feat in the masculine-driven world of the CVPD Homicide Unit. She had been next in line for Captain before her career had pretty much died with Greg. She'd been lucky enough to keep her job, but there were others that weren't as lucky. Ivy hoped her career would see a second life if they caught The Suicide Killer, and everybody forgot about Greg Burns long enough. York waved again, and Ivy almost walked into the door while trying to open it.

"What the hell are you doing out there, Chandler? Looked like you were afraid to come in here. Where have you been?"

Ivy looked down, cleared her throat, and closed the door behind her.

"I was having another go at the vic's boyfriend."

"How'd that go?" York asked, as she flagged somebody else into her office.

Ivy didn't turn, even when the door opened, and they stepped into the room.

"It didn't. He wasn't there. I spoke to the woman he works with. She seemed to think highly enough of him."

"Did you go to his house?" The voice behind her asked incredulously.

Ivy knew the voice before she turned around. Brandon Carson stood behind her, rocking on his toes with a big stupid grin on his face. Why was he even in here? Detective Carson was the biggest pain in the ass in the entire department. Everybody called him Johnny, but Ivy didn't think he was that funny and refused to call him that. She started to speak to him, but he shouldn't even be in there with them, so she didn't have to answer his questions, though Lieutenant York would be wondering the same thing. Ivy stepped in front of Carson so he'd know her back was to him.

"I was about to say that I was planning on going over to his house, but something more important happened," Ivy said, and let it hang in the air long enough for York to kick Carson out of the office. When she didn't, Ivy rolled her eyes up and slightly nodded back at the intruder. York followed her movement, and the hard look on her face dropped.

"Oh. Don't worry about Johnny. I called him in here to tell you that you'd be working the case with him since Don won't be able to work it."

Ivy deflated. She knew they wouldn't allow her to work the case alone, but Carson was the last person she wanted to work with. She closed her eyes and tried not to let on that she didn't want to work with him. York sensed it, though. Carson excused himself as he slid behind Ivy and sat in the far chair in front of Lieutenant York's desk. He crossed his right leg high and let in fall on his left. She wouldn't have been surprised if he'd propped his feet on the desk and kicked back. That's the way he was. Always calm and relaxed, no matter what was going on. It irritated her.

"Yeah, don't worry about me. Go ahead and tell us what happened that was more important than speaking to a witness," he said. He emphasized *what happened* with both of his hands up. She wanted to kick the leg of his chair as he leaned back.

Ivy turned back to Lieutenant York.

"He called me."

Ivy waited for one of them to ask who, but she could tell by the looks on their faces that they both knew who she was talking about.

"What...," Lieutenant York started slightly higher than her normal register. Finally, she cleared her throat, casually sat down, and continued. "What did he say?"

Ivy remained standing, even though she wanted to sit down with them. The weight of this case had been on everybody in the department one way or another, but it wasn't until this moment that it really took hold of her.

"He wanted to introduce himself to me."

Carson laughed, and Ivy glared at him.

"Johnny, now is not really the time."

Ivy continued staring at him until he threw his hands up in surrender and sat straight.

"You're right. I'm sorry, Lieutenant."

Ivy wanted to point out that he should be apologizing to her but let it go.

"He said that he wanted to be friends."

"With friends like him ..." Carson said.

"That's what I told him," Ivy continued.

Lieutenant York straightened.

"What'd he say to that?"

"He told me he didn't kill Greg. Don did."

"Bullshit," York exclaimed and stood. She walked to the window that looked out across the downtown area. "He killed Greg. He was playing a sick game and killed him when he was about to lose."

Ivy felt for Lieutenant York. She'd lost a lot in the past few months, but she'd lost a friend too and was still grieving.

"What else did he say?"

"He said he didn't want Greg to die, but he'd been cornered, and that'd been the only choice he had left."

"I don't give a shit about his feelings. I want to catch the bastard. How did he sound?"

"He sounded obnoxious and arrogant."

York walked back to her desk and grabbed a pen and notepad. She wasn't going to sit back down now.

"Hopefully, that arrogance will get him caught. Did he say anything that would let you know where he was calling from? Do you have the number?"

"I don't have the number. He blocked it."

"Let me have your phone, and I'll have the IT guys see what they can do."

"They don't need to do that. I already know where he was calling from."

"And how do you know that?" Carson butted in.

"Because he told me."

A burst of laughter erupted from the corner. Ivy turned to face Carson and could see everybody in the vicinity looking at them through the window.

"Why ... why would he tell you where he was?"

"Because he wanted me to know. I have no idea what's going on in his head."

Carson slid down in this chair.

"And you believe him?" Carson asked.

"He has no reason to lie."

Carson let out another round of insufferable laughing, followed by, "Of course he has a reason to lie to you. You're a cop and supposedly a good one."

Ivy let the dig at her ability go.

"He's arrogant. He got away with it once and believes he'll get away with it again. He doesn't fear any of us. And I'm willing to bet there's something he wants us to find," Ivy said, turning to York, "that's why I want to ride out there and see if I can find anything."

"Hopefully, it's not another body," York said.

"I don't think so. He didn't mention anybody else and he would have wanted to rub that in my face too."

"Geez, you sound like you already know him. Maybe you will be good friends," Carson said.

Ivy started to speak, but York broke in before her.

"Damn it, Johnny. This is serious shit. I'm giving you a chance to turn things around and show everybody you're not a complete fool, and you're going to screw it up before you even get out of my office."

"Yes, ma'am. I'm sorry."

Ivy felt a pang of sympathy for Carson, but it quickly dissipated. Nobody took him seriously because of the way he acted, but he fed into it and made things worse. It surprised her that York was taking a chance on somebody the department didn't take seriously. It was even more surprising that higher brass allowed her to. Hopefully, they weren't giving her enough rope. Ivy wasn't going to let Carson mess the case up anymore and let York take the fall.

"Where did he tell you he was calling from, Ivy?"

"He said it was a small town he'd already forgotten the name of, but he was close to Scarsville. Some dirt road with a creek running across it."

"Because that sounds real," she heard Carson say under his breath.

She started to say something to him but decided against it when she heard Lieutenant York sigh.

"If we could get a map of the area, I'm sure we could find it," Ivy said.

"No, that'd take too long," York countered.

Ivy let her shoulders drop. Lieutenant York wasn't going to let her go. Ivy needed to get out there before any evidence was washed or carried away.

"I'll make a call. I'll have to give Sheriff John Brown a call to let him know you'll be in his backyard. He'll know the place and can meet you there."

Ivy straightened up. She was going to get to go, but the last thing she needed was a country sheriff who slept his shift away in his patrol car to slow her down.

"With all due respect. I don't have time for small town politics. The sooner I can get out there, the better."

"He sounds like your stereotypical hick sheriff. Looks like one too, but he might surprise you."

Ivy finally sat down. There wasn't anything she could do, and calling the sheriff before traipsing through somebody else's county was the right thing to do, but she didn't have to like it. Lieutenant York pulled a black notebook from her desk and flipped through a few pages until she found the page she was looking for. She hit the speaker button and dialed the number. Several digital rings filled the room. Ivy feared he wasn't going to answer and she'd have to wait until tomorrow to go when the phone clicked, and a gruff voice with a strong Southern drawl answered.

"Thrill me."

Ivy looked up and rolled her eyes, and York tried to stifle a laugh.

"The Suicide Killer is back."

"Yep. That'll 'bout do it. How can I help you with that, Debbie?"

Ivy and Carson looked at each other. Carson mouth Debbie, and Ivy shrugged her shoulders.

"One of my detectives received a call from him," York said.

"Well, damn it, man. That can't be good."

"I didn't think so either, but they believe he was on a dirt road out that way."

"There's a lot of those out here. Goin' to need to be a little more specific," Brown said.

"He said there was a creek running through it. Does that make any sense?"

There was a long pause followed by a loud squeak like the Sheriff was sitting up straighter in his chair now that they had given him some information he could work with.

"Yea, I know the place. Name's Tim's Creek Road. It's an interesting place. Have to pull teenagers out of it every time it rains. Damn, kids think them big trucks can go through anything. Hit that water at the wrong angle, and the next thing you know, you're stuck on a fallen tree. Had to pull a little red truck from there just last week when that storm blowed through."

"That's where we think he was calling from. I wanted to send a couple of my detectives out there to have a look around if it's alright with you."

Ivy moved to speak, but Lieutenant York put her hand up. York had been playing these territorial games for many years and knew how to handle the egos that came along with wearing a badge.

"I suppose I could do that. Just promise me one thing."

Here it was. He was going to want something that York wouldn't be able to do.

"Just promise me if we get out there and find a body, you'll let my guys help on this side of things. They need a little excitement every now and then."

"Done."

Ivy started to protest again, and York shut her down again.

"Great. Tell your detectives to meet me at Crackerland Country Store in Howard in about an hour."

"Seriously?"

"Yep, that's the name of the place. I'll be there with lights on."

"Thanks, John."

Lieutenant York hung up the phone, and Ivy jumped to her feet.

"They can't help with the investigation. They've probably never worked a murder in their career."

"Relax. They won't mess anything up, and besides, you said there wasn't going to be a body out there anyway. They won't steal any of your spotlight."

Ivy stepped back and disengaged from the conversation. It hurt for Lieutenant York to think she was chasing headlines to further her career. Sure, it would be nice, but that wasn't the reason she was here. She hadn't even tried to get this case; they'd put her on it. The look on York's face said she realized that was an unwarranted low blow, but she didn't apologize. She most likely never would, especially in front of Carson. She couldn't show any sign of perceived weakness, or some in the group would be ready to pounce.

Ivy turned to leave the office when York broke the silence.

"Take Johnny with you," and then, as a way of explanation, "you might need back up that you at least know."

Chapter Eleven

Bobby pulled back into Crystal Valley weary. The excitement of finally engaging with a new friend had taken it out of him, but he also hadn't been sleeping well lately. Emily wouldn't leave him alone unless he were too busy to be bothered, though he could still hear her faintly in the background. He couldn't think of any way to get rid of her besides jerking the wheel of his Bronco into oncoming traffic or going to the top of a building and leaping off. But where would the glory be in that? He'd be gone with no one to remember or mourn him.

He thought about eating when he couldn't remember the last time he'd eaten. His stomach growled, agreeing with his thoughts. Instead, he fell into the comfortably worn recliner in his living room and like most people, pulled his phone out. He'd left it sitting on the arm of his recliner. He didn't want to take it with him and risk the cops figuring out his phone had been on the same dirt road as the one he'd called from.

There were several social media posts about the return of The Suicide Killer, ranging from those who were scared to be home alone at night to the tough-guys who wished the killer would try to do something to them or their loved ones. Bobby thought it might be fun to find out where one of these guys lived and take them out. That would shut them all up. Even the ones who said he was only killing women because they were all he could overpower. Bobby believed that was a bit sexist. He'd come across many strong women. Taking out one of these alpha male wannabes could ramp up the fear factor, or it could make more of them speak out. Everybody was tough behind a keyboard. Thinking of keyboard warriors reminded Bobby about Jonathan Leonard's website, and he opened the web browser on his phone.

Leonard's website loaded with a flash of white, and The Suicide Killer's extended N insignia popped up on the screen in blood red, then it was stamped in a red circle with a slash through it. It was a bit much but caused an effect on the viewer. No doubt, Crystal Valley's citizens were thrilled and cheered on their new champion, but Bobby saw red. It wasn't the fact that they wanted him caught. That should go without saying. There'd be something seriously wrong with a person if they wanted him to get away with it. What infuriated Bobby was they had no idea where the N came from. He didn't know why he used it the first time or even remember doing it. The extended N was his grandfather Nicholas Cotton's initial he'd seen many years ago scrawled on his suicide letter when his cancer had made him too sick to continue fighting. Somehow, it'd fought its way out of his subconscious that night, and Bobby had used it ever since. But Leonard and his group weren't only attacking him. They were attacking his grandfather's memory, too.

Bobby squeezed his free hand open and closed, and blood ran to his face. He calmed his breathing, clicked on the logo, and read the first entry on the page.

The Beginning of the End for SK
by Jonathan Leonard

Hello everybody, and welcome to my blog. It seems my last report for WRRL ruffled more than a few feathers downtown. I'm glad they're finally paying attention; I just wish it wasn't to me. Some are calling for my job, but WRRL isn't that stupid. They know they'd have a hell of a court case on their hands if they did. So instead, they have decided to censure me. That doesn't mean much in the grand scheme of things. But that's what it is, isn't it? A conspiracy to keep me quiet while they continue to do nothing and a crazed psycho kills young women in our city. But I say no more. Somebody has to do something, and since it looks like it won't be any of them, I'll have to do it myself.

That's right, as of eight am, I have stepped down from my position at WRRL, and I'm launching my own news website with my own brand of investigational journalism to root out the evil and corruption of our beautiful city. But I can't do it alone. That's why I'm asking any proud red-blooded citizen who wants to take this city back to join me in my fight. I know everybody can't be involved, but the kinds of changes we expect to make cost money. Donations for our cause will be accepted through the website or by mail at the address below. And what exactly is our cause, you might be asking? Our first assignment will be to rid this city of the vermin calling himself The Suicide Killer. But we won't stop there. Oh no, after we bring him to justice, we will drag all the skeletons from the closets of the mayor and all those who have stood idle while crime has taken over our fair city. Anybody interested in joining the fight should contact us at the link below.

Bobby's anger had subsided enough for him to look away from the phone. He still wanted to hunt Leonard down and hang him from the newsroom by his intestines, but from the looks of it, the newsman would have plenty of other angry people to deal with first. It would be wise to wait for the shit storm that he'd no doubt had stirred up to calm down a bit. Too many people would have eyes on him right now. Unless there was another way to get to him?

He put his gloves back on, picked up the Amanda Cramer file, and set the picture and phone on the end table beside his chair. Like her sister, Amanda had been a beautiful woman. Dark black hair and pale blue eyes that sparkled with life until she was found floating face down in Lake Oliver. At first, they had treated her death as an accident when she'd been discovered in a popular and equally dangerous section of the lake, but they quickly ruled it a homicide when they performed an autopsy. Bobby gripped the folder tight as he read how there were signs of a struggle and that she'd been raped. What DNA, if there had been any, had been washed from her being in the water for two days. Morgan might not want the guy dead, but Bobby wanted to find out where he was and destroy his life and break him down before he finally put him out of his misery. Maybe she'd let Bobby devastate him before she turned him in to the cops. The mixed emotions of depravity and empathy both confused and exhausted Bobby. He pulled a little white candle from the end table drawer, placed it by the picture, and lit it.

He leaned back in the recliner and flipped the footrest out. The scent of gardenia coated the stale living room air. After a few minutes, he went back to the file. The only thing found on her body was a white limestone-based chalk that they could not locate a source of on the banks of the lake. Additionally, when they pulled her out of the water, she only had one earring in her ear. The earring was the horizontal figure eight infinity symbol with an A on it. The missing earring looked the same, except it had an M on the symbol. Greg had three suspects but could never get any of them to confess, even after multiple interrogations with each one.

Walter Longway had worked with her, and according to fellow employees, he had a huge crush on Amanda, but she shut down all of his advances. A lot of her coworkers pointed to Walt because of the unwanted extra attention he showed Amanda. But also because Walt had finally had enough and caused a scene at the company Christmas party, where is drunkenly called her a tease and said he would get her one day whether she wanted it or continued to act like she didn't want it. The company fired Walt, and he yelled he'd get her and everybody that helped her get him fired for no reason. This is the guy who Greg believed, if it were one of the three suspects, would be the guy. He had an alibi for the night Amanda died. He was at his mother's house in Hawthorne County.

Jimmy Yates and Amanda had been dating off and on for the previous two years. According to her sister, Morgan, Amanda wasn't serious about Jimmy. She only called him when she was lonely, but Jimmy saw their relationship differently. He believed they were soul mates and meant for each other. Morgan had told her sister she shouldn't string him along, but Amanda told her she wasn't, and he felt the same way as she did about their relationship. Then Jimmy proposed. He didn't cause a scene when she turned him down in the large crowd at her favorite restaurant. He pulled himself up from his knee and quietly left, never saying a word. Morgan is the one who suggested the police should look at Jimmy. He was always nice, but he gave Morgan an uneasy feeling when she was around him. He didn't have an alibi, but Greg had interviewed him numerous times and believed he was innocent, embarrassed, and heartbroken, sure, but he didn't kill her.

William Kirk lived with his mother across the hall from Amanda in Valley Summit Apartments off Red Rock Road. Bobby froze when he read what apartments Amanda and William lived in. That was the same apartment complex as Danielle. He didn't think he could go back there and question Kirk. It was hard enough going to work where he first met her but going back to the place where he had killed her was too much. He'd deliberately avoided Red Rock Road since Danielle's death. Plus, it looked like Greg had ruled Kirk out pretty quickly. He was a hermit who lived in a small two-bedroom apartment with his mother. The only friends he had were the people he met while online gaming. People thought he was strange and pointed him out when Greg and Don had questioned her neighbors, but being strange wasn't against the law yet.

The other two guys looked like better candidates. Bobby would have to see about visiting one or both of them later that night. If he couldn't get anything out of one of those two, he'd wait for Kirk to leave the apartment one day and corner him. It wasn't that he was afraid of the apartments, but Kirk was the only one of the three that Bobby quickly dismissed. Kirk was a weird shut-in who rarely left his room. No doubt, the apartment residents blamed him for anything out of the ordinary that went on in that complex.

Bobby had a few hours before it got dark out, so he laid the recliner back as far as it would go and drifted off, trying not to laugh at the thought of Ivy going through that creek looking for anything she could that would lead her to him. He only left them one clue, but it would lead them in a completely different direction than they would have guessed.

Chapter Twelve

As promised, Sheriff John Brown sat waiting in the Crackerland Country Store parking lot with his lights on. Ivy pulled off the dusty one lane road and into the dirty parking lot of the small store. A shopping cart sat upside down beside three lawn chairs in the back corner of the lot. The metal wires on the cart were charred black like somebody had been using it as a makeshift grill. Her car came to a gravel-crushing stop beside the sheriff's car, and she rolled the window down.

"Thanks for the warm welcome, Sheriff."

"Aw. There's no need to thank me. Didn't want you to miss the place."

"With a name like that, how could you miss it?" Ivy asked and jerked her thumb in the direction of the country store.

The sheriff looked over, then said, "It's not what you think," but offered no further explanation for the store's name.

She'd just met him, and she'd already offended the guy. This was not going to go as smoothly as she'd hoped. If she were lucky, he'd only hold it against her for half the time she was out here.

"The boys and I had a pool going on how many times you'd pass the turnoff before you found it or you gave up and called for help. So if you wouldn't mind indulging me."

Ivy gave her best shit-eating grin and said, "Two times."

"Damn. Matt's not going to let us hear the end of it. He always seems to get these things right. Though I guessed one if that makes you feel any better."

"Glad you seemed to have more confidence in us than we did," Ivy said and grinned larger.

"Would you like to step inside before we go? They have fresh coffee all day long if—"

"We'd like to see the road now," she said, more forceful than she had intended. A short embarrassed laugh escaped her lips, and she continued, "It's been a long day, and we would appreciate it if we could get there so we can get back home before too late."

The sheriff returned her smile.

"Yes, ma'am. Straight to the point. I like that. Not much of one for pleasantries myself."

Ivy couldn't tell if he was telling the truth or if she had slighted him. He pulled a pack of cowboy killers out of his pocket, then patted the other pockets looking for the lighter. Even though he was in his car and no breeze blew, Sheriff Brown covered the flame with his free hand as he struck the lighter, and the flame licked the tip of his cigarette. He inhaled deeply and pulled out of the parking lot. Ivy turned their car around and followed him. A large cloud of smoke pushed its way out the driver's side window of his car. Ivy looked at Carson sitting in the passenger's seat. The look on his face said he was trying not to bust out laughing in the sheriff's face.

"Not now, Carson. We have to hold it together long enough to get through this without any issues."

Carson threw his hands up in mock surrender.

"Don't worry about me. I'll be on my best behavior."

"Somehow, I don't believe that."

Ivy put the car in gear and kicked dirt up behind the vehicle as she gunned it, trying to catch up with Sheriff Brown.

They kept up with the sheriff, for the most part. It struck Ivy as odd that a small county sheriff's department could afford brand new Dodge Chargers, but maybe the sheriff was the only one to get one. They drove down a few paved roads before they hit a long-forgotten highway to nowhere. It felt like an eternity, but after a few miles, the sheriff's car pulled off the main road and onto a dirt road. Why had the killer driven all the way out here? He said he'd happened upon it, so maybe he'd been out for an afternoon ride. Though, he didn't seem like the leisurely or country type. A deputy, also in a Charger, sat at the stop sign and pulled in line behind them. There was a sudden urge to drive faster than she usually would have as soon as the tires met dirt. She tried to fight it, but the sheriff seemed to have the same idea as his car pulled away from them in a cloud of red dust.

Red brake lights cut through the cloud of dust ahead of them, and Ivy reluctantly applied the brakes. As the dust settled, she could see why the sheriff had suddenly hit the brakes. Up ahead, the road had a sudden sharp curve down and to the right. A canopy of trees enclosed the road, so it was already a bit darker than the daylight would allow, but everything grew even darker as they descended.

The sheriff's car slowed to a crawl as they reached the bottom of the hill and eased into the creek bed running across the road.

"Huh? Guess water really does run through it," Carson said.

Ivy ignored him because she saw something that pissed her off. On the other side of the creek sat another deputy's charger with his lights on. Blue light cascaded across the top of the water and rippled through the trees and hanging foliage, but Ivy only saw red.

"That son of a bitch and his guys have already been out here. They've contaminated the scene just so they can find something before us."

"Calm down, Ivy. Maybe they haven't gotten out of their car yet?" Carson said.

Ivy looked down at his hand hovering a few inches above hers on the gear shifter. She hoped he wasn't taking this moment to make his move. Though, she hoped he never tried to make his move, even if it were at the appropriate time.

They made eye contact, and she looked down at his hand again. Finally, he must have gotten the hint because he quickly pulled his hand back and massaged his palm.

"Or maybe they've tainted any evidence we could have gathered, and the killer will be loose long enough to kill somebody else."

"Either way, it's not a good idea to blow up and cause unnecessary tension between the departments. Especially when the sheriff is on a first name basis with the Lieutenant. I just think—"

"Screw what you think," Ivy said, cutting him off and jumping out the door.

The sheriff, the offending deputy, and the one who followed them down the road, were already out of their cars.

"Sheriff. I thought we had made it pretty clear that we were fine with your guys being here and helping if we found a body, but we needed to canvass the area on our own."

The deputies looked from Ivy to the sheriff and back to Ivy. The one who had been waiting at the bottom of the hill had a giant grin on his face, like what was about to go down excited him. But nothing apocalyptic came. Instead, the sheriff removed his hat, scratched his head, and then replaced it back on his head.

"Detective Chandler, is it?" he asked and continued without waiting for a reply, "My men here are expecting for me to lose my temper, to tell you off and then escort you to the county line, but that's not what I'm going to do." He looked back at the crestfallen deputies, who had no doubt heard their boss go off on many people who had crossed him in the past. "Seein' as you're highly regarded by your Lieutenant, and you're under a lot of pressure to catch the S.O.B. before he kills again, I'm going to give you the benefit of the doubt, but I'm going to need you to do the same thing for these back-woods redneck deputies and myself. We haven't disturbed your crime scene, if that's what you'd call it. George, here, hasn't even gotten out of his car. We've been blocking the area for your arrival, so nobody goes splashing through here."

Ivy could feel her face turning red. Carson stood in front of the car, trying to hold back a laugh. She hated him so much more now. She'd judged the sheriff and his men without knowing anything about them. She had written them off as stereotypes. The sheriff's words hurt more than if he had gone off on her. But that would have fed into the stereotype she'd been expecting them to be. Lieutenant York had been right; they had surprised her.

"Sheriff, I'm extremely sor—," she started but was cut off with a flick of his wrist.

"There's no need to apologize, detective. It goes with the terri-tory. We can handle it. We only have a few more hours of daylight if you want to get started.

Ivy nodded and searched around the surrounding area. She pulled out her cell phone to check the time. The clock read 5:30, but she noticed there was no signal if she needed to make a call. That reminded her of something the killer had told her when they were on the phone.

"Hey, Carson. There's no cell service down here."

"So?"

"So, he told me he had to go to the end of the road so he could get service to call me. One of us should go back to the stop sign at the beginning of the road and see if there's anything up there."

"And I guess you think that someone should be me, huh?"

Ivy sighed loudly.

"It doesn't matter to me who goes. I'll do it if you'd rather I do it."

Carson rolled his eyes.

"No. It's no problem. I'll go."

The sheriff butt in before Ivy had a chance to go back at him.

"Matt can take you back up the hill and help you search," he said.

Carson walked toward the cruiser and waited for Matt to join him. He drummed his fingers on the top of the car. Matt showed no signs of speeding up on account of him.

After they'd turned around and the taillights were out of sight, the sheriff said, "He thinks the sun come up just to hear him crow, don't he? I'm surprised he even let you drive."

"He didn't want to, I assure you."

Sheriff Brown didn't give any indication that he held a grudge against Ivy. She hoped it would stay that way, at least until they left. There was no telling what he would tell *Debbie*. She walked to the edge of the water.

"What's that over there?" she asked.

"That there is where teenagers turn around in old man Johnson's pasture. It didn't use to bother him until they knocked down his fence and some of his cows got out. Now we get a call from him every couple weeks about kids tearing up his pasture. If he sees all the lights, he's liable to come down here with a shotgun. Hopefully, he can see who he aims to shoot at."

Ivy looked down at the flowing creek. It didn't look like it was moving too quickly or that it was that deep.

"If you want to come over on this side, we can see if it looks like your guy left any tire marks."

Ivy took a step toward the water, then stopped, pulled her shoes off, rolled up her pants legs, and stepped into the creek. Icy cold needles attacked her exposed flesh as she walked through the water. It barely came mid-calf but cooled her entire body. She hurried across the fifteen-foot expanse of water, trying not to let on how cold it was.

"I imagine that water is pretty cold. Might not want to wade around in it for too long. Hate to have to explain to the CVPD how one of their detectives caught pneumonia while they were out here."

Ivy closed the distance, walked on the rocky bank, and shook her feet dry enough to put her shoes back on. She walked to the spot where the pasture was trampled on the edge of the road. The tall grass was crushed and matted flat in a large area. Some of it had already turned brown. She had no doubt the killer had used this pasture to turn around in when he went back up the hill to call her. He might have even used it multiple times as he splashed back and forth through the water, but there were no discernable markings that would be worth making a cast of to track down what kind of tire they were. Then, as if reading her mind, Brown spoke.

"Don't look like you're going to be able to figure out what tracks are his or anything about the tracks."

"I can't, but can you?"

"No. I wish I could. I truly do, but it all looks like a tangled mass of tall grass to me. Even the tracks in the mud are messed up. Probably a dead end. I don't know of anybody who would be able to tell you anything about those except what type of grass it is, and I can do that."

"And what kind is that?"

"Aw, that's just timothy grass. Most of these fields out here are full of it. Farmers use it for hay to feed their animals. They bale it and sell it to the local feed and seed stores 'round here."

"So just basic grass. Hopefully, Carson and your guy will be luckier than we've been, but I doubt it. This guy is always careful."

"They're all bound to slip up at some point. They can't be meticulous all the time. There's always a point where the smartest person in the room makes a mistake or misjudges his opponent."

"I hope you're right, sheriff," Ivy said as she watched the water flow from a canopy of trees and bramble on one side of the road through rapids made by various vehicles, including the killer's, only hours ago. The other side of the road had been cleared away from the stream, and a large fallen tree lay across the water but didn't stop the current.

She dropped her shoes on the water beaten clay, pulled at her pants leg to make sure it was firm above her knees and walked back into the creek toward the clearing.

"That side of the creek is cleared out from a red pickup truck that got stuck out here. It was stuck up on that downed tree. Those teenagers spent two hours trying to dig it out in the middle of the night before they called us. Had to bring my truck out here just to pull it off that tree."

Ivy continued toward the edge of the road. The icy water now came to her knee. Any sudden movement caused the water to splash her pants. Finally, she reached the edge, the water now just above her knee, soaking her pants. A soft ray of light cut through the tree branches and gleamed off something under the water.

"I found something," she called back over her shoulder.

She heard the sheriff approaching the creek bed, not entering the water behind her.

"It's probably just an old Coke somebody throwed out."

Ivy pulled a rubber glove out of her pocket, then rolled her right sleeve up and plunged it into the icy water.

"I don't think so."

"You ought to be careful rootin' around like that. You're liable to reach in and pull out a moccasin."

Ivy hesitated at the mention of a snake. The last thing she needed to do was look up and be eye to eye with a venomous snake. Head parallel with the water, she looked around for any threatening creature. The tips of her fingers brushed against the object. It wasn't aluminum. It felt like plastic. She reached further. A few strands of hair fell from behind her ear and floated on top of the water. She touched it again, but it was just out of reach. There wasn't anywhere else for her to go. The fallen tree blocked any other possible angle. She looked down at the water, held her breath, and leaned forward far enough to dip her face below the surface. The plastic object slid further, and she leaned deeper. She almost lost her balance as she wrapped her fingers around what she was diving for. The force from abruptly changing directions quickly sent her stumbling back. Pinwheeling her arms, she caught her balance before tumbling over. The last thing she wanted was to fall into this nasty creek with all these men watching her. The ride home with Carson would be unbearable.

"I got it," she said, holding the crumpled plastic in the air.

"Yeah, but what is it, and was it worth swimming in a creek to clean up litter?" Carson asked.

When had they gotten back? Ivy hadn't heard their car drive up. She was too focused on getting the thing she'd seen out of the water.

"It's a phone. It's the phone he used to call me."

All the men looked at each other incredulously. The sheriff was the first to break their shared skepticism.

"Chances of that being the killer's phone are astronomical. It could belong to anybody. I just said I pulled two teenagers from that exact spot. It could be one of theirs."

"It could be," she conceded, "but I don't think it is. I think he left it here for me to find. He told me where to find him. Unless you found anything around the stop sign, he made that call and then drove back down here and threw it in the water."

"I still think it's a reach, but it might be worth looking into. Couldn't hurt if you've got nothing else to go on right now," Sheriff Brown said.

Ivy gave a slight nod to the sheriff, and he returned it. A slight twinge of guilt flitted in her stomach for judging him before she met him properly. She could tell he had the trust and loyalty of the people who worked for him. And for good reason.

Carson gave her a hand out of the creek and handed her an evidence bag for the phone. It had grown dark suddenly from the time she'd found the phone and climbed out of the creek.

"Well, it looks like we've done all the searching we're going to be able to tonight. Unless you want me to send somebody back to get the big flood lights we have at the station."

"No, I don't think that will be necessary, sheriff. But thank you for showing us the way out here. I don't know that we would have found it otherwise."

Carson kicked the dirt behind her. No doubt he thought he'd be able to find it on his own without stopping to ask for directions.

"Me and a couple of the guys will come back out here in the morning and look around to make sure we don't find anything or anybody else. I'll call you if we do."

"Thank you. I'll let you know what we find out about the phone."

As they parted, Ivy tossed the keys to Carson. She'd rather be driving herself, but it'd been a long day, and she wasn't above being chauffeured around while she laid the seat back and rested her eyes.

Chapter Thirteen

Walter Longway's house sat at the end of Dillingham Street in the Historic District of Downtown Crystal Valley. His house was one of the few that, to the dismay of the city, had not been completely renovated. As a result, the avocado green house with a sagging roof, and rarely cut knee-high grass, was an eyesore to everybody who walked down the road.

Bobby stood on the front porch dressed in his solid black death clothes. He pulled his mask up long enough to feel a slight breeze and possibly the freshest air he'd be smelling for a while, and it wasn't even that fresh with all the rotting and decaying wood on the porch and siding. He took one final deep breath, pulled his mask down, and knocked on the door.

Nobody answered. Bobby carefully leaned over the railing. Light jumped and moved through the cracked mini blinds. A low murmur emanated from the interior, but he couldn't make out what they were saying. He contemplated leaving and coming back another night in case Longway had company, but before he turned, he pounded on the door one last time.

A voice called out to him from within.

"Come on in. It's open."

A smile forced its way onto Bobby's face as he tried to stifle a laugh. The easiest way to deal with evil is to invite it in before it forces its way inside. He turned the doorknob, and the smell of filth assaulted him before the door fully opened. It would be days before anybody knew this guy was dead. Not that Bobby had any plans to kill the man, that is, unless he forced him to.

Thankfully, Walter was in the den, which was the first room you came to after walking through the front door. He was lucky because it would have taken Bobby forever to find him if he'd been in any other room. It also helped in case the guy decided to run instead of answering his questions.

Walter sat facing a computer screen with his back to the door. As Bobby approached, the sounds of violent sex filled the room. Walt turned around in his desk chair, and Bobby couldn't help but see the violent pornography on the screen. Walt left the video running and jumped to his feet.

"Who the hell are you? I thought you were somebody else."

"Yes, it'd probably be better for you if I were."

Walter backed up against the desk and reached behind him for anything he could use as a weapon.

"You don't have to search for a weapon. I'm not planning on hurting you."

Walter stopped and put his hands down by his side.

"Then what the hell do you want?"

"I have a few questions to ask. If you answer them, then I'll leave, and you'll never see me again."

"What if I don't answer them?"

Bobby moved closer.

"If you don't answer, it will still be the last time you see me, but it will also be the last time you ever see anybody again."

Walter licked his dry lips and ran a dirty hand through his greasy hair.

"O ... okay. I'll answer whatever you want me to."

"Great. And will you please turn that shit off?"

Walter tilted his head back to the briefly forgotten video on his computer.

"What? A little porn bothers you. You can stand there and threaten me, but you draw the line when it comes to sex?"

"I don't have any issues with sex, but only a truly deranged mind would watch rape porn."

"Different strokes, man, different strokes."

This guy was getting too comfortable with Bobby. It was either a ploy to get him to let his guard down or how he survived in the normal, everyday world.

Bobby grabbed an empty beer bottle from a pile against the wall.

"I said turn that shit off," he screamed and threw the bottle at Walter's computer.

The bottle missed wide and shattered against the wall.

"Okay, okay. Calm down. I'm turning it off," Walter said and hit the power button on the computer.

"Good. Now the first question is, how in the hell do you live like this?"

"I ... uh, well, I get distracted and forget to take it out. Are you from sanitation? Did the neighbors call again?"

"No, I'm not from sanitation."

"So you broke in here to ask me why I don't take my trash out?"

Bobby walked closer to Walter, but not so close that he got a full whiff of him.

"I don't care how you live. You can be as revolting and live in as much trash as you'd like. I'm here to ask you about Amanda Cramer."

"Amanda? I don't know no Amanda."

Bobby pulled back and slapped Walter across the face. Tears immediately filled his eyes, and he stumbled backward and fell back into his chair.

"Don't fucking lie to me. I should just kill you right now and put you out of your misery than spend another minute in here smelling you. I know you worked with Amanda and that you asked her out multiple times."

Walter put his hand to the red mark on his cheek and rubbed it.

"Put your hands down," Bobby said and pulled a small roll of duct tape from his back pocket.

Walter saw the tape, and his eyes grew large. He was ready to talk straight.

"Yes, okay, yes, I knew her. Damn. You didn't have to hit me like that, and you don't have to tie me up."

"Apparently, I did, since you chose to lie to me instead of telling the truth, so this can all be over. And the tape is for your protection, so I don't think you're reaching for something."

Bobby wanted to say to hell with Walter, cut his throat and go on to the next guy, but pulled a long strip of tape from the roll instead. Walter jumped at the sound. He tapped his arms to each armrest and then taped his feet together. After checking to ensure the bonds were strong enough, Bobby threw the nearly empty tape roll onto a nearby pile of trash.

"I won't lie anymore. I promise. Yes, I knew her. We worked together, but that's it."

"Do you still work there?"

Walter sighed.

"No. They fired me a couple months after Amanda died. I really cared about her. It messed me up when she died. I haven't been the same since."

Bobby couldn't imagine Walter being in a better situation. To him, he had always been like this and always would be.

"My heart breaks for you," Bobby said and mockingly put his hands to his heart.

"Thank you."

"I wasn't ... you know what? Never mind. When was the last time you saw Amanda alive?"

Walter struggled against the tape.

"I saw her the day she died. Look, man, I already told the cops this two years ago. I didn't kill her, and I don't know who did," Walter said.

"You were infatuated with her, and she didn't want anything to do with you, but I'm supposed to believe that you didn't have anything to do with her death?"

"We were friends. I wasn't always like this."

"You were friends?"

"Well, work friends. She always turned me down when I asked her out. Even if it was to go out with a group of coworkers."

"All those times, and you never got the picture? Did you stalk her?"

Walter sighed and looked down at his protruding belly.

"I didn't tell this to the cops, but only because I didn't want to get in trouble."

"Naturally," Bobby said, and motioned with his hand for Walter to continue.

"Yeah, well, I wasn't stalking her. But there were a few times that I did follow her after work. Just to see where she was going. I was bored. I didn't have anything else to do."

Bobby crossed his arms.

"You realize that's the definition of stalking, right?"

"But that's not what I was doing. I swear," Walter said, and tried to stand up to further plead his case.

"I'm not judging, but that sure sounds like stalking to me."

"It was only a couple of times. I didn't mean to do it either. We both happened to end up at the same grocery store one day, and I followed her to see what she bought. Then she left, and I was curious where she lived, so I followed her home."

"You know you're sick, right?"

"And what the hell are you? Breaking into my house and tying me up."

"You invited me in," Bobby said.

"I thought you were somebody else, and I sure as hell didn't invite you to tape me to my chair."

"You got me there, but I'm still not letting you up. Did you follow her any other times?"

"Yes, but most of the time, she just went to her sister's house. They look so much alike I thought about leaving Amanda alone and taking a shot at her sister."

Bobby laughed but played it off as a cough. He didn't want to let on that he knew anything about Morgan or their family. Of course, he didn't know Amanda, but if she were anything like her sister, this guy would have been so far out of his league, and he'd never know it.

"Why do you care about Amanda? You a private investigator or something?"

"Or something, but I'm the one asking the questions. Did you see anybody different in the time leading up to her death?"

Walter closed his eyes and squinted like a five-year-old, thinking hard.

"Now that I think about it. I did see her going out with somebody in a fancy SUV."

"And you didn't think the cops would want to know that?"

"Like I said, I wasn't going to admit to them that I was following her. If I lied about how I knew, and the guy in the SUV ended up innocent, they'd be all over my ass."

Walter was right. As much as Bobby despised the guy, he would have done the same thing if he had been put in the same position. Though he'd be following the woman for a different reason.

"What can you tell me about the SUV and the driver?"

"Nothing really. The windows were tinted, too dark to see inside, and the driver never got out when I saw it. I don't know what kind it was, but it was large like a Navigator and black."

"Anything else?" Bobby asked as he pushed off the pile of trash behind him and got ready to leave.

"That's it, honest. It looked like the type of car a rich guy would drive, so I did tell the cops they should look into her boyfriend, Jimmy. I can't remember his last name, though."

"Yates?"

"Yeah, yeah, that was it. Jimmy Yates. He was some rich bastard with a trust fund. They were off and on for the longest time. I think they had just hit one of their cold periods just before she died."

"I guess that's all I have for now."

Bobby said before he turned and walked to the front door.

"For now? What the fuck is that supposed to mean? Are you going to just keep showing up at my house and holding me hostage?"

"I haven't thought about it, but I'll do whatever the hell I feel like doing."

He opened the door, and Walter started screaming for help at the top of his lungs.

"Shut the fuck up, or I'm going to kill you."

Walter continued screaming and didn't stop until Bobby kicked him in the shin.

"If you don't shut your mouth, I will kill you. If you don't believe anything tonight, believe that."

Bobby walked back toward the door, and quieter, Walter called out to him.

"Hey, are you going to just leave me like this?"

Bobby turned back to face him.

"Yeah, that was the plan."

Walter struggled against the tape.

"You fucking asshole. I told you what you wanted to know. You can't leave me here like this. I have to piss."

"I'm the asshole?"

Maybe sensing that he'd gone too far, Walter licked his lips before continuing.

"Yes, you're the asshole. You come in here demanding information that I don't know, and now you're going to leave me tapped to this chair. You're the asshole."

"You might not have killed Amanda, but you're still one sick fuck with all the rape porn you watch. That's not a kink. It's disgusting."

Bobby's anger was at a tipping point and was ready to boil over. He concentrated on his breathing and let out a long, steady breath. He was ready to leave, but Walter had other ideas.

"Fuck you, and fuck that Amanda bitch and her sister. Whatever her name is. I hope she ends up just like her."

The calming breath caught in Bobby's throat and choked him. Anger surged through his system, and a whirling dervish of light-headedness made him sway on his feet.

"What did you say?" he asked, much calmer than he felt as he walked toward Walter.

Being taped to the chair didn't cool Walter's bravado at all. He acted like he didn't think Bobby would actually do anything to him. That was the problem with most men. They never thought they had anything to worry about. Even when cornered like a possum in a trashcan, they'll continue to lash out the same.

"You heard me. Fuck all of you. If I—"

The punch to his left temple shut him up and left him stunned. Bobby was tired of listening to the garbage he spouted. Walter spit a wad of snot and sweat at Bobby's feet.

"Not really a fair fight for a man when he's taped to a chair."

Bobby leaned in close enough to smell the tangy sweat radiating off the man's skin. It repulsed him.

"Most of the time, life's not fair."

Bobby reached into his pocket and pulled out a cigarette lighter. He didn't smoke but always carried one. You never knew when one would come in handy. He quickly snapped his hand on top of Walter's and pushed it against his chair arm until they were splayed.

"What the hell are you doing?"

Bobby didn't say a word. Instead, he struck the lighter and held the flame up so Walter could see it.

"No. Wait. Don't."

Sweat poured down Walter's face as panic set in. He licked his lips and tried to stand, but the tape held him in place.

"Do you think that's what she said before he forced himself on her? He never stopped either, though."

He held the lighter under Walter's pinky finger. The flame licked the air and blistered the pad of the finger. Walter screamed and tried to wrangle away. The screams were getting loud enough for a curious neighbor to call the police, so Bobby looked around until he found a dirty sweat-stained undershirt lying forgotten against the baseboard of the room. He twisted the shirt, shoved it in Walter's mouth, pulled the ends behind his head, and tied them into a knot. Walter tried to speak through the gag, and Bobby looked at him.

"What's that? I can't understand you with that gag in your mouth. It's not like the ball gags in those movies you watch, but it'll do."

Bobby grabbed his hand again and thrust the flame under his ringer finger. Walter jerked again and tried to stand up. Bobby lifted the lighter and engulfed the finger in the flame. Walter pulled and twisted away, causing the flame to sear the sides of his other fingers. The scent of piss filled the air as it ran down Walter's leg and splashed on the floor.

"Damn it, man. Did you just piss yourself? This is going to make things a lot less pleasant for me. And I was just starting to enjoy this."

He wasn't lying. Torturing this man gave him a feeling he had never experienced before. He liked it but didn't want to get too used to it. Like a bad drug, he would keep coming back for more if he did it enough. He'd get sloppy trying to get another hit, and then he'd get caught. There was no rehab for that darkness.

Bobby torched the final two fingers until they were as bloody and charred as the others.

"Oh, look, I forgot one," Bobby said.

He reached down and grabbed Walter's thumb. Their eyes met, and Bobby could see the pain and fear in the man's eyes. Then, without breaking eye contact, Bobby snapped the man's thumb back until it touched the top of his wrist. Bobby felt the bone break and the tendon and muscle stretch beyond the snapping point.

Walter didn't scream that time. Instead, his head bobbed and swayed.

"No. Don't you do it. You don't get to pass out from the pain," Bobby said, and playfully slapped Walter's face.

Bobby removed the gag from Walter's mouth. He tried to say something, but Bobby couldn't make it out.

"What's that? I can quite hear you."

He leaned in closer to hear what Walter was trying to say. Even after all the pain inflicted on him, Walter was still able to move quickly. He snapped his head up and smashed the crown of his head into Bobby's chin. Blood filled Bobby's mouth where he bit into the side of his cheek. There was nowhere to spit. He didn't need to leave any trail for the cops to find and connect him to anything else. He swallowed and stood up straight. Though he hadn't removed the gag, he could still see the wide grin on Walter's face, and the rage he had felt earlier reignited.

Bobby grabbed Walter by his hair, gripped the lighter in his fist, and punched him in the cheek. He didn't move much, and Bobby jumped in the air and came down with his fist on the side of Walter's face. He didn't listen for anything from Walter; he continued to pound his hardened fist into Walter's lower jaw. Bobby lost count after ten but continued beating Walter's face. When he grew tired from the barrage, he stepped back, put his hands on his knees, and caught his breath. He stepped back and looked at Walter's ruined face.

It was no longer symmetrical. The left eye was swollen three times its normal size, and his jaw fell broken to the right. What looked like a molar protruded through the ragged cheek skin. Walter's chest slowly rose and shuttered and hitched when he inhaled. He was still alive, and that's the way Bobby intended to leave him. He smiled at his work and walked out the door. He thought about calling the guy an ambulance but thought better of it. He'd be too tempted to wait until they showed up to take him to the hospital. Maybe he should take him to the hospital? That could be an adventure. Just wheel him over in the chair he's strapped to and—.

I wish you'd fight that hard for me.

Bobby almost flipped at the sound of her voice. She couldn't be here. He hadn't heard from her in days, and he hadn't killed anybody. At least he didn't think Walter had died. He thought about going back into the house to check on him when she answered his question.

I'm glad you didn't kill him, though. It would have been horrible to be stuck in his body.

"No. Go away! Leave me alone," Bobby yelled with his hands on his head.

His face stung from stretching his cheeks when he yelled, and more blood leaked into his mouth. Maybe Emily could now appear when people were on the verge of dying. He walked toward the Dillingham Street Bridge. His Bronco waited just across the bridge in an old mill parking lot that nobody frequented anymore. If he could get to the truck, he'd be able to go around the other way and not pass back by Walter Longway's house. Her voice continued to follow him as he made it to the bride.

I don't understand why you don't want me anymore. I used to be enough for you, but now you don't want me around. Why don't you let me make it up to you?

"There's nothing to make up. I'm through with you. I want you out of my head. I can't take it anymore. I feel like jumping off this bridge."

No. Don't do that. Please. I'll do whatever it takes. Just don't jump.

Bobby looked up and realized he was already in the middle of the bridge. A little further, and he could be away from her, but he knew she would find him again. He couldn't keep his urge to kill in check. He would kill again, and it'd be soon.

A homeless woman walked toward Bobby. She looked around erratically but couldn't seem to make up her mind if she was going to cross the road or try to get past Bobby as quickly as she could.

"Yes, we're going over the bridge, and everything will be better."

Don't do it. Talk to me. You haven't even been listening to me. I don't want to leave again.

"I can't handle it anymore."

The woman made up her mind to try to skirt around Bobby as best she could. When the woman got beside Bobby, he yelled, "One of us is going over, and it won't be me."

He grabbed the surprised woman and slammed her face into the steel bridge beam. Broken teeth bounced across the bridge like dice in a back alley craps game. The violent impact killed her instantly. Bobby held her upright to make sure she was dead. Emily called out to him again from the broken woman.

Why did you do that? What are you doing? You can't leave me here alone.

"Like I said, it won't be me."

Bobby grabbed the woman by the hair and threw her over the railing. She splashed into the water and quickly sank as her heavy clothes, filled with supplies for the streets, weighed her down.

He looked over the rail and caught a glimpse of her as she sank.

Bobby. Please help me. Don't leave me here. It's cold and dark. They ... sa ... yo ...

He heard Emily calling out to him, but her voice was water-logged and sounded further away until finally, she fell silent. Bobby finished his trek across the bridge and fell into the front seat. He didn't find Amanda's killer, but he could at least mark one name off the list.

Chapter Fourteen

It had been too late to give the damaged phone to the IT guy to look at when Ivy and Carson got back to town. She had left it on their incoming table with too much urgent red tape and a large hand-written note to call her as soon as they found anything out. She then went home and tried to get some sleep instead of daydreaming about what breaks the phone could give them. After flipping through the channels trying to find something to fall asleep to, she'd given up and gone into the living room, curled up into her recliner, and stared out the large front window until she woke up with a severe crick in her neck. She'd spend the rest of the day trying to work that one out.

Now, she sat impatiently waiting at her desk, willing the phone to ring, but it'd been quiet all morning. Half-written notes with quarter thought out ideas spread across her desk. The only way they were going to catch this guy was if he screwed up and left evidence at the scene or if he let something slip while he had her on the phone. She hoped it was the former; she'd spent all the time with him on the phone that she cared. It was amazing that Greg had been able to talk to him that much. The killer saw them as friends, but there was no way a once highly respected detective would think the same. Stranger things had happened, no doubt, but she couldn't believe it. Wouldn't believe it until she saw irrefutable proof.

Ivy's thoughts had wandered from one useless topic to the next all day. And none of it was getting her anywhere. She hit her computer mouse with a disinterested flick of her wrist, and the screen lit up. She might as well look like she was doing some work since she was here. Carson had made himself scarce all day. Lunch with the guys and checking in with some CIs on a different case she wasn't privy to. It'd been nice and quiet, but that's not what she wanted. Something else she didn't want was waiting in her inbox when she logged in to see if maybe they had emailed her instead of calling.

Instead, she found an email from Jonathan Leonard's bring-SK2justice.com website. Everybody knew and had varying opinions of Leonard and his work. Ivy had never been a fan. She'd been too young when he'd started at WRRL to understand most of the stories he talked about on the evening news, but her grandmother, who lived with her family, watched him every night. When she was old enough to want to pay attention to the news, he seemed normal enough, but after internal fighting and a sudden change in politics, he became more and more extreme in what he said. The station had suspended him a number of times for things he'd said on air, but that seemed to be all they would do to him. He had too large of a following in the city and the surrounding area to do anything else. That is, until recently, when he went on a diatribe about anybody he could think to go after in the city. Now, he had his own news blog that, sadly, had a large following within the community and the department.

Ivy, however, was not one of those acolytes. She couldn't stand the man or his brand of guerilla journalism that was often wrong and misleading, so it was surprising that she'd find an email with the latest post in her inbox. Though she didn't sign up for the email, she had to admit, she was more than a little curious. She looked around the station to make sure nobody was around, angled her monitor so she could see anybody walking toward her desk, and clicked on the link.

The screen flashed white, and the red N signature that The Suicide Killer left on all of his faux letters materialized in red. A red circle with a slash through it stamped across the N. They certainly weren't subtle about anything they were doing. Ivy clicked on the most recent post, checked her surroundings, and read.

Investigations Are Tough ... and Expensive
by Jonathan Leonard

Hello everybody, and welcome to the latest edition. There have been many developments going on around the office. We have been hard at work, doing our best to find out the truth, so everybody will be able to sleep a little sounder. Even those who'd rather not hear it. There have been some exciting developments in The Suicide Killer case that I'm sure the mayor and police chief couldn't care less about finding out. But I assure you, fine reader, we have made great strides in this investigation. It's quite spectacular how much you can accomplish when you actually try to solve crimes. Things can get done. They no doubt move slower than we would like, but nowhere near as slow as those in charge would like for you to believe. For those keen readers we have (aren't you all?), you have no doubt read the title of this article and wondered what we were talking about. Like the title says, investigations are hard, not too hard for us, but like it also says, they are expensive.

We have had many of you reach out to us, wanting to know how you can help. So many people wanted to give us money, but we felt it was wrong to take your money without anything in return. That's why we have opened up an online shop that is full of custom hats, bumper stickers, t-shirts, and pretty much anything else you can possibly think of, we have. The koozies are the most popular choice around the office. Right now, everything in the store is boldly emblazoned with the insignia N of The Suicide Killer with a bright red slash through it. If you've wanted to help us out, but didn't know how, or if you just want to show this killer that we will not cower in our homes at night, but are ready and willing to meet him head-on, then I encourage you to visit the store and pick something up. Different styles will rotate in with availability, but we intend to have custom merchandise for the cases we work on and solve.

Ivy closed the website and sat back in her chair. She'd heard it was bad, but she had no idea. She'd thought it would burn out pretty quickly, and Leonard would find himself in a larger news market, and that would be it. But this was worse. He was actively investigating her case and was now marketing it to the people in the city. Setting them up to be targets of a deranged killer who would have no second thoughts about taking out somebody who had put a target on their back or car. There were too many ways this could go wrong. Hopefully, the mayor or chief, who so far had ignored him, would get involved and stop him before he got somebody killed.

The worst part was that he sounded like he'd made some progress on the case. He could be and doubtless was lying, but you never know. If it progressed any further without the higher ups stepping in, she'd track him down and see what he had. Or threaten him with interfering with a police investigation charge. It was bad enough that he claimed to be making progress that she wasn't, but she hadn't seen him anywhere, let alone at one of the crime scenes, so threatening him would come off hollow.

The phone rang, and Ivy jumped to answer it. She snatched her phone from the desk and knocked over half a cup of cold coffee. She answered the phone while jumping to her feet to avoid the deluge.

"Shit. Sorry. Detective Chandler."

"Yeah, hey, this is Wade from the lab."

Ivy pulled wadded balls of paper from the trash and tried to soak up as much coffee as possible from the desktop.

"Do you have something for me?"

"Yeah, yeah, we'll send the final report to you later."

Ivy was getting impatient. If it was important, she needed to know fast, and if he didn't have anything to tell her, he was building up for a letdown.

"Fine, but want can you tell me now?"

"Well, the phone was pretty waterlogged when we got it."

No shit. Tell me something I didn't know almost slipped from her lips, but she held back.

"And?"

She hoped he could feel her frustration.

"And there wasn't too much we could get from the phone, but we were able to find out who the phone belonged to."

Ivy grabbed her purse and headed toward Lieutenant York's office. When she heard the name, she hung up on Wade and started running.

"The phone belonged to Morgan Cramer," she yelled, stepping into York's office.

Chapter Fifteen

Ivy arrived at Morgan Cramer's house at the same time as Brandon Carson and the Rapid Response Team. CVPD vehicles filled the small road, blocking traffic on both sides. Ivy snatched the bulletproof vest from the passenger seat as she jumped from her car. The RRT had already lined up with uniformed police officers falling behind them. Ivy was reminded of Sheriff Brown's remark about Carson as she saw him strutting along the curb in front of the house. He wasn't going to be the first in, but he'd be in right after the threat had been neutralized. The tree he hung around would provide good cover if he needed it quickly.

The heavily armed and protected squad approached the house with military procession. This is what they trained year-round for. Ivy only hoped they weren't too late and weren't about to storm a house that had become a crypt days earlier.

An officer with a battering ram prepared to run up the steps and smash the door when he dropped back, yelling something that Ivy couldn't make out. All the officers fanned out with their weapons pointed at the door. Uniformed cops backed up the line, pistols drawn. Ivy looked from the officers to the door, and a black slash cut the white door in two. She shielded her eyes from the sun and realized somebody had opened the door to the house. All the officers screamed at a woman as she stepped from the house, keys in hand. It was Morgan Cramer, preparing to leave her home.

Ivy screamed and ran toward the house. Two officers turned in time to be knocked to the ground as she ran by.

"Hold fire. Don't shoot. Stop."

The sudden change of events surprised the officers, who continued to yell for the woman to get on the ground. None of them saw Ivy streak past until she was already in front of the firing squad.

"Don't shoot. She's okay," Ivy screamed with her hands held out.

She didn't know what she was thinking. They could have just as easily shot her as Morgan. Adrenaline flowed through her body, and pulses of fear ran under her skin.

A few of the team looked at their captain, who finally raised his hand and lowered his weapon. Ivy released her pent-up breath heavily and put her head between her knees to steady herself.

Carson ran up, yelling at her.

"What the hell are you trying to do? You trying to get shot?"

Ivy snapped and stood up quickly. The top of her head only came to his chin, but she pushed her finger into his chest.

"I'm trying to save this woman's life before these testosterone-fueled assholes kill her for going grocery shopping. What the fuck are you doing?"

The Rapid Response Team walked up to the detectives. Ivy could easily tell who was in charge. He was the man with the reddest face in the group.

"Johnny, what the hell is going on here? She almost got herself killed," the captain yelled.

Why was he asking Carson? She could answer for herself and certainly didn't need Carson doing the talking for her. She pushed past him and read the name on the officer's vest.

"I can speak for myself, Captain ... Ramsey. Somebody had to stop you guys before you ended up shooting a terrified woman who has no idea what is going on out here. She's obviously not in any distress. You should have put your guns down when you realized she was no threat."

"That's not our procedure. And I'm not going to stand here—"

"To hell with your procedures. That's the problem with all of you. Makes the rest of us look bad when you screw up," Ivy said, and turned on her heels before Captain Ramsey could say another word. She heard them talking to Carson again when she walked off. No doubt saying she was being an emotional woman.

To Ivy's surprise, Morgan was still standing on her bottom step, keys in hand, like she didn't know if she should be running toward or away from them. She walked up to Morgan and introduced herself.

"Ms. Cramer, my name is Detective Ivy Chandler. I'm sorry about all of this. Do you mind if I have a few minutes of your time?"

Morgan didn't take her eyes off the men with guns. Fear filled her eyes. Ivy had seen that look many times, but this time it seemed a little different. She wouldn't get anything from her if they continued to stand in front of the house with all the commotion going on.

"Ms. Cramer. Why don't we step inside and talk?"

Ivy gently put her hand on Morgan's elbow, and Morgan let herself be guided inside the house. They walked inside, and as Ivy tried to close the door, Carson stuck his hand inside. Morgan jumped, and Ivy had to force herself to stop from slamming the door on him. She stuck her head outside.

"She's pretty shaken up. Might be better if I did this one alone. You and the boys can go compare the size of your guns," she said, and shut the door before he had a chance to respond.

"Why don't you have a seat, Ms. Cramer?"

Morgan backed out of the mudroom and then backed to her seat at the kitchen table. She fell into the chair and continued to stare. It made Ivy uncomfortable to see Morgan so vulnerable.

"I thought they were him, at first," she finally said.

"Who did you think they were?"

She was in shock. Ivy hoped nobody would hang around outside. The revving engine of the Rapid Response Team's tactical vehicle rumbled, causing Ivy to relax, but Morgan tensed.

"I wasn't paying attention when I walked outside. I rarely let my guard down."

"You should be able to let your guard down in your own home."

"But I can't. Not since that night he was here."

Ivy walked into that one. She knew the killer had been here, and Morgan was lucky to have survived the encounter.

"I'm sorry. I should have thought about that before I spoke."

"It's not your fault. I know it sounds stupid, but I thought they were him when I walked outside, and I froze. Even when you ran in between us, I still hadn't grasped that there was a group of them, not just one dressed in all black and wearing a mask like that."

She was clearly still suffering long-term effects from PTSD. She might not end up being the best witness, but right now, she was all they had. The good news was that she was alive. Ivy had feared the worst when Wade told her whose phone she'd found in the creek. She tried to tell Lieutenant York that the RRT would be overkill. Send a lot of back-up, by all means, but going in like the killer was actually there would be too much. Worst-case scenario, they walk into another one of The Suicide Killer's tableaus, and best-case scenario, she'd be perfectly fine like nothing ever happened. Nobody had expected her to be alive. Automatically jumping to that conclusion made Ivy feel queasy, but more often than not, best-case isn't what they got, especially when it came to this killer. The best-case scenario for Ivy now would be for Captain Ramsey to leave and forget the entire scene she'd caused had ever happened. Ivy wasn't that lucky, and she'd hurt his pride. There's no way he'd leave to lick his wounds and let everything go. However, until they reprimanded her, Ivy still had a job. She pulled out her notebook and tried to get everything back on track.

"Ms. Cramer, I'd like to ask you a few questions, if that would be okay."

"Okay, and Morgan is fine."

"Okay, Morgan. When was the last time you left the house?"

Morgan laughed.

"That's the same thing my mother asks me when she talks to me. I don't leave the house too often nowadays, but I had to go to the grocery store two days ago. I was on my way to the office when you showed up."

"The office? Are you still writing for the paper?"

"Yeah, while we still have one, anyway. I don't do the crime beat anymore."

Ivy scribbled the important parts in her notebook. If she hadn't left the house in two days, then the killer must have gotten her phone when she was at the grocery store.

"What grocery store do you use?"

"I just ran down the road to Hiwatt Foods. Why is where I get my food important?"

Ivy looked at the confused woman. It would be strange that a person would not notice their phone had been missing for two days. But, on the other hand, maybe it was cloned, and she had no idea what was happening.

"It's not. I don't think, anyway. This is going to sound like a strange question too, but do you happen to have your cell phone with you?"

Morgan's features changed. Was that recognition she saw in her eyes? Does she know where her phone is? Or is she just helplessly confused?

"I ... well, I don't know where it is. I haven't been able to find it."

"Don't you think it's a little strange that somebody wouldn't know where their phone is? Everybody is practically attached to them nowadays."

Morgan sat back in a defensive position in her chair.

"I guess it's a little weird, but I don't stay on my phone all day like most people. Guess I'm just old-school like that."

"You do still work at the newspaper," Ivy said, and laughed, trying to reel her back in before she got suspicious and stopped talking.

"That's true," Morgan responded, and laughed awkwardly.

Both women sat silent. Ivy attempted to will Morgan to continue speaking. She didn't think she would get anywhere with her when Morgan finally spoke.

"I hope a lost phone isn't the reason you were ready to bust down my door."

Ivy expected the same cordial laugh after that statement, but there was none. She wanted a real answer.

"No. We haven't gotten quite that bad," Ivy said, and laughed uncomfortably while adjusting in her chair.

"We were worried about you."

"Why?"

There was no surprise in her question. It was accusatory. Morgan, no doubt, had issues with the police in this city. Her sister was killed two years ago, and they still didn't know any more than they did the first day. She had a right to be mad. Hell, Ivy was the new detective on the case, and she had hardly cracked the spine of the thin file, and now a serial killer is back killing people. She would never have admitted it to anybody, but Morgan's sister was forgotten. A lot of people would have thrown her out and would have been hot to do more than file a few complaints after the stunt they pulled today.

"Because we found your phone."

"That's still weird. Where did you find it?"

"That's why we were worried. I found it in a creek bed out near Scarsville."

Morgan leaned forward in her seat. Now Ivy had her full attention. Couldn't keep the journalist out of her for too long.

"Scarsville? I can't remember the last time I was out there. And even then, I was only passing through to go somewhere else."

Ivy let the air sit between the two of them. She wanted to see her reaction when she told her who had the phone. She didn't think she was involved in any way, but a lot about this case wasn't making sense.

"I received a call from your phone yesterday."

Morgan's eyebrows furrowed.

"I'm not following."

"I received a call from your phone from somebody claiming to be The Suicide Killer."

Morgan raised her hand to her mouth but only touched her lips with her index finger. She was thinking, and Ivy was waiting for the horror to dawn on her, but it never did. Instead, she sighed loudly. It was Ivy's turn to be shocked. That's not the reaction you would expect when you tell somebody that a serial killer has stolen their phone. The same serial killer who had attacked her in her home a few months prior.

"It was him," Morgan said coldly.

"What do you mean?"

"I mean, it was The Suicide Killer."

Ivy stared at Morgan. Not a single worry line formed on her face. She had been through a lot, but there was no way she was this desensitized.

"How do you know it was actually him?"

Ivy asked, even though she knew it was the killer, but she wanted to know how Morgan knew.

"Because he was here at my house, and now that I think about it, I haven't seen it since he was here two days ago."

Ivy didn't understand. If she was an accomplice, she was a pretty bad one. She remained far too calm.

"That doesn't scare you? That you knew he was in your house again?"

The blank look on her face finally changed, but instead of fear, Ivy only saw anger.

"Scare me? It fucking terrifies me."

"Why didn't you call the police?"

"Why bother? Would they actually be able to help me? Were you able to help my sister? Cause I haven't seen anything on that in I can't remember when."

Ivy had lost her. She went from talking about the police as *they* and started calling them *you* when she brought up her sister. She stuck Ivy in the same rudderless boat as the rest of them.

"I don't think that's entirely true or fair," she stuttered as she lied.

Morgan stood with her hand firmly planted on the kitchen table.

"Fair? Don't come in here and tell me what fair is. Nothing that happened to my sister or me has been fair."

"I'm sorry. That was a poor choice of words. I truly am sorry," Ivy said with her hand on her chest, "and the only thing I can speak to about the past is my inaction since taking over the case."

Morgan scoffed.

"I'm here now, and I want to do what I can to make sure this doesn't happen again. You shouldn't have to live in fear of somebody coming through your door whenever they want to."

She wasn't sure Morgan believed her, but at least she relaxed and sat back down.

"What do you want to know, now that you've found the time to finally show up?"

"Why was he here?"

Morgan sat back.

"I have no idea. I guess he wanted to scare the hell out of me."

"Is there anything you can think of that could help us catch him?"

Morgan crossed her arms.

"Not off hand, no. He came in here with the same obnoxiously hyper attitude he always has, wanting to know who was on his case."

"What did you tell him?"

"Said I had no idea. I didn't work the crime beat anymore, so he'd have to find another way."

Ivy shifted in her seat. She was about finished with Morgan for now. She wasn't going to be too much help at this point. Ivy could tell Morgan had given up. It was in her eyes.

"Aren't you afraid he'll come back when he finds out you lied and had my number?"

Morgan didn't flinch.

"He's coming back if he wants to, and there's nothing you can do to stop him. He knows that too. That's why he's so damn cocky."

Ivy felt the same way. She hated how cocky and sure of himself he was. It would feel great to rub it in his smug face that he wasn't the smartest person out there. Sensing Morgan was ready to be finished with her, Ivy stood, and Morgan stood with her to confirm. Ivy pulled a card out of her pocket and handed it to Morgan. She expected a tremble or something, but Morgan's hand was as steady as hers.

"Do you think it'd make you feel better if we put a car outside to watch the house for you?"

"And do what? I'll be fine. I don't expect he'll be coming around for a while."

"Why's that?"

"He got in touch with you. There's nothing else I can give him."

"True, but I think I'll have patrol increase the number of cars in the area."

Morgan quietly led Ivy to the door.

All the excitement had died down, and everybody had gone home when Ivy stepped outside. Carson sat in his car on the phone, throwing his hands up when he saw her, and shrugged his shoulders at Ivy. When Ivy shook her head, Carson cranked his car and drove off. She should have told him what they talked about, but it wasn't anything that she couldn't let him know later. He looked more interested in who he was talking to on the phone.

Ivy hadn't gotten much information out of Morgan, but she still felt like there was a lot she wasn't telling her. She just didn't know if it was because she had blocked most of the experience out of her mind or if there were darker motivations.

Chapter Sixteen

Bumper stickers? Everything that he'd done, and they were making light of it. They were mocking him and making him look like a fool. Instead of cowering in their houses at night after a citywide curfew, like they should be doing, the city wasn't doing anything, and this sorry excuse for a local celebrity was using him as a marketing ploy. He didn't care any more than the powers that be. This was Leonard's opportunity to have everybody know his name and to make money off the deaths of those he swore to avenge. He was playing the same political game they all were.

Bobby slammed his fist on the counter. Anger and hatred radiated off him. His entire body felt white hot as blood slammed through his veins and adrenaline dumped into his system. It was bad enough they were openly mocking him, but they also somehow believed they were making progress on the case. That didn't make sense. It all had to be lies. There was no way they knew anything. He'd been too careful, they didn't have any of the labs the cops had, and the cops were still clueless. Either way, they were trying to make a fool of him.

The bottom of the counter exploded as he put his foot through the thin wood. His nonskid shoe got stuck in the opening, infuriating him even more. Sharp spikes of cheap wainscoting pinched at his exposed ankle. Every movement caused the points to dig deeper into his skin, making him angrier the more he moved it.

"Fuck this shit," Bobby screamed as Jody walked around the corner from the back of the store.

In one swift movement, he jerked his leg from the splintered wood. The sharp edges pierced his skin and pulled down, ripping the skin more as he pulled back. Blood ran down his ankle and soaked into his no-show sock. He screamed and pounded the counter wildly as Jody, and a customer who had walked in during the commotion stared in silent horror. Bobby screamed a primal, guttural yell toward the ceiling and knocked the tip jar and straw canister across the room, landing at the appalled customer's feet. She backed away with her hand gently pushed against her chest but didn't leave. Everybody enjoyed a car wreck, Bobby thought, and then gave her a show she'd never forget.

Jody backed away as he turned in her direction. He stepped to the back counter and ran an outstretched arm across it, sending all the containers of coffee beans, nutmeg, cinnamon, and various syrup pumps crashing to the floor. Jody took a step toward him.

"Bobby. Please stop. I don't know what happened, but you're scaring me. Please stop."

He kicked the broken containers on the floor and got in Jody's face.

"I should scare you," he growled.

Jody's face dropped, and the frightened look Bobby had seen many times before swam in her eyes. It gave him the same exhilarating and electrifying feeling that flowed through his body just before he took the life of the person staring at him like that. He grabbed the butcher knife, used for chopping up the overpriced salads they sold, and walked toward Jody. She didn't move. She must not have thought he would hurt her. She was wrong. They'd worked together for years, but he could just as easily slice her throat and let her blood mix with his own on the tile floor as the random woman staring at him on the other side of the counter.

His nostrils flared, and he forced deep breaths polluted with coffee grounds from his lungs. He wanted to kill her. The knife swung from a chopping position down to a stabbing position as he loosened his fingers enough. Jody trembled but didn't move. The woman on the other side of the counter was pulling her phone from her purse. Bobby screamed in Jody's face and plunged the knife down.

The knife dug into the wood counter. Bobby and Jody locked

eyes. She made a move like she wanted to hug him. He snapped the tip of the blade off into the counter, and she stopped moving toward him. Bobby reared back and threw the knife at the large window he'd seen Danielle walk past so many times before. The glass did not shatter as he'd thought it would. It withstood the impact, and only a nickel-sized star marred the glass like a rock hitting a windshield.

Bobby calmly removed his apron and dropped it on the counter along with his Daily Grind hat. He'd need to find a new job. The owner, Randy, probably wouldn't even fire him over this. He didn't care about the store. As long as Bobby cleaned up the mess and paid for any damages, he'd be allowed back after a week or two off. Bobby would rather find a new job, but he had more important things to do, like finding a phone.

Chapter Seventeen

Ivy slouched in her chair and counted the dots on the squad room ceiling tiles above her desk. The sudden and fleeting urge to spin around until she made herself sick crossed her mind. It had been a long day. She was confident she'd saved Morgan Cramer's life even though she was the one they were there to protect. The Rapid Response Team had seen several complaints under Captain Ramsey, ranging from excessive force to wrongful death, but he and his team continued to rack up accommodations from downtown. Captain Ramsey should have been higher ranking, but he'd held himself back. He thrived on the adrenaline rush of storming into something he wasn't completely sure he knew the outcome. Most of his lackeys were the same way. Ramsey might not hold the highest rank within the department, but he had the respect and pull of high-ranking officials.

And to that end, Ivy found herself in Lieutenant York's office when she returned to the station. There had been a lot of yelling, mainly by York, but Ivy did interject a few highly charged jabs early until she realized it didn't matter what she said or what really happened out there. The only thing that mattered was that she interfered with a Rapid Response Team action plan and could have gotten herself or Morgan Cramer hurt, and she'd been the one they were trying to protect all along. It didn't matter what it looked like to Ivy or that this wasn't a protection mission. They were either going to find Morgan dead or utterly clueless as to what was going on. Luckily for her, it was the latter.

Ramsey wanted her off the case and suspended, but by some miracle, they left her on. Reprimanded, but still on the case. Ivy wasn't sure how she'd managed that, though. She knew they'd try to pull her before she even walked into York's office. She had no high-ranking friends and hadn't done anything to prove herself yet. The only thing she could think of was that the killer had contacted her personally, and they didn't want to disrupt anything they could get from those conversations. They knew the killer wouldn't care who they put on the case. He would still call Ivy because he'd fixated on her like he did Burns. The only thing that saved her from being taken off the biggest case of her career was the person she was chasing.

There wasn't anything else she could do from the office today, so she decided to go home early, get some rest and start again fresh in the morning. She stood and pulled her purse off its perch, hanging on the edge of her cubicle.

Her phone rang.

She sighed, dropped her purse back on the corner, and pulled her phone from her pocket. A tingle of excitement ran through her body when she didn't recognize the phone number. She fell back into her chair and answered the phone.

"Detective Chandler."

"Bumper stickers," the barely constrained voice said.

Maybe it was the wrong number.

"Excuse me?"

"I said, bumper stickers. Fucking bumper stickers."

Ivy sat up straight. It was him, and he'd obviously read Leonard's article.

"I...uh... What are you talking about?"

She kicked her cubicle wall. That had to be the worst response, and his laughing confirmed it. Though it wasn't his typical, over-the-top, I'm smarter than everybody maniacal laugh. There was anger and hatred barely hiding behind the laughter.

"You know what I'm talking about, detective. I know you and your bosses keep tabs on Jonathan Leonard's search party. He's calling everybody in the CVPD incompetent and can't wait until he can rub your pig noses in your mess. I'd be rooting for him if it wasn't me that he was hunting."

"You don't seem like the Leonard type."

"I hate his politics. He's an unseemly monster that only cares for himself. He's not anti-cop, just anti-CVPD. If the higher ups were composed of people he liked, he would be their biggest fan."

"You don't like the CVPD?"

"That doesn't mean anything. I don't like any cops. The only thing special about your department is that you're the ones failing to catch me."

"But we will."

Ivy pulled the phone away from her ear as the laugh erupted from the receiver. She'd managed to get him back to normal. Normal for him, anyway.

"No, detective. I don't think you will. But that's not the reason why I'm calling."

"Then why are you calling?"

"Because I had to vent to somebody before I lost my mind and made a rash decision. It was one thing when they formed their little city neighborhood watches to find out who I am, but now they've gone too far."

"Why? Do you think they're on to you? They said their investigation was progressing."

"Ha. They haven't made any more progress than they had the day he left the TV station. All that posturing was for a damn commercial."

Ivy didn't disagree with him. It made sense. Like anything, the motivation behind it sounded like it was money.

"There's no need for me to worry about anything. Nobody will ever catch me. I know you hate to hear it because you hoped catching me would make your career. Sorry, but it's not going to happen."

"Being conceited is going to trip you up."

"I'm not conceited. I'm convinced, and that's all that matters, but that's not the issue."

"Then what's the issue?"

"Try to keep up. It's been a long day."

Ivy gripped the phone tightly in her hand.

"The issue is that this third-rate reporter is making money on my brand."

"Your brand?" Ivy asked with just enough condescension to keep him talking. They'd been tapping her phone since the first time he'd called, and they'd be tracking where this call was coming from as they spoke.

"Yes. I know you've seen the article, so I know you've seen all the merchandise he's selling. You can't be that dense. How does he know about it, anyway? I've never seen any news about it on there. There has to be a leak within the department. It isn't you, is it, detective?"

He was right. They hadn't shared any information on the case with anybody, so how did he know?

"Of course it's not me. I'd never do anything to jeopardize my case."

"No. I didn't think so. And it wasn't Greg. Apparently, he didn't tell anybody anything."

Was there a leak in the department? She didn't think anybody in the homicide unit would do something like that, but there were a lot of other people she couldn't speak for.

"Anyway, that's your problem, not mine. My problem is this guy is making money off my name. He's seen my genius, and now he wants some of it for himself, and without thinking, he's taken it and packaged it and slapped it on some merch, some popular around the office koozies, and now he's selling it. He's selling me. Except it's not my message. It's his. It's his bastardization of what I'm doing, and I don't like it."

Ivy heard an opening and went for it.

"What is your message? What are you doing that he's mocking?"

"I don't expect you to understand."

"That's not an answer."

"No, it isn't. But suppose I broke everything down for you and explained every thought and move I made. It wouldn't matter."

"Why do you think that?"

"Because nothing I told you would ever be good enough. I could tell you every minute detail of what I've gone through and what I've done, but it would never justify it in your eyes. Even if I told you the truth, you wouldn't believe it. Because you can't understand it. Nobody can. Why do you think true crime books and podcasts fascinate so many people? It's not because they're killers in training trying to glean any tips or tricks they can learn from what's happened in the past. So I'll just say because I like it."

He was right. There was nothing he or anybody else like him could say that would make too much difference. Murder was wrong, and that's all there was to it. Nothing could justify cold-blooded murder in Ivy's eyes. But she had managed to calm him down, it seemed. That was good for everybody, and none more than Jonathan Leonard.

"I have to say, detective, this is not how I anticipated this conversation going."

"What do you mean?"

"I thought I would rant and rave, and you'd try to calm me down, and I wouldn't listen. Then I'd hang up, track Jonathan Leonard down, make a noose out of his intestines and hang him by the neck from whatever building he is hiding in, but now I think I'll just go home instead."

Ivy recoiled at the mental picture he'd given her.

"I'm glad I could do that for you."

"Don't pat yourself on the back too hard there, detective. Leonard is a marked man, no doubt. You haven't saved his life. You've just given him the gift of a few more days."

Air rushed from Ivy's lungs. She felt deflated. She hadn't saved anybody tonight; she'd prolonged the inevitable. Though maybe there was a way they could use it to their advantage. She didn't like the idea of using a civilian as bait, but Leonard wasn't an ordinary civilian, and he'd gotten himself into this mess on his own.

"I guess that's all for now. I'm sure your friends have had plenty of time to track me to the Lonesome Pines subdivision. I stole the phone from some kid in Rusted Lakes Park."

Ivy's breath caught in her throat, and a strangled choking sound came out.

"Don't worry. I didn't kill the kid. I'm not a monster. I would never hurt a child. I just made him realize that the phone was more important to me than him."

Ivy relaxed in her chair again.

"As I was saying, that's about all I have time for today. I have an old friend to look in on."

The phone clicked before Ivy had a chance to respond. She stood and walked briskly toward Lieutenant York's office. Having listened to the conversation, York was already standing at her door, waiting for Ivy with her arms across her chest. She spoke before Ivy even had a chance to tell her where she was going.

"Good job calming him down. That could have been a volatile situation if you hadn't."

"Thank you."

"Don't thank me. You haven't saved the day yet. You need to get to Leonard now and tell him that he's gotten the killer's attention and is in danger. He's not going to want it but offer to put a few extra cars in the area."

Ivy turned and walked down two rows of cubicles and out the homicide unit door without saying a word. York hadn't meant to praise her, but it was the first step to getting back in the lieutenant's good graces. Detectives tended to stay on the outs with her for extended periods of time and never truly knew when they were officially off her shit list.

She thought about calling Carson to fill him in and see if he wanted to go with her. She didn't want him around, but having two arrogant men in the same room together would either make them neutralize each other or start a fight. Either way might be interesting. In the end, she opted to go alone. She was done peopling for the day, and the fewer she had to encounter, the better.

Ivy sat in her car, slid the key into the ignition, and froze. Something was off. It didn't make sense. The killer had called to complain about Leonard, but she'd been able to talk him down. She shouldn't have been able to do that. Once he made up his mind to do something, he would do it then. It's a compulsion. It'd drive him crazy until he did it. She finally cranked the car and sat back in the seat while the air conditioner cooled the interior.

She closed her eyes and thought back to her conversation. There was something she was missing. Leonard could be in trouble now if she were wrong, but she didn't feel like that was the case. What had he said about an old friend?

She couldn't remember, then it came to her. He said he had an old friend to look in on. But who was he talking about? Ivy hadn't confirmed with York, but he'd said they'd already figured out he was in the Lonesome Pines subdivision. York would have told Ivy if he'd been lying to her, and they'd have gone to where the trace led them.

Lonesome Pines sounded familiar because she'd almost driven through there to question Bobby Cotton when he wasn't at work. Her brain felt sluggish as it finally dawned on her. The killer had seen Bobby Cotton at Meadow Butler's house, and now he was taking care of loose ends.

Ivy threw the car in reverse and dialed Lieutenant York's number. She'd have to talk to Jonathan Leonard later. The only eyewitness they had was in danger.

Chapter Eighteen

Ivy's car slid into the Lonesome Pines subdivision and almost took out the neighborhood sign. She had killed the sirens before approaching and now killed the lights. York had insisted they send a few units to check on Leonard in the off chance she was wrong. It pissed her off that York was second-guessing her, no matter how many times she told herself that it would be better safe than sorry. If she was wrong, and somebody high profile died who they could have saved, there would be no saving her job. It wouldn't matter if the killer called and asked her to dinner. They wouldn't care anymore.

She had been instructed to wait at the entrance to the cul-de-sac for backup and the Rapid Response Team. Ramsey would love to have another chance to show her up or make her look foolish. Anything he could do to get her canned would be good for him at this point. She pulled in behind a squad car and waited in the dark. The neighborhood was gloomy and quiet. The only sound was the crack of the radio with units checking in. The RRT gave their position as turning off Hawthorne Springs Road into the subdivision. Ivy would be able to hear their military engine at any moment. She never understood why they needed a vehicle like that. If they all wanted to ride together, they could use a van. They didn't need a decommissioned military vehicle that had been cruising around a foreign desert two years ago.

Alex North and his partner checked in that they'd made contact with Jonathan Leonard at his place of business. He was fine and had refused any security from the city. North responded they would stay in the area for a while.

The RRT pulled into the cul-de-sac without waiting for anybody else to show up. Ivy rolled her eyes and stepped from her car. She walked down the street with the cops who were parked in front of her.

The RRT members filed out of their truck and fanned out across the front yard. Ramsey led the charge up the front steps to the door. They flanked both sides of the door and waited for confirmation before breaching.

The officer with the ram stepped in front of the door. Ivy held her breath as she waited for him to smash the door open. Then he did something that surprised her. He reached out and turned the door-knob. The door swung open, and the RRT funneled into the house.

Ivy listened as each member said "clear" on the radio. She had given up hope of finding anybody alive at home. Bobby had been the only eyewitness who'd seen the killer. There was no way he would let him live like nothing ever happened. She kicked herself for not checking in on him sooner and trying to convince him that it would be in his best interest to stay elsewhere for a while. If the killer had been watching Meadow Butler for a while, he knew about Bobby and where he lived. Screams to get on the ground came from inside the house and startled Ivy from her thoughts. They'd found some-body alive in the house, and no shots were fired. That was a good sign.

The yelling finally stopped, but they hadn't emerged from the house yet. Ivy walked through the dead grass of the front yard and climbed the rickety stairs to the porch. When she reached the front door, Ramsey came out with a red-faced and handcuffed Bobby Cotton.

"What are you doing, Ramsey? He's not the suspect."

"He resisted and wouldn't tell me his name."

"I'm not telling you a fucking thing. This is my house."

Ramsey twisted the cuffs on Bobby's wrist until he winced.

"You'll tell me everything I want to hear."

"I'll tell you to kiss my ass," Bobby said through gritted teeth.

"Let him go," Ivy ordered, standing behind Ramsey.

"Nah. I don't think I will. You might have jumped in the way earlier, but this one is mine."

Great. Ramsey would make everything a pissing contest between them from now on, and right now, Bobby Cotton had to suffer because Ramsey had to be the Alpha.

"I sense there is some animosity between you two, and I want no part of it, so if you'd let me go, I'll go back inside, and you can all fuck off."

Bobby winced again as Ramsey pulled the cuffs.

"Let him go. He's not the suspect."

"He looks guilty to me."

"Why would he make those calls from his house?"

"Criminals are stupid."

Bobby's shoulders sagged. He almost looked bored, like a child stuck in the middle of their parent's fight, and he didn't understand.

"Criminal? I was in my house minding my own business. Now that I think about it, which one of you assholes has a warrant?"

"We don't need one."

"The hell you don't. You can't bust in and arrest whoever you want."

"We thought you were in imminent danger. We don't need a warrant."

Bobby fought against the cuffs until he was face-to-face with Ramsey.

"Then why am I the one in the fucking cuffs?"

Ramsey squared around like he was preparing to hit Bobby. The entire situation was getting out of control, and there wasn't anything that Ivy could do to stop it. Bobby hadn't done anything wrong, and everything he said was true. Ramsey had no cause to hold him. If Ivy said anything, he would double down. She turned to the road, wishing York would pull up and stop everything before it got any worse.

"Cause I think you're guilty. I think you killed all those girls, and are screwing with us, so we don't think it's you."

"I don't know what you're talking about, but you can go fu—"

An officer came around the corner of the house and said, "We found something in the backyard."

It wasn't the interruption she'd hoped for, but it would have to do. Ramsey stood nose to nose with Bobby.

"If I find a dead girl back there, I'm going to be very upset. Watch him and try not to let him get away by the time I get back."

"What the hell is he talking about?" Bobby asked Ivy.

Ramsey pushed past Bobby, walked down the steps, and disappeared around the corner. Ivy watched the side of the house and Bobby from the corner of her eye. He didn't speak. He stood there with the same bored look on his face. Then, as if he needed to prove how uninterested he was in everything going on, he yawned and leaned against the doorcase.

Ramsey finally came back around the side of the house. He stomped up the stairs and got in Bobby's face again.

"What size shoe do you wear?"

"What kind of question is that?"

"It's the one I'm telling you to answer."

Ivy tried to step between the two men, but Ramsey jerked away from her hand.

"Why do you want to know what size shoe he wears?"

Ramsey sighed and turned his ire toward Ivy.

"Because we're doing actual police work here. There were boot prints in the flower bed out back like somebody was peeping through the window."

"Wait. Somebody was looking through my window? You don't think it was The Suicide Killer, do you? Oh shit. He could have been getting ready to kill me."

"Shut up."

"I guess I should be thanking you for scaring him off. If you take the cuffs off, I'll give you a hug."

"Shut the hell up."

"Come on. Let's hug it out. No hard feelings."

Bobby had the same playful gleam in his eyes when Ivy spoke to him at Meadow's house. It unnerved her. She couldn't stop Ramsey from being an ass, but if she could get Bobby to cooperate, Ramsey might back off.

"Mr. Cotton, I'm sure you have more important things to be doing right now. If you could please indulge Captain Ramsey in this one question, he can be on his way."

Bobby didn't answer. He stared Ivy down. She was about to break eye contact and look away, and he dropped his head to the side like she had confused him and he wanted to study her closely. It made her skin crawl.

"Okay, I'll bite. I wear a nine and a half."

"Can you tell what size the prints are, Ramsey?"

"It's not exact, but they're bigger than mine, and I wear a twelve."

"Wow. You know what they say about guys with big shoes? The bigger dicks they are," Bobby said, and laughed quietly to himself.

Ramsey growled.

"Can we see your shoes?"

"Sure, I don't have anything to hide. They're right inside the door."

Ramsey tipped his head toward the door, and one of his team ran up the stairs and grabbed the shoes.

"They're nine and a half, sir."

"See. I wasn't lying. Can you take these things off now?" Bobby asked, and twisted his hands toward Ramsey.

"Can we search the house?"

"Now that, you're going to need a warrant for."

"Why? I thought you said you didn't have anything to hide?"

"I don't, but I can't have you tearing up my house for no reason since you're not going to find anything here."

Ramsey took the cuffs off Bobby and walked back to the truck without saying a word. The rest of his team knew it was time to go and marched to the truck. Within minutes, they were gone. Bobby sat on the porch while Ivy took pictures of the boot prints outside the window.

She walked back around the house, and he was still rubbing the red marks on his wrists.

"Okay, Mr. Cotton, we got everything we need. I want to apologize for the way Captain Ramsey acted. Everybody is on high alert until we catch this killer, but that is no excuse for how he treated you."

Bobby didn't respond. He continued to rub his wrists. It was a half-assed apology, but she shouldn't have been the one apologizing in the first place. She'd thought about leaving without saying anything to him and hoped he'd file a complaint against Ramsey, but the department didn't need any more bad press in the news if they could help it.

"Don't worry. I'm not going to try to sue the city or anything. You don't have to smooth things over. I have better things to do than fight losing battles in court."

"Given that we did find boot prints in your flowerbed that aren't yours, I still think it would be a good idea if we had a car stay with you until this is over."

Bobby shuffled his feet and looked around. She could tell he didn't want the protection but couldn't think of a good enough excuse not to accept it.

"I appreciate it. The police department obviously has the citizens' best interests in mind as they try to find this killer, but I'm not worried about him. If he had planned to kill me, he would have done it before you got here."

"I hope you're right, Mr. Cotton, but if you change your mind, you still have my card."

"It's on the fridge."

"Okay, then, have a good evening. Somebody from the department might drop by in a few days to check in on you."

Bobby nodded and walked inside the house. Ivy didn't want to turn her back to the house but didn't want to look ridiculous walking backward, either. She couldn't shake the eerie feeling whenever she was around Bobby Cotton. Ramsey must have felt the same way if he'd taken such a considerable risk with the way he acted. It couldn't have only been to upstage Ivy, could it?

Ivy didn't want to think about it anymore. There was still a killer on the loose in the city who would be more than happy to take advantage of them being distracted on dead ends. She was hungry but decided she'd rather drive home and go straight to bed. This case had taken a lot out of her so far, and she had another asshole to deal with tomorrow when she went to talk to Jonathan Leonard.

Chapter Nineteen

Ivy pulled into the parking lot of a square two-story building. The bricks looked like they had recently been whitewashed and made the building stand out in stark contrast to the deep green forest flanking the back and right side. Three men stood on the side of the building, facing the avenue that led to a once prominent neighborhood. Ivy parked her car in the front of the building facing the Wynnton Road traffic. She walked toward the front door but changed direction when she heard one of the men on the side of the building speak. It was easy to recognize the person calling out orders. She'd been hearing that voice on her TV for years.

She turned the corner, and the two men working were the only ones to acknowledge her presence. The man barking out orders continued facing the other direction. It was clear he was irritated at their lack of initiative and how they were easily distracted from their job. Ivy covered her eyes from the blinding sun and the reflection it caused, bouncing off the bright white brick. A large red N covered the middle portion of the wall. Its legs extended to the ground on one side and to the roof on the other. They hadn't completed the slash through it yet, but it looked garish and out of place surrounded by past decadence.

The man in a brown suit and fedora finally turned to see who stood behind him. He made a double take, removed his hat, and wiped the sweat from his reddening brow. Jonathan Leonard walked up to Ivy, still holding his hat in his hand. A slight breeze blew what was left of his hat hair in all directions.

"These guys act like they've never seen a pretty woman before," he said to Ivy, then turned to the men and yelled, "We don't have all day to fix this mess, so let me know what your *expert* opinion is soon." He made air quotes and emphasized expert.

Leonard held his hand out and ushered Ivy toward the front door. She quickened her pace so he could not rest his hand on the small of her back. When they got to the door, he skipped in front of her, grabbed the door, and held it for her to enter. After scrubbing his shoes on a worn doormat, he followed her inside. The air conditioner chilled the air, making her shudder as the built-up sweat cooled on her skin.

Large off-white tiles covered the lobby floor and led off to three side rooms. The only fixtures in the entrance were the gloss black wrought iron stairs leading to the second floor landing and a battle scarred desk. Behind the desk sat a woman busying herself with the computer.

"Well, Darlin', I'm not sure if we had an appointment today, but if you'd like to check in with Bernice here, I'm sure she'll get you settled while I clean up."

Leonard's smile was like a hyena, too large for its face and waiting to pounce at the first sign of weakness.

"It's actually detective, not darlin'. Detective Ivy Chandler. And I don't have an appointment."

Leonard's smile faltered, but only slightly. Years in journalism trained him not to let anything get to him, but she could still tell he wasn't happy to see her. However, she didn't know if it was because he didn't want any police around or if it was because he didn't want her specifically around. With all the propaganda he was spreading, he had to know that the police would eventually show up, though he was undoubtedly hoping for somebody a bit higher up so he could sensationalize it in his next article.

"Well now, why didn't you say so, Detective Chandler? The CVPD doesn't need to have an appointment. They are welcome here any time."

"That's not the way it sounds in your articles."

"Got to rile up the base. Otherwise, you're just pissing in the wind. Plus, it's not like anything I've said was a lie. They haven't done anything to protect this city in a long time. I'm sorry if you took what I said about you being a rookie the wrong way, but the way I see it, they need to have their most tenured detectives on this case."

"Like you said, the way you see it."

"Right. I'll be glad to answer any questions you have if you'll follow me to my office. Bernice doesn't like it when we talk about the gory details around her."

Leonard didn't wait for a reply. He turned and walked up the black staircase. He talked to her over his shoulder as they ascended the stairs.

"I'd like to thank ya for sending some boys in blue over here to check on us last night. That officer North is a nice fella."

Ivy didn't like the implication. When they reached the top, he stopped and faced Ivy.

"Give me just a second. I want to check on those two outside," he said, and walked into the room directly off the landing. He went to the window and made a clicking sound with his tongue as he shook his head.

"I can't tell what they're doing out there, but it's not work because they aren't even looking at the building."

"Are they painting your merchandise logo on the side of the building?"

"Oh, heavens no. That would be tacky."

At least he drew the line at some point.

"Then what are they doing?"

Leonard walked across the landing to the other side of the floor and entered an office with a large frosted window like old detective movies. His name in gold-leaf was in the middle. He opened the door, ushered her inside, and closed it behind them. It was noticeably warmer in the office. Two large cherry wood bookshelves lined the back wall behind an ornately decorated cherry wood desk covered with scattered papers. Organized chaos, she assumed he would tell her if she asked about the mess. Pictures and post-it notes covered two of the walls. Red yarn connected a number of the pins. Her initial reaction was that Leonard was just another conspiracy theory nut who'd taken things too far. She only wanted to warn him of the potential danger he and all of his followers might be in.

"They're trying to figure out the best way to get rid of it. My first reaction was to put a slash through it, but Bernice pointed out how gaudy and unprofessional that would look. So I got those two guys out there to tell me what the best way to cover it would be. Unfortunately, I'm afraid they're going to have to whitewash everything all over again."

"Did you file a report for the vandalism?"

Leonard let out a deep belly laugh as he walked around the desk and fell into his chair. He wiped tears from his eyes and slapped an open hand on his desk.

"Thank you. I needed that."

Blood flushed Ivy's face. Why the hell was he laughing at her?

"If I don't trust the cops to catch a serial killer, what makes you think I'd call them to catch somebody vandalizing my building? And even if I did call them, they wouldn't do anything about it after everything I've said about them. But that's sweet that you still believe in the good of mankind and all that. We'll see how you are when you reach my age."

Ivy wanted to be mad at him, but she had walked into that one. There was such a thing as stupid questions. People only said that when they needed engagement from an audience they weren't getting it from. She decided to play along with him and laughed at herself.

"Good point. Kind of walked right into that one," she said and looked down as she shuffled her feet.

Leonard rocked back in his chair and gestured to the empty one in front of his desk.

"Ah, don't worry about it. We all have our moments. This isn't as nice a neighborhood as it once was. Not by a long shot. But that doesn't really matter. We got the vandal on our security camera. He was wearing a mask, but we know it was The Suicide Killer not some neighborhood kid."

Ivy perked up in her seat. Leonard didn't move. He watched for her reaction, enjoying every minute of this conversation. He wanted to see the police department squirm, and she was the department proxy. She rubbed her sweaty palms down her pants like she was trying to straighten out the wrinkles.

"How uh ... how do you know that?"

"Would you believe me if I told you it was a reporter's intuition?"

Ivy stared at him with a blank face.

"I didn't think so."

She continued staring at Leonard until he finally opened his desk drawer, removed a folded piece of paper, and handed it to her.

"He slid this under the front door. Now, we're not handwriting experts around here, but it would seem to match the handwriting from the letters he's left at the crime scenes."

Ivy stared to open the paper but stopped.

"How do you know what those letters say? We haven't released any of those."

"I obviously can't divulge a source, but I know what they look like. I also know he's been contacting you. I'm glad you did the smart thing and told your lieutenant about it instead of hiding it like Burns did."

"That's actually the reason I came out here. He called me yesterday and was more than a little angry about your last article with your merchandise."

"We gotta keep the lights on."

"Yes, and you're using him to do it."

Leonard sat up in his chair and leaned his elbows on the desk.

"Whose side are you on? Nobody was doing anything productive in this city, so I decided to do something about it."

"Whatever you need to tell yourself to justify what you're doing. I'm not on his side, but I also don't think you should be getting yourself or anybody else around here involved in any homicide cases. Somebody is going to end up getting hurt."

"I'm not forcing anybody to do anything they don't want to do. As my article said, I don't want everybody trying to get involved. Aside from Bernice downstairs, I only have eight volunteers who are helping in various capacities. Now, why don't you have a look at that letter and see if I know what I'm talking about."

Ivy carefully unfolded the letter.

This is The Suicide Killer speaking,

I bet you think you're clever with your merchandise scam. I'm sure it makes you feel like a big man while you steal from all those people who have watched and trusted you over the years to provide them with the news. It's sickening. I am demanding that you stop this game at once. There is no way you can win, and the price of losing is death. Using my signature is not smart or cute. It pisses me off and makes me want to wait for you in a dark corner of your office, peel the skin from your sorry body, and then hang you upside down from the front window for all who drive by to see.

How long do you think it will take them to realize you're real and not some Halloween decoration put up a little too soon? I don't think anybody would take too much notice until Bernice comes in just before lunch. That's right. I know your routine as well as your secretary's. I also know when the two cops and the other six people who work with you show up. I could go into names and times, but that would be boring. Just know that I know, and I can end it any time that I want. I am the one in charge. Not you. I don't care about your investigation or your articles. They humor me. So you can continue them and say whatever bullshit you come up with, but I draw the line at my signature. It's my identity, as I'm sure you understand.

Sincerely,

N

Ivy folded the note and placed it on the desk.

"Can I have a copy of this?"

"I'll make a copy for you. I'd ask Bernice, but I don't want her reading it."

"Why not? It involves her. She's not safe here. There's no telling what else he knows about her or anybody else that comes here."

"I know, but you read the letter. He doesn't care what we're doing here. He just doesn't want us using his identity."

He had a point. From what she knew about the killer, he lived by some demented set of rules and didn't seem to break them unless somebody forced him.

"Then you're going to stop selling everything?"

"I don't think so."

It confused Ivy how a deranged killer could directly threaten you, and your first response was to not comply with a basic request to stop doing something that was in bad taste in the first place. It was one thing for Leonard to put himself in danger, but now he was putting other people in danger who didn't have any say.

"You're endangering the lives of everybody here."

"I plan to let Bernice work from home until this has blown over. The rest of the guys know what they're getting themselves into."

"This is crazy."

"Maybe. But it could all be over real soon."

"How's that?"

Ivy shifted in her seat. Leonard was just as cocky as the killer and half as dangerous, but it intrigued her to find out if he actually knew anything or if this would be another ploy to bait the killer.

"Like I said, we got him on camera."

She wanted to grab the cup on his desk overflowing with pens and throw it at him. She rocked forward, then settled for an exaggerated sigh. A loose strand of hair fell in her face, and she blew it away from her nose.

"Not impressed, I see. Subtle."

"Are you going to tell me, or is the letter the only thing you have?"

Leonard laughed to himself.

"We are a small group of journalists and cameramen, but we are growing. Soon we will be a formidable foe for the criminals in this city."

"The one thing you always forget is that you're not police. Even if you solved a case, there isn't anything you can do about it. You still need us to finish the job."

"Yes, that is true. For now."

For now? What the hell was that supposed to mean? Unless he was attempting to recruit cops to do his dirty work for him. The last thing Crystal Valley needed was a loud-mouthed reporter who had his sights set on the mayor's office with his own special police. From the killer's note, it sounded like he'd already recruited two cops into his group. Downtown would not be happy if they heard about two of their cops moonlighting with Jonathan Leonard. Not to mention the issues it could cause with any court case they could eventually have. Ivy wanted to argue that point but realized it wouldn't get her anywhere, and she was ready to be anywhere else than in Jonathan Leonard's office.

He leaned over, opened the bottom desk drawer, removed three manila folders, and dropped them on the desk in front of Ivy. She didn't immediately pick them up and waited for him to speak first.

"In those folders are the names of three suspects we have come up with."

Ivy's breath caught in her throat. She coughed to keep from choking but was unable to hide her surprise. There had to be a leak in the department. That would be the only way, except they didn't have any suspects or strong leads on the case, so he had to have been working on it long before the Burns controversy broke.

"I see you're surprised. Maybe even a little jealous? Huh, detective Chandler?"

Shock and ineptitude were more what she felt, but she'd never give him the satisfaction of hearing her say it. He might have been able to read it all over her face, but she'd never say it. She moved toward the files and hesitated.

"Go ahead. You can look at them. Hell, I'm feeling so generous today. I'll let you have those copies."

Now she really had to get out of there. He would be a condescending prick for the rest of the conversation.

"How?" was all she managed to say.

He leaned back in his chair with a widening grin on his face. He was proud of himself. She doubted he'd done any of the legwork in the files, but the pictures and yarn hanging on the wall said he was the brains.

"Just doing our job. We have three suspects, but that first one has moved to the top of the list after this episode outside."

Ivy flipped the file open.

"Why's that?"

"After he got done defacing our building and sliding his love note under the door, he ran back around the side and got into a dark-colored SUV. That fella in the bottom file was tied up and beaten pretty badly the other night. They're surprised he lived. A young woman who happened to be on the bridge at the same time as our killer wasn't so lucky. He smashed her face on the rail and threw her over. She drowned in the river."

"I haven't heard about either one of those cases."

"Can't say I'm surprised you guys haven't connected the cases, but I'll give you the benefit of the doubt here. He didn't leave no note or any calling card."

"Then how do you know they're connected?"

Leonard already had a smile on his face, like a child waiting for his parents to ask how he did something so he could show them how smart he was.

"We've started a few neighborhood watches in a few areas, and it just so happened that one of our team leaders was on patrol that night and saw the suspect run from the house, attack the girl and then get into an SUV. Just like the one in our video feed."

He was really proud of himself. He leaned over, flipped his hat in his hand, and gently placed it on top of his head. Then, he stood and walked around the large desk, prompting Ivy to stand with him. Now, he was the one in a hurry.

They walked in silence down the stairs and across the titled lobby floor. As they reached their cars in the parking lot, he called out over the roof of his freshly washed Cadillac.

"You know, I was surprised to hear from you. Most of the police around here look at my brand of investigative journalism like it's one step above asking a psychic for help. What changed your mind?"

"I came down here to warn you, and I'd be lying if I said I wasn't a little curious if you knew anything about the case."

Leonard smiled.

"So you don't think I'm a joke?"

"I didn't say that. I figure this case had gone on long enough before I got involved, and it's ramping up again. I want to stop him before he hurts any more people. And besides, you're my last ditch effort before I give the psychic a call," she said and ducked into her car before he had a chance to respond. He was still smiling at her when she pulled out of the parking lot.

Chapter Twenty

A blinking streetlight in the distance let Bobby know his turn was coming up on the left. He was beginning to get used to talking to Ivy. She'd never replace Greg, but she was a worthy successor, and it was time to fan her flame before it faded to embers. Michelle Parker was the next name he pulled from his stack of files. It would be another two hours before she got home, but it gave him enough time to plan everything out. There had been plenty of times when he thought it'd be a good idea to prepare what he would do once the target got home, but he'd grown to love the thrill of winging it. Like a skilled musician, he knew every part of his song from front to back. There was nothing he hadn't planned for, but he did like to improvise the solo. Jazz it up a bit. It kept things interesting and him on his toes.

He turned onto Wagner Lane. The hood of the car he'd recently stolen flashed in the orangish blinking street light that welcomed everybody to Wagner Estates. The neighborhood wasn't too far from Jonathan Leonard's headquarters. It'd taken a small miracle for him not to drive by there again.

Something was wrong. He sensed it as soon as he turned off the main road. The neighborhood didn't feel right. The welcome light was the same, but he couldn't figure out what was different as he slowly drove down the street and waved at two people walking down the road. It finally hit him when he turned onto Wagner Circle. The streets were too bright. It had been a few weeks since he'd driven these roads, but it was noticeably brighter. They had the streetlights fixed. Before, almost all the streetlights in the neighborhood didn't work, or the power was turned off because this used to be one of the darkest neighborhoods in Crystal Valley. It was one of the things that had initially drawn him to it. Getting away was a lot easier when they helped you out.

He drove to the other end of the loop and threw the car into park. The engine clunked and knocked a couple of times before it finally died, leaving him in silence. It would have been smarter to case the place before he'd decided to show up, ready to kill. Michelle's house was two from the end of the loop, where it rejoined Wagner Lane. The light on the corner, plus the one newly awakened in her front yard, lit up her house like she'd added spotlights. It didn't help that she always left the front porch light and the two hanging at the entrance to the garage on at all times. It didn't matter what time of day it was; they were always on.

Two walkers came around the bend in the road. They were both wearing black t-shirts with a red logo on the front. They looked similar, but not quite the same as the two people he'd seen when he entered the neighborhood. As they got closer, he realized what was on their shirts. It was the same shirts he'd seen for sale on Leonard's website. Rage boiled through his body, and he grabbed the door handle. He put his shoulder against the door and prepared to swing the door out and hit the passersby. He'd teach them to listen to that man. Leonard's words seemed a bit cultish, but now that he was recruiting followers, there was nothing else to call them. The city was supposed to be cowering in fear, not parading around town wearing their false bravado on their chests. These two thought they were some half-assed neighborhood watch protecting their community, but they'd both piss themselves if they knew how close they were to death right now.

They cautiously approached the backend of the black Plymouth that'd seen too many dirt roads in its life. Bobby prepared to jump out of the car, but something caught his attention at the last moment. One of them carried a radio like you'd see the police have. Bobby slouched, hoping the tinted windows were dark enough to hide him from their prying eyes.

They backed up and walked to the rear of the car. Bobby watched in the rearview mirror as the one carrying the radio moved it to his lips. The woman with him looked back and forth across the street. They were taking this seriously. Too serious for Bobby to talk his way out of, and the neighborhood was lit up like the festival was in town. It was too risky to get out and handle them. There were no doubt a number of security cameras watching the streets from all angles.

He couldn't see the couple anymore and slowly slid up in the seat. The couple stood on the porch of the house he parked in front of. The man beat on the door as his partner nervously watched the car and street.

A blinding beam of light blasted him in the face, and he ducked to protect his eyes. When he looked over the steering wheel, the two people he'd seen walking earlier ran toward the car. He hadn't noticed before, but they both wore the same black t-shirts. He closed his eyes and prayed to the god he didn't believe in that the piece of junk he sat in would start up as soon as he turned the screwdriver. If it stalled, one of them might try to be a hero and stop him. Eyes still closed, he turned the flathead, but nothing happened.

He sat up straight, and yelling erupted from outside. They'd seen him. Two ran toward the front of the car while the man jumped off the steps and charged the side. Bobby pulled the screwdriver out and jammed it back into the ignition. The engine clicked but wouldn't turn over. He put both hands on the wheel and screamed at the dashboard as he rocked back and forth. The man hit the side of the car and started beating on the window, yelling something unintelligible through the glass. Bobby could take him, but the other two were about to reach the car, and that would be a little harder for him. Plus, he didn't know how far out the cops were.

He jammed the screwdriver back into the ignition and turned it as hard and far as he could. The shaft started to bend when the engine roared to life. He revved the engine a couple of times, put it into drive, and floored it as the other couple came within a few feet of the car. One of the men must have thought Bobby would stop if he acted like he was going to step in front of the car, but Bobby clipped him with the steel front bumper.

Bobby looked back and saw the man rocking on the side of the road, clutching his knee. He wouldn't be playing in the community flag football game again. The big car chugged through the stop sign, coughing out clouds of blue smoke. Many people in the neighborhood must have had a radio because they all stepped on their porch as Bobby floored it down the street. He didn't let off the gas until he'd driven to the other side of town and crashed into the chain link fence surrounding an out-of-commission forestry watch tower. He jumped from the car and ran to his waiting bronco.

The ride home was quiet in the truck and in his head. He drove home on autopilot. There would be plenty of time for contemplation later. The neighborhood watch sign with a figure wearing a black hat and trench coat now covered with a slashed out N barely registered as he turned on his street.

Chapter Twenty-One

It had been a long day, and all Ivy wanted to do was get home and climb into bed. She was hungry but not enough to worry about stopping to grab something on the way home, and there was no way she was going to cook anything. She slowed and turned on her blinker, and her phone rang. It was Brandon Carson. She turned her blinker off and continued slowly past her neighborhood, longing for the bed she knew she wouldn't be seeing for a while now.

"Ivy Chandler," she answered.

She then pushed the speakerphone button and stuck the phone between the sun visor and the roof of the car. The unmarked car she drove still didn't have Bluetooth. They wanted the public to drive hands-free but hadn't gotten around to doing it themselves.

"Ivy, it's Johnny. Where are you?"

She rolled her eyes at the fact that he thought he needed to tell her who he was like she wouldn't have his phone number saved.

"I was about to be home, but I'm guessing you're not going to let me do that."

"Not me. The Suicide Killer."

She jerked the wheel off the road and snapped awake. Now adrenaline would be controlling the next part of her evening.

"What do you mean? Did he kill somebody else?"

"Well, not exactly."

He dragged each word out like he was trying to add to the weirdness of the situation and build intrigue. It pissed her off.

"What the hell is that supposed to mean? Where are you?"

"He didn't kill anybody, but we have what we think would have been a crime scene."

He wasn't making sense. Ivy hoped they hadn't called him to the scene after he'd already downed a few. And why had they called him first? She sighed deeply into the phone.

"Where are you?"

"Wagner Loop in the Wagner Estates subdivision. You know where it is?"

Damn it. She was just over there warning Jonathan Leonard that he was playing with fire. Now she had to drive all the way back downtown.

"Yeah, I know where it is. I'll be there in a few," she said, and hung up the phone before he had a chance to respond.

Ivy flipped the blue dash lights on and headed back from where she'd come. The more she thought about it, the angrier she got. She'd just been right there. Had he been watching her, waiting for her to leave? Or was it all a coincidence? There'd be no way for the killer to know that she'd been there unless he'd happened to be there for Leonard and saw her. Of course, he was full of himself, so it was more likely that he'd defaced Leonard's building and then caused trouble in a close neighborhood to show him he wasn't afraid.

Ivy squinted her eyes as she pulled into the subdivision with the blinking streetlight. Blue and orange hues bounced and reflected off each other, and she made a blind turn. The second entrance to Wagner Loop was awash in blue lights, and nosey neighbors dressed alike in Leonard's t-shirts. She pulled her car up to the edge of Carson's pants leg. He turned as she stepped from the car.

"Did you call the entire department?"

"No," he said, then pointed his pen at a group of people standing off to the side, whispering amongst themselves, "they did. Apparently, they are one of the new neighborhood watch groups that are starting to pop up in a number of the neighborhoods around the city."

"Guess we have Leonard to thank for that."

"It's not that bad of an idea. Look how bright it is out here. Nobody is getting away with anything. I bet crime as a whole will go down everywhere."

Ivy's mouth dropped. At first, she couldn't believe Carson would actually think anything Leonard was doing would be a good idea. Somebody was going to get hurt. Though she had to admit, more eyes and ears would lower the chances of crime regularly happening. She tried to ignore him and go about the scene like she typically would. She looked suspiciously at all the uniformed cops who had also arrived before her. Maybe they all were sympathetic to the movement because it might make their jobs easier. Or, the crime would move to another part of town that wasn't as fortunate enough to have people to look out for everybody or afford the fancy security cameras that worked worth a damn and recorded at the right time and have a clear enough picture to look like anything other than a blurred out face like it was protecting the guilty instead of the other way around.

"So, if nobody was killed, why are we here?"

"Damn, Ivy. That's cold."

"I didn't mean it like that, but we're homicide cops."

Carson exchanged pleasantries with several cops as they worked their way through the growing crowd. None of them said a word to Ivy. They noticed her, some more than she'd like, but none said a word. She was walking through the boy's club tonight. They reached the corner of a pale green house everybody congregated in front of, and Carson spun on his heels.

"The neighborhood watch group said they were doing their rounds when they came across an old black Plymouth sitting in front of this house."

Ivy followed Carson's finger as he pointed toward the road. He was thinking, and it looked like it was starting to give him a headache. It must have been hard when you finally had to start acting like you wanted to do your job. She didn't particularly care for Carson, but she did have to admit, he'd been more serious around the office lately. At first, she'd thought he was jealous the killer called her instead of him, but now she felt it was personal for him like the victims finally had names and faces and families to him, where they were a toe tag number before. Ivy started taking notes.

"Did they see anybody?"

"Yes, and no."

"Please make sense."

"They saw the strange car but didn't see anybody inside. They walked up to the house and tried to get somebody to the door, but nobody was home. About that time, two more watchers came around from the front. Then the car started and drove off."

"I thought they didn't see anybody."

"That's why I said yes and no. They didn't see anybody at first, because the windows were so dark, but they saw one person in the car when they drove off. They tried to stop them but weren't able to. One of the other watchers got clipped by the bumper and had to be taken to the hospital. They don't make 'em the way they used to. Solid steel bumper shattered his kneecap."

And that was the problem with everything Leonard was stirring up. People who hadn't been trained and had no business patrolling the streets would continue getting hurt until he stopped with all his propaganda. They were scared, and she understood that, but now was not the time to do it themselves. She only hoped none of them were dumb enough to walk around with a gun.

As of now, one person who'd gotten too close to a car had been injured, but what would they say if an innocent person got shot because they locked themselves out of their house and looked suspicious as they tried to find the spare key? And God forbid a child gets caught in the crossfire. As responsible as they believed they were with guns, none of them had been through the same rigorous training that police have to go through, and hell, the police still made the wrong decision far too often. She wanted to say all of this to Carson but waited for him to continue so she'd find out why they were here instead of ending up in a philosophical debate.

"You don't want to know what all this has to do with us?" he asked

"Yes, I just didn't want to ruin your grand revelation."

"There's no need to be that way."

"Did they get the number on the tag?" she asked.

"Yes, but the car was reported stolen a few days ago," he said.

Ivy exhaled loudly.

"Then I don't see what the point ..."

Her mouth continued to move, but no words came out as Carson stepped back with a Vana White flourish and revealed the final consonant in the puzzle. An N with extended legs the size of a baseball had been carved into the siding of the house. The deep gash cut through the outer layer and had been colored in with a red marker. He'd been here. But when?

"Did he do that and get back in the car when the neighborhood heroes showed up?"

Carson made a disgusted face. She could tell his patience was wearing thin.

"Don't be so cynical. It's unbecoming."

"Let me guess; I should smile more, too."

"It wouldn't hurt."

She opened her mouth to tell him exactly how she felt about that, but he raised his hand in surrender. Or was it to silence her?

"Sorry. I take it back. It was only a joke because I knew it'd get you riled up. But seriously, these people just want to protect themselves and their community. I don't think we can fault them for that."

Damn it. He was right. When had he become the one to have everybody's back? He almost sounded like he was buying into the stuff that Leonard was peddling, but not on as dangerous of a scale, yet.

"But to answer your question. No, I don't think so. The two standing by that squad car over there are the ones who knocked on the door. The other two who came around from the front of the car saw it when it drove into the neighborhood, and that had only been ten minutes before."

"So there's no way to know if this was him or not. For all anybody knows, it could have been somebody who got lost and pulled over to look at their directions, and neighborhood watch scared them."

"Except the car was stolen, so it could have been."

"If that's true, then he'd been here before and had already cased the place. He was ready to kill somebody tonight."

Carson left Ivy staring at the symbol and walked around to the front porch. The N looked like it'd been there for a while. He could have been watching the house for months. That would make sense so that he would know their routine. Ivy realized she was alone, staring at the side of the house. She walked back to the front of the house and joined Carson, who was standing with Lieutenant York.

"So, do we think it was him?" York asked as Ivy walked up.

Carson didn't acknowledge her presence. Ivy could have sworn he turned his back and stepped between her and York like he was trying to freeze her out. This was her damn case, and she wasn't going to let him do that to her. She walked around to the other side to face both of them, and Carson couldn't squeeze her out without making it painfully obvious.

"There's no way to tell for sure, but given the carving on the side of the house, we think so. The neighborhood watch groups probably saved the couple's lives tonight. They didn't know how close to death they were."

Now he sounded like he was in charge. But what he was saying didn't make any sense.

"They weren't the targets. If it even was the killer," Ivy said, stepping forward.

Carson rolled his eyes and exhaled loudly.

"Everything that Johnny is saying sounds reasonable to me," York said.

"That's because it's pretty obvious that's what was going on. It's also pretty obvious that Ivy has a problem with citizens protecting themselves from a brutal killer. If they hadn't been here tonight, there's no telling when we would have found their bodies," Carson said, no longer trying to hide his contempt for Ivy in front of their boss.

Ivy stepped back and rested her weight on her back leg like she was preparing to pounce.

"That's not what is going on here at all. You know as well as I do that there is more than a good chance that somebody is going to end up getting hurt, or worse, because of Leonard's garbage."

"Sounds biased to me," Carson said, crossing his arms over his chest, resting his case.

York looked at her, imploring her to give her more than that as a response.

"None of this looks right," she said, waving her open hand around.

"Why?"

"I'm not saying it wasn't him. It probably was, but he wasn't here to kill anybody in this house."

"I gotta hear this. Did he tell you that on the phone over your morning coffee?"

"Fuck you, Carson."

York stepped between the two arguing detectives before they drew any more attention.

"That's enough. Both of you," York said, looking from one to the other, "now, tell me what you're seeing, Ivy," York finished, saying Ivy's name while staring at Carson.

Ivy took a deep breath.

"Because serial killers tend to either be organized or disorganized killers."

"Great, now she wants to be an FBI profiler."

York spun on Carson fast enough to make him take a step back.

"Damn it, Johnny, I'm not asking you again to keep your mouth shut. One more outburst and you're out of here," she said, and looked back at Ivy.

"But The Suicide Killer is the most disorganized organized killer I've seen."

York narrowed her eyes and cut them over at Carson when he scoffed.

"How so?" York asked.

"He's organized in how he sets up the scene. He shows us exactly what he wants us to see when he's finished. He's disorganized in how he kills his victims. It's almost like it wings when he gets there to add some sort of excitement to the process. It's like two people are raging inside his head."

"Come on, lieutenant, we don't have to listen to this. Now she's saying there are two of them, or one with multiple personalities. You going to give him and his lawyers their defense strategy now?"

"You're wrong, Johnny. You don't have to listen to this, but it's my job to listen to all plausible scenarios. It'd be a good idea for you to remember that if you ever want to be in my position."

The day Brandon "Johnny" Carson was her boss would be the day she'd transfer from her dream job or look for a career change. The thought made her shudder, and she forced the thought from her mind.

"The main reason none of this feels right is because of them," Ivy said, snapping her head back in the direction of the homeowners. Her ponytail whipped her in the face from the force. York and Carson's eyes followed her movement.

"He's killed different types of people. There's possibly a lot we don't even know about. But when he is setting up a scene, he only kills single women who live alone."

Ivy looked at Carson, who only shrugged his shoulders.

"This isn't his M.O. He wouldn't have bothered with them."

"Then why did he mark their house?"

Ivy looked at the front of the house. A security camera on the end of the porch was positioned to look out across the yard and the driveway but wouldn't be able to see the side of the house. The house next door had a few cameras, but the closest one on the end of their home pointed back in the opposite direction.

"Because he got bored waiting for his target to get home. It was safer for him to stand in the shadows against the house because, between the two houses, there is a security camera blind spot. So he could stand in the shadows and not worry about being seen."

"Then who was he watching?" York asked.

Ivy went back to the corner of the house and stood by the carving. From where she stood, the three houses across the street were in full view. Her eyes darted from house to house until movement under a large magnolia tree caught her attention. She waited until the figure reemerged. It was hard to tell from this vantage point, but the figure looked to have long swaying hair that wafted out just past the small of their back when the wind blew. Ivy pointed the figure out to York and Carson, and all three walked to the house directly across the street.

Chapter Twenty-Two

The three officers approached the timid woman hiding behind the tree. Ivy had expected her to turn and run back inside her house. She looked around like a cornered animal but had undoubtedly stayed where she was because she knew the cops would follow her back to the house, and then they'd be in her space. The open front yard felt safer and unviolated.

"I didn't see anything. I just got home," she said before they'd even made it all the way across the street.

None of them spoke until they were a few feet from the woman. She was a small mousey woman with long brown hair down her back. She wore a solid green skirt and a maroon sweater that had to be uncomfortable just stepping outside in the sweltering heat. Ivy didn't even want to think about walking around in it all day long.

"That's fine, but we'd still like to ask you a few questions if you don't mind, Ms..." Carson trailed off while attempting to give her his borderline flirty smile.

The smile didn't impress her.

"Parker, Michelle Parker," she said, pushing her glasses higher on her face with fingers from an open hand.

Carson opened his mouth to speak again, but Ivy cut him off. She couldn't let him run the interview when he didn't even believe her theories.

"Do you live alone, Ms. Parker? I know it sounds strange, but it could really help us out."

"I don't see what that has to do with anything, but yes. It's just me and my cat, Mr. Whiskers."

Mr. Whiskers? How old was this lady? She didn't look any more than twenty-two or twenty-three. How did she even afford a house in this subdivision? Ivy's mind raced with questions she had to filter out because they didn't matter.

"Have you noticed anything or anybody out of the ordinary in the neighborhood lately?"

"No, not really. Unless you count the ones walking around the neighborhood at all hours of the night in their matching uniforms."

"They're the ones who have been keeping you safe. If it weren't for them...uff," Carson started before Ivy and York, who stood on each side of him, smashed an elbow into his ribs.

Carson stepped back from the conversation.

"What was he talking about?"

"There was an unknown car parked in front of your neighbor's house across the street, and somebody carved something into the wood on the side of their house. We just want to make sure it's vandals and not somebody more dangerous."

"Like a gang?" she asked, her eyes widening.

"The gangs around here tend to stay a few roads back. I don't think you have anything to worry about from them."

Her eyes grew even wider, and her hands went to her mouth.

"Then you think it's The Suicide Killer."

"We're not sure who or what we're dealing with."

"Oh, my God. He's been outside my house. You think it was looking for me! I can't stay here anymore."

York sighed and looked at Ivy for help.

"We're not saying that's who it was. For all we know, it could have been some kids playing a prank. But if you have somewhere else to go, it might be a good idea if you and Mr. Whiskers stayed somewhere else for a few days."

"My dad is allergic to cats, so we can't go to my parents' house."

"Anywhere else?"

"I guess I can call my sister. I'm afraid to go back in my house alone. Do you think one of you could go with me until I get packed?"

Ivy turned to look at Carson, but he had already looked the other way and shuffled toward the mailbox. Guess he didn't hold the same values he thought the neighborhood watch people did. York was in charge so that automatically counted her out.

"Sure, I can do that. It looks like I'm finished out here, anyway."
Michelle smiled and walked to the house, with Ivy close behind.

147

Chapter Twenty-Three

The knock on the door felt like it came as soon as he'd closed it behind him. It was so soon he thought he'd imagined the sound until the knock came again. He sighed and looked out the small window beside his front door. Jody stood on his front porch wearing her Daily Grind uniform, though she'd ditched the hat. The porch light reflected off her bright red hair. Stray hat-hair strands illuminated in an unnatural glow around her head. The radiance mesmerized Bobby until she reached up and knocked on the door again, breaking the spell. He took a deep breath and opened it.

Jody took a step back as the door opened.

"Hey ... hey, Bobby, I um, how you doing?" she stuttered.

She was clearly nervous and was having second thoughts, and he didn't feel like being around anybody, but he also didn't want to scare her off, so he smiled. It was fake, and they had worked together long enough that she knew, but her tense shoulders relaxed, and she returned the smile.

"Hey, Jody. I'm doing fine. How about you?"

"Oh, I'm great. I'm not a stalker or anything, I swear."

Bobby laughed.

"That thought never crossed my mind."

Jody squinched her eyes, shook her head, and looked at the ground.

"That didn't come out right. It was supposed to be a joke because

I knocked right when you walked inside. I pulled up right behind you. Guess you didn't hear me."

"Guess not. You're pretty good at sneaking around for not being a stalker," Bobby said, and laughed.

Jody's face reddened.

"It's too damn hot to stand outside talking. Do you want to come in?"

Jody hesitated but nodded and walked past Bobby into the foyer. She let out an audible gasp and stopped in the middle of the room.

"It look that bad?"

"What? No, this is great. I love this. Older houses have so much personality," she said and ran her hand across the lumpy cerulean blue wall.

"If you like this ugly stuff, you should go check out the bathroom down the hall. It's pink. Straight up seventies pink. Everything in this house is still decorated like the seventies."

"I'll have to check it out."

"Be my guest," Bobby said, and held his hand out to lead the way.

"I didn't mean to interrupt your evening. I didn't like the way we left things the other day."

"You're not interrupting. I'm sorry for the way I acted. I don't know what came over me. But I had to leave before I made a bigger fool of myself."

"I get it. That place makes me want to throw something through the window two or three times a day. I've never acted on it, of course," Jody said, and let out an embarrassed half-laugh.

"Of course. A normal person wouldn't do that," Bobby said.

Jody's face reddened again. She tilted her head and scrunched her nose.

"That was supposed to be a joke. I'm not really good at this."

Bobby walked into the kitchen. What was this? He wasn't good at much either when it came to dealing with people. A clean butcher knife lay on the counter. It was hard, but he finally pulled his attention away from the gleaming metal and focused on Jody.

"This place really is great," she said, looking around the room at the white and harvest gold flower wallpaper.

Was she serious? There's no way anybody in their right mind would like the way the house was decorated. It still looked the same way it had when his grandparents bought it in the seventies. He still didn't know why she was at his house in the first place. He'd worked with her for years, and nothing like this had ever happened. They'd always been friendly, but that was about it.

"Thank you. Would you like something to drink? I'm afraid I don't have much. Just water. I might have some coffee."

She laughed. He liked the way her laugh lit up her entire face and the house.

"Water is fine. I'd be up all night if I had coffee now."

Bobby made her a glass of water. Their fingers brushed against one another and lingered for a beat. Had she tried to touch him, or was he imagining everything? It wouldn't be the first time.

"I'm sorry I destroyed the store and left you to clean up the mess. That was fucked up. I shouldn't have done that."

"It's okay."

"No, it's not. I shouldn't have reacted like that and should have cleaned it up myself."

Jody leaned against the counter, held her elbow in the palm of her hand, and took a gulp of the water.

"No worries. It was a slow day, so it gave me something to do to make the day go faster."

They laughed together.

"Randy said there'd be no hard feelings if you wanted to come back to work."

"Damn. He must be hard up to find somebody to work, so he doesn't have to."

Jody took another sip and licked her lips like she was working up to something.

"He is. I turned in my notice, so he's going to be down two people."

"Oh, I'm sorry. I hope it's not because of what I did."

What was he saying? Of course, it wasn't because of him. Nobody wanted to work in the food service industry for the rest of their lives.

"It wouldn't have been the same without you, but I was leaving anyway. I just finished nursing school and got a pretty good job at Crystal Valley Medical Center."

A twinge of jealousy hit him. He wouldn't have minded if it was because of him. He'd always thought she'd had a thing for him, but she was too shy to act on it, and he was too focused on Danielle.

"That's great. Got you a real job."

Jody set her glass on the counter, took a deep breath, and stepped in front of Bobby.

"I'm excited and nervous. What do you plan on doing? I saw that your neighborhood is starting one of those Suicide Killer watch groups. Do you plan on joining it?"

Bobby tightened his grip on his glass. Condensation threatened to send it shooting through his fingers.

"No. Not at all," he growled, and slammed the glass on the counter.

The sharp rattle startled Jody, and she took a tentative step back. He'd scared her and tried to soften his features but wasn't sure he was pulling it off.

"I'm so sorry," he said and reached his hand into the expanse between them and grabbed nothing but air. "I don't know what came over me. I didn't mean to scare you. I just don't like what that reporter is doing. He's calling out a dangerous serial killer like he doesn't expect any reprisal."

She was still frightened. It was his voice. He may have fought to keep the stern look off his face, but he could hear it in his voice. Sharp and biting. He wanted to kill Leonard, and if he weren't careful, Jody would find out about the side of him she never knew existed. Then what would he do? What choice would he have? He cleared his throat and tried to swallow the hard rock of anger.

He stepped close to her again. She didn't move, but he could tell her breath had quickened.

"It seems like I'm apologizing a lot tonight. I'm sorry," he said, softly. "I guess it's easier for me to say something like that since I am me, and you're beautiful."

Bobby took another step closer and put his palm on her cheek.

"You're more in his demographic than I am."

Jody put her trembling hand on his and nuzzled her face against his hand.

"I won't be joining any watch groups, but I guarantee that as long as you're with me, you won't have to worry about him."

"You're going to protect me?" she asked. Her voice was breathy and heavy in the cool kitchen.

"Yes. He'll never hurt you. I promise."

She pushed up on the tips of her toes and slowly brushed her lips against his. A hint of cherry from her lip gloss floated in the air between them. Bobby wrapped his arms around her, pulled her tight against him, and kissed her deep. They stayed in that embrace for a few minutes until she finally pulled away. He didn't want to let her go. Mixed emotions flooded through him. Danielle was gone, and he should move on, but he'd hurt her and didn't want to break his promise to Jody. He wasn't even sure he'd be able to keep it.

"You left before I got a chance to try that, so I had to show up and hope I wasn't too awkward."

"I'm glad you decided to stalk me tonight."

A sly smile crossed her face, and she pulled him into another kiss.

"Why don't you give me a tour of your room?"

Bobby's voice cracked when he started to speak. He caught himself and cleared his throat.

"Right this way," Bobby said, and led her up the stairs.

* * *

Bobby woke from a nightmare covered in sweat. He searched the room for any evidence that the black-cloaked skeleton was still with him. Offering him a crown of ivy and heavenly blue flowers. He only saw darkness. The alarm clock on the nightstand changed to 3:00 am. Jody's red hair cascaded across the dark green pillowcase. Everything had been unexpected and entirely out of his control. Those people shouldn't have been waiting for him when he got to Michelle's house, and Jody shouldn't have been waiting for him when he arrived home. Though, she was a welcome distraction. He ran his hand down her nude back. She stirred and pulled the covers up to her neck.

Bobby slipped out of bed and slid on his clothes. It had been a while since he'd bothered to watch out for the squeaky stair, but he still managed to navigate down the stairs without stepping on it. The door creaked as he stepped out into the humid night. It didn't matter what time it was, Georgia was always ridiculously hot in the summer. Sweat dripped down his forehead before he'd made it down his front yard, through the cul-de-sac, and stepped into the forest leading to Rusted Lakes Park.

The humidity felt like it doubled as he stepped under the pine and oak canopy. He wiped the sweat from his brow and started down the steep embankment that led to his favorite spot. Or what was once his favorite spot. He didn't go to the muddy bank as much as he once had. Too many memories, good and bad, great and horrible.

When he reached the shore, he skimmed his shoe across the

ground until he'd cleared Danielle's final resting place, and then he cleared a place for him to sit. The compacted earth didn't give when he sat down. Jarring pain shot up his spine. He attempted to stretch it out in all directions, but it left him feeling sore.

He'd enjoyed his night with Jody but couldn't help feeling somewhat guilty because of Danielle. She undoubtedly wouldn't care if she'd still been alive after everything he'd done that she knew about, so there was little doubt that she would care now that she was dead. He leaned back with his hands behind him and watched the moon play on the surface of the water while being serenaded by a bullfrog song.

A tear slipped and slithered down his face. He missed them both so much. Ivy hadn't been good enough to replace Greg, and he doubted Jody would ever replace Danielle. He'd seen a lot of death in his life and had caused a lot as well. The difference between them and Greg and Danielle were they didn't matter. They weren't lost to him.

Losing somebody cuts like a dull knife. It doesn't pierce the flesh. It rips as it pulls from the point it enters the body until its final destination, creating a wound that never heals. It's our choice whether to let it scab over or fester and bleed until it kills us too. Ivy and Jody didn't mean as much to him, but he was willing to let them try. You can choose who you love, and even if you didn't choose them, you allowed it to happen.

Bobby stood and knocked the dirt from his hands and the seat of his pants. The sun would be coming up in a few minutes, and he didn't want to miss the purple and black sky change to pink. He looked around the area for the best vantage point and hesitated before carefully walking around Danielle's grave and hopping up on the fallen tree. Emily's tree.

He pulled his phone from his pocket to waste the last remaining minutes of the night and saw there was a new article by Jonathan Leonard waiting for him from the night before.

The Mask is Beginning to Fray
by Jonathan Leonard

You read that right. We have been working diligently around here, and the mask is indeed beginning to fray. I believe The Suicide Killer will be unmasked very soon. Don't think we haven't noticed all

153

the wonderful work you've been doing around your neighborhoods with the watches. I'm sure they've stopped a number of crimes from being committed; some of you may have even saved lives. The crime numbers have gone down throughout the city, and the mayor and police chief will be taking credit for it soon. But don't forget, it was you who saved the city. You all are the real heroes out there. Our merchandise has been a huge success around the community, and everybody loves it, well, almost everybody. I say almost because The Suicide Killer contacted me right after he defaced our headquarters with that large red N. You no doubt saw if you've passed our headquarters recently. He threatened me for using his identity. You read that right. He's mad and lashing out over our merchandise. He hasn't seemed to have had a problem with anything else that I've said, but he draws the line over some t-shirts and koozies.

We are dealing with a sick mind here, folks, but as I said, that mask is beginning to fray, and we have a couple of suspects. One of those suspects was brutally beaten and left for dead a few nights ago, and we believe it was the killer who did it. He messed up, folks. He ran onto the bridge, smashed a poor innocent girl's face beyond recognition, and threw her over the rail into the river below. I'm sorry for being so graphic, but this is the kind of animal we are dealing with here. I need everybody to know that and to be vigilant while you're out there. Keep each other safe, and this will all be over soon. Oh, and for those who are curious, I'm not stopping the sale of anything. In fact, for the next week, we will be having a 25% discount on everything in the Justice Store. So join us in telling this monster that we will not be afraid and we will not let him control what we do.

Bobby missed the sunrise.

He jumped from the fallen tree and twisted his hands like he was trying to rip his phone in half, but it wouldn't give. A building scream erupted from his lungs as he yelled to the sky. A rabbit tucked back into its hole shortly after emerging, and two squirrels paused from chasing each other around the trunk of an old oak tree long enough to decide they wanted no part of what was happening and jumped to a tree further away.

He picked up any loose rock and branch he could find and threw them into the water. That son of a bitch didn't know who he was messing with. He thought he was playing the game on the same level as Bobby, but he didn't even know what game they were playing, let alone the rules. Bobby screamed again and jerked at a branch still connected to a live tree. It wouldn't give, and he threw all of his weight into it. The young branch bent but did not crack at the trunk. The unwillingness of the branch enraged him more, and he pulled harder. The slender wood slid through his fingers and sliced his palms.

Yes. Let that rage out, baby. It's no good for you to keep all of it inside. You have to let it out, but you're using the wrong target for that rage. You know what you have to do.

Her voice came and went so quickly that he almost missed it. He froze and scanned the woods, hoping to find a lost hiker who'd wandered too far off the path. The embarrassment of a stranger witnessing his half-assed assault on a tree would be better than the alternative.

You can keep looking, but you know there's nobody out there. I'm everywhere.

"No. No, you're not. I killed you and got rid of you. You can't be here now."

Bobby flinched as a sudden burst of Emily's haunting laugh echoed through the trees.

You can't get rid of me that easily, lover. And besides, I don't think you really want to be rid of me, anyway.

"Yes, I do. I want you gone. Now. Forever."

Why? So you can have that little coffee whore? You know I'm the only one for you. Look at what happened the last time you tried to replace me.

Bobby looked down and realized he was standing where Danielle's head should be. He jumped back and bounced against Emily's tree.

See, that's where you belong. You need to dig her up and bury her in the landfill with the new girl.

"I'm not killing anyone else for you. And I won't kill Jody. Nothing you can say will make me do that again."

I didn't make you kill anybody. You knew you couldn't trust her, and that was the only thing you could do to stop her from telling the police. She didn't love you. Nobody can love you the way I do.

"That's not true. You're the one I can't trust anymore. I want you out of my life."

You don't mean that.

"Yes, I do. I want you out of my life, and I don't want to hear from you again."

Whatever you say, honey. You know you need me to continue what you're doing, to live. I'm the only one who understands you and what you need. I'll back off, but you're going to cry to have me with you, and I don't know if I'll come back to pick you up when you're on the ground because you can't function without me. Jody won't be able to help you the way I can.

A strong breeze blew through his hair, and she was gone, or at least she was quiet, but the air felt different like a weight had been lifted from him. Maybe she was gone. He wasn't going to hold his breath or get too excited about it because she would show up again when he least expected it. He didn't think he'd ever be rid of her for good.

Bobby's shirt was soaked through with sweat by the time he climbed back up the hill and entered the cul-de-sac. Jody's car was no longer by the street. He wouldn't have blamed her if she'd woken up and decided to leave before he got back, so she wouldn't have to see him or exchange uncomfortable pleasantries as she bolted for the door.

A note surprised him when it fluttered to the ground as he opened the door.

Hey Bobby,

I guess you went for a walk or something, and I missed you. Sorry, I had to leave before you got back, but I have a lot of errands to get done this morning. I had an amazing time last night, and I really hope we can do it again. Call me later if you'd like to. Oh yeah, I checked out the bathroom. So much pink. I love it.

Jody

Bobby laid the note on the counter and got a large glass of water. It didn't quite quench his thirst after being outside, but it helped a bit. He was wrong about Jody. She did want to see him again. Now he needed to decide if he wanted to see her again. He was pretty sure he did, but he had bigger issues to deal with at the moment.

Chapter Twenty-Four

Two birds dive-bombed a squirrel hanging from the wooden privacy fence by its hind feet while it stretched out to steal seeds from the birdfeeder. Normally, Ivy would have run it off for messing with her feeders, but the birds seemed to be holding their own this morning. A mockingbird spun in the air, then swooped in, clipping the squirrel's ear. It fell to the ground and escaped from the backyard through a hole under the fence.

Ivy laughed and took another gulp of her cooling coffee. After dropping Michelle and Mr. Whiskers off at her sister's house, Ivy came home, collapsed into her oversized armchair, and stayed there all night. She woke once and thought about setting her alarm but changed her mind and rolled back over.

She decided to go into the office a little later than usual. The past few days had been physically and emotionally draining. The case was taking its toll on her and the city. Something had to give before Leonard and The Suicide Killer collided, and people got hurt. The sad thing is one of them might be taken down, but there were going to be other innocent people dragged into it, and they were the ones who would end up being hurt the most. It was the innocent people she worried about. They were blindly following Leonard in a game of chicken with a serial killer who didn't care who got in his way. She wished there was something that could be done, but he hadn't broken any laws that she knew of yet. But his quest for his own brand of justice and personal brand would eventually lead to his downfall. Ivy hoped he wouldn't take too many people with him. Her cellphone rang and danced across the table to the staccato rhythm. She thought about ignoring it for a while but relented at the last moment.

"Ivy Chandler."

"You realize he has to die, right?"

The straightforward statement caught her off guard, but it only took her a moment to be pulled from her serene moment and back into the real world with a real killer.

"I realize that's what you believe needs to happen, but nobody else needs to get hurt."

Ivy pulled her legs under her in the cushioned chair.

"This one's not on me. It's all on him. I've given him plenty of opportunities to back off. I thought I was rather nice about the whole situation."

Venom dripped from his voice. This was the first time Ivy hadn't heard the playful, I'm the smartest person in any room I walk into, persona. He was pissed. And anger was not the best state of mind for him to be in for anybody's sake, especially Leonard Johnson. Ivy needed to calm him down before he acted rashly, and more people ended up hurt. But she didn't know how to handle the situation. She was a homicide detective, not a negotiator or therapist for psychopaths.

"Definitely nicer than I had to be."

"Vandalizing his building was being nice?"

"Better than slitting his throat like I wanted to do."

"Yeah, I guess that is better."

The killer sighed heavily into the phone.

"Yep. I'm done humoring him. I thought he would be a necessary evil, and help spread my reputation, and cause fear in the city, but all he has done is riled up his base against me. That's not fear. It's fake bravado. He can say whatever he wants, but if he saw me coming, he'd run like hell, and so would most of his acolytes."

Ivy downed the rest of her cold coffee and made a face.

"So you want to kill him because he's not afraid of you, and he's not making the public afraid of you, either?"

"No. Fear is what I wanted, but ridicule and mockery are what I got. He's still going to help me spread fear, but now it will be his blood that causes it."

"Or you can ignore him?"

"Whose side are you on, detective? He's made a mockery out of you and all of your bosses. I would think, if anybody, the police department would want to shut him down."

Ivy leaned forward in her chair. He was rationalizing what he wanted to do and was trying to get her to agree with him. Why did he care? He seemed to kill indiscriminately, but now he sounded like he was seeking permission.

"We do want him to stop what he's doing. It makes it harder for us to do our job, and it obviously upsets you. But we don't want him dead."

"Aww, detective, you care enough not to want me upset."

She cringed at the thought, but at least he was coming around a little.

"Yeah, but not in the manner you're thinking."

"And what manner is that?"

"You think it means I care about you, but honestly, you're easier to catch if you're not upset. Leonard thinks making you mad will cause you to make a mistake. I don't believe that, though."

"And what is it that you believe, detective?"

"I believe you're more dangerous when you're upset. Being upset will cause you to lash out at people who you wouldn't have ordinarily had anything to do with. You won't make more mistakes because you're mad. You'll kill more innocent people, and that's the one thing I don't want."

"I do thrive under pressure. It causes me to focus more. So you got me there. Too bad he underestimates me. You know you'll never catch me, right?"

"I don't know that. We'll find something in all the evidence already collected, or you'll get sloppy because of your confidence. You're not that much different from Leonard."

"Watch yourself, detective. Those are fighting words, and I don't think you could handle me coming directly at you."

The blood in Ivy's veins ran cold, and a chill ran through her body that she couldn't stop despite the high ninety-degree morning temperature. She'd almost pushed him too far. As much as she'd like to say she'd wished he'd go after her and leave everybody else alone, she didn't mean it. The thought of having the killer's attention when it came to who he wanted to blow steam off with on the phone was a far cry from having him actively hunting you. She was stunned into silence.

"Stung you with that one, didn't I? Don't forget who your friends are, detective. The last thing I want to do is end this relationship before it gets fully started, but I've had to find new friends before."

There was a click, and the line went dead before she had time to respond. Her hand shook as she placed her coffee cup on the table. The phone vibrated in her lap, and she jumped to her feet. Tears flooded her eyes but did not fall.

"What do you want from me?"

"I'm ... sorry. Did I call at a bad time?"

Ivy winced at the sound of the feminine voice. She pulled the phone from her face and saw Morgan Cramer's name on the screen.

"Ms. Cramer. I'm so sorry. I thought you were somebody else, and I didn't even look to make sure before I answered the phone."

"No worries. He has that effect on people. If you're talking about who I think you are."

"Yes, he does. It's very unfortunate too."

"I bet he's a hit at parties," Morgan said with a laugh.

She was attempting to make light of the situation for Ivy's sake, but it was also a cover for herself. Ivy could hear the exasperation and fear in her voice as well. Ivy had only spoken with him on the phone, but he'd been in Morgan's house and attacked her, though he said he didn't want to kill her. That was an entirely different level that Ivy hoped she'd never reach with the killer. She didn't know if she'd have been as strong as Morgan had been when she stabbed him. Now that Ivy thought about it, Morgan was the only person to survive an attack from the killer when she tried to protect herself. What made her different?

"I'm sure he is, as long as he's allowed to believe he's the smartest one there and nobody challenges him."

They were falling into a casual conversation, but Morgan had obliviously called for a reason. Ivy hoped it wasn't for the status of her sister's case. The Suicide Killer had taken up all of her time, and as long as he was active, she'd be actively chasing until she caught him.

"How can I help you, Ms. Cramer?"

"Morgan, please. I'm calling because I wasn't completely honest with you when you were here the other day."

Ivy knew she was hiding something. She'd thought it was because of Ramsey and his men, but maybe there were other reasons. She hoped she didn't sound overly excited when she responded.

"Oh, really," she said and paused long enough to soak in, but not long enough for Morgan to respond, "what do you mean?"

Morgan audibly inhaled on the other end of the phone.

"He's been in my house."

"I know. I have it all in your statement from when he attacked you."

"No. That's not everything."

Ivy's pulse quickened.

"He was in my house a couple nights before you and the swat team showed up."

That excited feeling quickly left Ivy.

"We know. That's how we assumed he was able to get your cell phone and call me. Since you hadn't been anywhere, we assume he stole it from your house."

"I know he did because I spoke to him in my kitchen before he stole the phone."

Chapter Twenty-Five

Ivy pushed past Morgan before she had time to open the door all the way and invite her inside. She left the mudroom and looked around the kitchen in wide-eyed surprise, like she'd expected the killer to be sitting at the kitchen table, enjoying a freshly cooked brunch.

Morgan followed quietly behind her and took her seat at the kitchen table.

"There's fresh coffee if you want some."

Under normal circumstances, Ivy wouldn't have accepted the offer from a witness, but she felt like she was going to need the extra burst of caffeine while deciding if Morgan was still a victim and not an accomplice at this point. She grabbed a Crystal Valley Times mug from the dish rack, slopped the dark roast in the cup until it splashed over the edge, and burnt her hand.

"Damn it," she said, and ran her hand under the cold tap.

Morgan shuffled behind her.

"I wasn't trying to hide anything from you. I was scared. First, by the killer and then by your guys when they about busted in here."

Ivy understood her reluctance, but it could have helped to know that he had already come back and confronted her again. She was the only person to survive an encounter with him twice.

"What did he want? I'm sure he didn't show up to discuss the weather."

Morgan looked hurt. Ivy needed to back down, but it was hard. She felt like she'd been lied to this entire time, and somebody else had paid for it with their life. Two more people, if you believed what Leonard and his group had to say about everything.

"I'm sorry. But this has come as quite a shock to me, and I'm trying to remain calm and levelheaded about the situation. That's why I haven't told anybody else yet. But I will have to. It wouldn't be a good idea for me to hide anything, as you can imagine from what's happened with this case in the past."

"You have to understand. This isn't what I wanted to happen."

"Then what did you want?"

Ivy took a sip from her coffee.

"I wanted my sister's case solved."

Ivy almost spit her coffee across the table.

"What in the hell does that have to do with this?"

Morgan hesitated. Ivy could tell she was having second thoughts now like she shouldn't have called at all.

"I'm sorry, but I'm failing to see the connection between the two."

Morgan looked down at the table and spoke barely above a whisper. Ivy leaned in closer so she could hear her.

"He said he would find out who killed my sister."

How did he think he'd be able to do that?

"What did he want from you? I'm sure he didn't agree to do it out of the kindness of his heart."

"He wanted me to find out who the new detective was on his case."

What? Morgan had been the one to unleash the killer on her. Why would she do that? Ivy thought about jerking her up from her chair and arresting her for endangering an officer. She slowly counted to calm herself. 1 ... 2 ... 3... She couldn't do it, though. 4 ... 5 ... 6 ... Morgan looked defeated and like she hadn't slept in a couple days. 7 ... 8 ... 9... The charges more than likely wouldn't stick, anyway. Ivy placed her palms flat on the kitchen table.

"What did you tell him?"

"I said hell no."

Ivy released a deep breath.

"At first."

Blood ran to her face.

"What do you mean, at first?"

"I wasn't going to unleash that monster on somebody else. Especially after he killed Greg, I wouldn't do that to anybody."

"What changed your mind?"

"I knew he would eventually find out just by following the news. They don't exactly keep your names private. Then that megalomaniac Jonathan Leonard started his shit, and I knew he wouldn't keep your name out of anything."

Ivy adjusted herself in the seat to seem more domineering like she was looking down on Morgan. It was a shitty power move, but she needed answers.

"So you decided to do it before anybody else had the chance so you could get what you wanted from him? Did it ever occur to you that he was lying or that he wouldn't care about due process while tracking down the person who killed your sister?"

Tears streamed down Morgan's face. Ivy could tell she felt bad about the situation, but Morgan was still able to raise a defiant face and meet Ivy's eyes.

"You have every right to be mad at me, but ..."

"Damn right, I do."

"But I didn't tell him. I said I couldn't do it."

"And he stole your phone?"

"Yes, but I didn't have your name saved in there yet. It would have been there with all the other random numbers I called or called me. So he would have had to call them all to find you."

He'd known who was going to answer the phone before he even dialed the number. Ivy believed Morgan, and more importantly, it wasn't a secret, so he would have found out anyway. Why would he set her on such a strange errand if he knew he'd find out?

"Is he still working on your sister's case?"

"As far as I know."

Ivy relaxed and sat back in the chair. Morgan followed suit and leaned back in her own chair. Now they could get back to calmly talking about the situation.

"Why do you think he'd still find her killer if you didn't give him my number, and he knows that you lied to him?"

Morgan sat quietly for a long time. Ivy was beginning to think she wouldn't answer when she finally did.

"I'm not sure. Everything is a game to him. This is just one more part of it. I think he has a thing for me and that this is his way of doing something for me, even though he knows it will never lead anywhere."

That was an interesting thought. They might be able to use that against him if he thinks Morgan is working with the police.

"What makes you think that?"

"I don't know any other reason a guy would do something for a woman he doesn't even know unless he was trying to hook up with her."

"Good point," Ivy conceded.

It was demented but not the worst thing she'd heard a man do to get a woman's attention. Morgan stood from the kitchen table and started pacing from the living room back to the kitchen. There was something else she wasn't telling Ivy and was working up the courage to tell her.

"Does he just show up out of nowhere when he's ready to talk?"

"Not exactly."

Ivy turned around in her chair so she could better see Morgan. She was now furiously pacing back and forth and wringing her fingers.

"What is that supposed to mean?"

Morgan turned to face Ivy. She had stopped pacing but continued with her hands until she had rubbed the skin red and raw. She didn't say anything.

"Morgan? What does not exactly mean?"

"It means ... it means that I fucked up. I didn't let him in my house again. He broke in and scared me to death. I thought he'd come back to finish the job, but he swore he'd never hurt me."

"And you believed him?"

"No. Not at first, anyway. Now, I'm not so sure. I don't think he wants to hurt me, but if I give him a reason to, like stabbing him in the back again, then I don't think he will hesitate to kill me."

Ivy stood and walked toward the visibly shaking woman stopping short of grabbing her trembling hands.

"Tell me what you know, and we can protect you."

"I'm not sure you'd be able to do that. If he wants to get to me, he'll find a way."

"If there's something you can tell me that will help us catch this guy, I need to know."

Morgan didn't respond. She continued to pace through the house. The worried look on her face deepened the further she made it into the kitchen before turning around. She wasn't pacing. She was trying to work up the courage to make it somewhere in the house. Ivy brushed the tail of her blazer from the butt of her gun. The more nervous Morgan grew, the more nervous she did, too.

Morgan took one more long lap around the house before she walked straight through the kitchen with a determined face and stopped by the back door. She stared Ivy in the eyes and flipped the switch closest to the door.

"What was that?"

"His invitation."

Chapter Twenty-Six

The door jerked back with enough force that the air pulled into the large house and whipped at Bobby's pants leg. Amanda Cramer's jilted ex-boyfriend stuck his head out the door. He didn't look directly at Bobby. Instead, he looked around him as if he wasn't there.

"What the hell do you want?"

"Jimmy Yates?"

"Yeah, that's me. What do you want?" Yates said, and stepped out to make sure nobody stood behind Bobby. He then walked to the edge of the porch and looked across the vast front yard. Though Bobby wasn't exactly sure what he was looking for or how he would see it in the darkness.

"My name is Stephen ... Stephens. I work for the Crystal Valley Police Department."

Yates made a coughing sound and spat into the front yard.

"'Bout time you people show up. I've made three complaints this week about somebody in my yard. They keep knocking on the door and running off at all hours of the night."

Bobby looked down the long, winding driveway he'd recently driven down. There was no way anybody would bother coming all the way down here to screw with somebody unless they really didn't like them. If somebody was out here tormenting Yates, they had an agenda that Bobby didn't want any part of. He also didn't want to risk being seen. He'd decided at the last minute to ditch the mask and try a different approach with Yates.

"I'm sure it's only kids messing with you."

"That's what they said on the phone. What did you say your name was? Stephen Stephens? What kind of name is that?"

Bobby smirked. It was the best he could come up with off the top of his head.

"My parents were big fans of the family name, I guess."

"That makes sense. I used to work with a guy named Bill Williams. Never thought about it until now. Do you mind if we step inside? I don't like being out in the open like this for too long."

"Sure thing," Bobby said, and followed Yates into the large vestibule.

The house looked large from the outside, but the inside was massive. They stood in a large marbled floored atrium with at least six dark hallways leading deeper into the enormous mansion. No sounds echoed from any direction. It was clearly only a skeleton of what it once had been. Built by his father as a symbol of the family's place and prominence within the community, no doubt. Now, it appeared to be as soulless as the man standing before him.

"If you're not here for the complaints, why are you here?"

"I'm one of the detectives assigned to solve Amanda Cramer's murder."

Jimmy's eyes glassed over at the mention of her name.

"Are you here to harass me too?"

Bobby was confused. Greg's notes indicated that Yates wasn't a suspect.

"I'm not sure what you mean, Mr. Yates. I don't know if you've seen it in the news, but the detective who was previously working the case died in the line of duty."

"Yeah, yeah, yeah. I saw that. I hated to hear that. Don't get me wrong, I was a little relieved when I read it, but I don't like to hear about anybody getting hurt. Especially the way he did, but you know he might have asked for it, the way he worked."

Bobby squeezed his fists until his knuckles cracked. He looked around the room but didn't see any place where cameras could be hiding. It was a mistake to come in here and be civil with this guy. It was an even bigger mistake not to anticipate that a house like this wouldn't be heavily secured, even if the lone resident wasn't paranoid that his shadow would creep up and choke him if he wasn't fully aware.

"Do you have cameras in or around the house?"

"Not at the moment, no. I got rid of the cameras I had because they weren't good enough to see any details of who was after me. I've been researching some new ones, but the alarm works. I'm thinking about replacing everything, though, and getting state-of-the-art equipment."

"That might not be a bad idea considering how big a place you have here. You can't watch everything all the time. They could climb through a window all the way at the other end of the house when you open the front door, and you'd never even know it."

"Yes, exactly," Jimmy said enthusiastically because somebody finally agreed with him, but his excitement quickly dropped when the ramification of somebody agreeing with him set in.

Bobby fought to hold his amusement inside. He was relieved there wasn't a high-tech security system that he'd have to track down and destroy after disposing of Jimmy Yates' body in the lake behind the estate. With any luck, and no more shots at Greg, Jimmy would make it through the conversation and live to hide from another day.

"As I was saying, I'm not here to harass you. However, I am a little surprised to hear that Detective Burns was harassing you. According to all of his notes that I've seen, you didn't have an alibi for that night, but he never considered you a suspect."

"That's news to me. He wouldn't leave me alone. I had to call the Police Chief and threaten to sue the city if he wouldn't leave me alone."

Maybe Greg had altered his notes in case there ever was an official harassment complaint made. That was shady, even for Greg.

"I hate that happened to you, but that is not my intention with showing up tonight. I've been speaking with everybody that Greg spoke to during his investigation."

"Investigation is not the word I'd use for it, but okay."

Bobby had to hold himself back.

"You seem to still be upset about your experience. Are you sure it's the way you remember it, or maybe you're just being—"

"Being what? Paranoid? I know I act a little weird, but I wasn't always like this. It was Amanda's murder that made me this way. I'll do whatever I can to help you catch who killed her."

He must have thought they were after him and his money instead of a girl like Amanda. He was a self-righteous coward, but Bobby didn't think he had killed her.

"Fair enough. When was the last time you saw Amanda alive?"

"I'm sure you already know, but we were pretty serious. I proposed to her, and she said no, right there in that restaurant in front of God and everybody. Embarrassed the hell out of me. I guess that's why they thought I had something to do with it, but the truth is, I hadn't seen her for a few months after that night."

He was holding something back. Bobby could see it in his eyes.

"But then ..."

"But then, what?"

Bobby wanted to yell and snatch him by his neck until he told him everything he knew.

"But then, you saw her the night she died. And you didn't want to tell anybody because the cops were already harassing you, and if they found out you'd seen her, they'd find a way to blame it on you."

Jimmy took a deep breath and exhaled slowly.

"Okay. Okay, you're right. I saw her that night. She was out with some other guy. She looked so happy with him. I'd never seen her look that way before. I thought if I told that to Burns, he'd never leave me alone."

"Did you ever think he might be able to tell you weren't giving him all the information, and that's why he thought it was you?"

Jimmy sighed and shook his head. Bobby almost felt sorry for him. Jimmy seemed like one of those people you marvel at how they'd gotten this far in life. It was always baffling. However, being a sheltered rich kid didn't help Jimmy none. Under other circumstances, he might have been a completely different person, a completely normal person.

"What kind of car do you drive?"

"So now you think I did it too?" Jimmy said. His calm demeanor changed to outrage quickly.

"No, I don't. It seems like Amanda was a pretty popular person. Another sus ... person said he saw her get into a black SUV. It was big, like a Navigator. That's a pretty expensive vehicle."

"So? Half the people in this town drive expensive cars they can't afford."

Bobby couldn't argue with him there. He'd seen a lot of people whose cars looked better than the houses they lived in.

"So you don't have a large black SUV?"

"No, I don't. All the cars I own are sitting out there in the garage. You can look all you want."

"All the cars?"

"There's ten out there, but only one is mine. The rest of them belonged to my father. There's no SUV, though."

"Okay. Is there anything else you want to tell me?"

Jimmy was still holding something back. Bobby felt like he wanted to tell him but wasn't sure if he would or if he'd have to tie him up and force it out of him.

"I can tell there's something else. So why don't you go ahead and tell me, so I don't have to come back out here?"

"I ... I saw the man she was with that night."

Son of a bitch knew the whole time and never said anything.

"Seriously? You could have told us who it was the whole time, but you kept your mouth shut."

Bobby clenched his fist and walked toward Jimmy, who stepped back quickly.

"Nuh ... nuh ... no. I don't know who he was. I just saw the black SUV, and the guy who got out was tall. Like six-four or something, and he had blonde hair. That's all I know. I swear. That could be anybody."

"Maybe, but it sure as hell could have narrowed the number down."

"It might not have been him. Somebody else could have killed her. I'm not even that sure he was blonde. It was dark out there, and I was paying more attention to Amanda than that guy."

"Okay, well, I think you've done enough. I don't think I have any other questions for you."

Bobby walked to the front door and flung it open. He'd half hoped whoever was terrifying Jimmy Yates, if it wasn't Jimmy Yates himself, would be standing on the other side of the door when he opened it. He would have stepped to the side and let them have him.

He heard Jimmy behind him on the porch as he stepped onto the crushed gravel driveway and turned to face him.

"Don't worry, Mr. Yates. Just because you're paranoid doesn't mean they're not after you."

Jimmy's face dropped.

"Wait, what? I don't think I ever saw your badge."

Bobby turned on his heels. Grinding rock covered all sound.

"No, you didn't, Mr. Yates. Have a good evening," Bobby said, turning on his heels again. A quick succession of four bolts being thrown closed made Bobby laugh. He watched from his Bronco as Jimmy ran from window to window and peeked through the heavy curtains. It was sad that he'd scared himself so much that he would rather lock himself inside most of the time. It hadn't been the best idea to drive his own vehicle, but he had been in a hurry to get over here and hadn't felt like stopping for another one. Jimmy wasn't going to call the police. Bobby hadn't threatened him. He told him he hadn't thought he did it, so Jimmy shouldn't be worried about him coming back. As for the phantom knocking on Jimmy's door, Bobby had no idea, but he wasn't against the idea of ghosts.

Bobby was ready to go home and get some sleep. He hadn't gotten that much the night before. But before he went home, he needed to make a stop by Leonard's office. According to his last article, they had a few suspects for the murders. If nobody were there, he'd sneak in, find out the information he needed and be on his way without anybody realizing.

Chapter Twenty-Seven

Bobby found a trove of information in Jonathan Leonard's office. They had intelligence on everybody that worked for them. That had been an enlightening list, but for some reason, they were also keeping personal information on everybody who donated money to them and bought merchandise. It had been hard not to trash the place or steal everything they had, but Bobby had held himself in check and had only taken pictures of the information he needed.

The excitement was too much to handle, and Bobby had driven past Morgan's house on the way home. For some reason, she had her porch light on. He thought it might have been a mistake; she'd accidentally left it on. But he'd driven past again tonight, and the light was still on.

He sat in a car around the corner from her house, going over everything he had from her sister's case. There was a new suspect in the case who, it seemed, Greg had never thought about questioning. It was a big break and excited him, but Morgan would not see it the same way. The news would devastate her all over again and rip open old wounds that were scabbed over. He didn't want to do that to her until he was absolutely sure he knew who'd killed her sister. The plan was to go to the suspect's house tonight, but that would have to wait now that Morgan's light was still on. He should have made his stop first, and then maybe he could have given her some news tonight.

Bobby pulled his mask over his face and stepped from the car.

The sweltering heat hit him before he was entirely out of the vehicle. Sweat slipped from his brow and attacked his eyes. He was beginning to rethink coming over to her house tonight when he reached the stop sign at the end of the road. The light on her front porch still burned, a pale orange star in an otherwise dark space.

All the cars that were usually on the street sat silently along the curb. There didn't appear to be any extra cars in the street or neighboring driveways. He leaned against an ancient oak tree and watched the house while fighting the urge to pull his mask off. It was too damn hot to be running around town wearing a ski mask. It didn't matter how late it was. The heat and humidity were killers.

A car pulled up to the stop sign beside him, and he ducked around to the other side of the tree so they wouldn't see his mask and call 911. He hadn't seen any of those obnoxious neighborhood watch stickers, but people did seem to be on higher alert. After what Bobby felt was too much time to look both ways, the car crossed the intersection and continued on its way, leaving the road quiet and dark again.

Bobby ran across the street but took care to stay just to the edges of the shadows cast by streetlights through tree branches. He didn't see anything out of place, but something felt off. He'd sensed it ever since he saw her porch light on, but the feeling that he should turn and run screamed at him from a primal region of his brain.

He walked slowly up the driveway and hopped up the first three steps.

Flashlights clicked on, and storm trooper armor clacks rounded the corner. Before Bobby could turn around, a hand landed on his shoulder and jerked him to the ground. Air rushed from his lungs when he hit the driveway. Broken concrete crumbs scattered across the driveway stabbed at him, causing instant stone bruises.

"Get on your fucking feet, or I'll blow your head off," a man cloaked in his own black mask yelled at Bobby.

Before he had time to react, two strong hands grabbed him under the arms and hauled him to his feet. Bobby staggered forward, fighting for breath, and the hand jerked him back.

"Hold still, or I'll put you back on the ground."

Pain radiated down his back and both legs. Small gulps of air forced their way into his closed windpipe, and a sudden blow to his kidneys made him double over.

"I fucking said to stand still. Put your hands on your head. Now."

The pain in his back was excruciating, but he could better catch his breath with his hands on his knees. The plastic clatter of mini blinds bouncing in a window case rattled above his head. She was watching him. She'd set him up. He was trying to help her and make up for scaring her in the past, and the bitch set him up. He'd be lying to himself if he said he hadn't expected it in some way before. Blue lights bounced off all surfaces as Bobby stood up straight and put his hands on the back of his head. He swayed as he awaited the inevitable. It would be too easy to let them have their way and take him in. The spotlight he'd always hoped for would be all his, and there wasn't anything people like Jonathan Leonard could do to take it away from him. It felt like he'd lost, but he'd still win the game of infamy. With a few exceptions, the person who caught the *monster* was rarely remembered.

"Turn that piece of shit around. I want to see his face."

One of the strong hands grabbed his hands, and the other grabbed his left biceps and pulled to turn him around. As of now, there were only two police standing with Bobby, but he knew that many more lighted the shadows on the dark street. He'd known betrayal many times in his life, but this somehow felt different. He grimaced at the pain as he was suddenly stopped in front of a tall, wide-chested officer in riot gear. A flash of blonde hair illuminated by blue light caught his attention. Ivy Chandler stood beside a dark car that wasn't there before he crossed the street.

"Hold him still," the cop, who was obviously in charge, yelled, and the hands gripped tighter.

The man yanked Bobby's mask from over his face. At first, he didn't say anything, only stared Bobby in the face as his eyes grew wide with recognition.

"I fucking knew it was you. You're nothing but a scared little bitch who only feels powerful when he's beating on women smaller than him."

Bobby smiled.

"Are you going to leave your mask on, or do I get to see what kind of bitch you are?"

The punch to the stomach came fast and hard. Bobby wouldn't have been able to react in time, even if the officer behind him hadn't been holding tight. He'd be lying on the ground again if they hadn't been holding him up. He heard a female voice yell from the street. It sounded like Ivy, but he couldn't be sure.

"Is that a no?"

The cop spit through his mask and pulled it off his head. He was the older man, hardened from years of training for moments like this, where he could be smug and proud that he was the strongest and the victor who had tried to arrest him at his house. Silver streaks ran through his dark hair, and a subtle five o'clock shadow popped in the light.

"There. Is that good enough for you, Nancy? You get a good enough look at a real man?"

"I was hoping the person to finally catch me would be remarkable in some way, but you're just as much of a faceless bastard on a power trip as the rest of them. I'm disappointed in myself."

"Cuff this piece of shit before I hit him again."

Bobby tried to pull his right arm away but couldn't budge. The first cuff slipped around his right wrist and clicked tight. A few of the other cops were starting to move up the driveway with their guns drawn, itching for him to make a run for it.

The hand moved to put the other cuff around Bobby's left wrist. For a split second, the officer released Bobby's right wrist, and Bobby pulled his hand from behind his head, tugging the cuffs from the officer's hand.

In one motion, he caught the open cuff in his right hand and swung it at the unmasked officer in front of him. The point of the cuff caught him in the soft skin of his temple and pierced the skin. The officer screamed as Bobby swung him in front of him by the cuff buried in his head. Blood poured from the man's head, coating Bobby's hands. He almost lost the slick metal and his new hostage. He pulled his mask down with the hand not handcuffed to the cop's face. Ten police ran up the driveway. Three tried to flank him from the side, but Bobby stood between Morgan's car and the side of the house. One acted like he was going to surround him, and Bobby kicked a dent in the driver's door.

"Stop right there. Looks like I hooked a big 'un. You make one more move, and I'll fucking kill him."

All the cops stopped but kept their guns trained on Bobby.

"Not so tough now, are you?"

Blood ran down the man's face. Bobby twitched the cuff when he didn't respond. The scream echoed through the neighborhood and made all the encroaching cops jump forward.

"Stop. I told you not to move. I'm leaving here tonight. And if you want your stupidly valiant leader here to live, I suggest you fucking listen to me."

They stopped, but Bobby still felt exposed and hid as much as he could behind the man's large bulk. He backed toward the back of the house where it was dark as pitch, hoping that Morgan wouldn't get any more bright ideas and turn on the floodlights. He put his shoulder against the brick wall and scrubbed against it until he'd reached the edge of the house.

"We ... we're going to fucking kill you," the man choked out.

Bobby stood at arm's length from the officer.

"You're the only person who has seen my face and lived this long. You know I can't let that stand, now that I have you like a little bitty worm on a big fucking hook."

"Fuck you," the man said, and swung a knife he'd slipped from a hidden sheath at Bobby's face.

The officer's reflexes were slower from the amount of blood he'd lost, and Bobby easily dodged the knife. He grabbed the man's arm and twisted the cuff in his head until it punctured his eye and forced it from the socket.

The man screamed in agony and tried to fall, but Bobby kept him up in front of him. He pulled the knife from his hand and slipped the cuff from his skull. The man screamed again, and Bobby plunged the knife into his other temple. The screaming cut off suddenly, and Bobby pushed him toward his friends and slipped around the corner as bullets kicked up dirt in the small hill behind Morgan's house.

Bobby ran the length of the backyard. His bloody hands slipped on the chain-link fence as he hoisted himself up and crashed to the ground on the other side. It wasn't long before flashlights filled Morgan's backyard, like tiny searchlights, looking in the tall grass and on the roof. He jumped up and ran to the neighbor's patio door. He pulled the handle, and the glass door slid open without a sound.

He closed the door and moved through the dark kitchen until he stood in the living room. The homeowner was apparently asleep, and nothing going on outside had woken them up at this point. Bobby moved around the arm of a worn loveseat and stood in the darkened corner. He parted the linen curtains and watched the cops as they ran across the front yard.

Two of them made their way up the walkway to the house. They beat on the front door, and he dropped to the floor. He sat in the corner and tried to stay below the arm of the loveseat. They beat on the door again, and the kitchen light flipped on. An old woman tied her light pink bathrobe as she shuffled across the floor, mumbling to herself. She left his small line of sight.

"Oh my," he heard her say, followed by the squeak of the front door.

"Ma'am, have there been any disturbances at your house tonight?"

"Disturbances? No, nothing has happened here all night."

"Are you sure?"

"Well, of course, I'm sure. I've been in bed for an hour or so, and nothing's disturbed me until you started banging on my door."

"We're sorry. Ma'am, but we have an escaped suspect that we're looking for."

The old woman sighed.

"I can assure you that he's not in here with me. I've a good mind to call your boss and let him know you're bothering a poor old lady in the middle of the night. Bunch of perverts."

Bobby had to smother the laugh building up in his diaphragm. He liked this woman.

"That was not our intention, ma'am. We're trying—"

"You keep calling me ma'am like that's supposed to make it better. Why don't you go on and leave me be?"

"Yes, ma'am. Sorry to have bothered you. Please stay in the house, and keep all of your doors locked. Do you mind if we check your backyard?"

"I make sure my doors are always locked. I don't let just anybody traipse through my house. And I don't plan on going anywhere except for back to bed, where I was. The gate is unlocked. I trust you can figure out how to open it and close it back when you're finished."

"Yes, ma'am, we'll be fine. Have a good evening, and sorry to have bothered you."

"I'm sure," the woman said, and closed the door before they could reply again.

She walked back across the kitchen, talking to herself.

"Scared me half to death just to find out if they can snoop around my backyard. They could have done that without waking me. Never would have known they were there no way."

She walked in Bobby's line of sight again, through the kitchen to the patio door. She looked out the window and flipped on the floodlights in the backyard.

"Hope that helps them, so they'll be gone quickly. Make sure you lock your doors. What kind of person do they think I am? Just go to sleep with my doors ... oh ... well, I ... well, I must have forgotten just this once. No reason to telegraph my mistakes to the world, though."

The woman slid the switch to lock the door and then padded off back to her bedroom.

Bobby waited ten minutes to make sure the woman was not coming back before standing up. He bent and twisted his sore body, stretching it out. Sitting in the corner for so long had given his muscles time to tighten up on him, and being slammed to the ground from the steps hadn't helped any. It still mystified him that Morgan would set him up like that. He wanted to go to her house right now and confront her, but blue lights still flashed outside of the house, and they wouldn't be going anywhere for a while. The wiser move would be to wait them out, but he didn't want to risk them staying all night and the old woman waking up early. He'd hate to have to kill her after she'd helped him without knowing it.

He crept to the front door and looked out the window. There didn't seem to be any cops in front of the house he was in or across the street. If he could get out and across the street, they might think he was a nosy neighbor trying to get a closer look. Though that wasn't a good idea for anybody to be out in the open right now, even if they were completely innocent. The cops were no doubt on the warpath because one of them had been killed or severely injured. Bobby wasn't sure if he killed the guy or only made him wish he was dead, but he hoped it was the former. He'd recognized Bobby, and his death would be the only thing that could make sure Bobby stayed free.

Bobby turned the deadbolt, unlocked the doorknob, and waited to make sure the old woman hadn't heard him before turning the knob. If it weren't for the humidity, he would have said the temperature in the house was as hot as the night air. He slipped out the door and pulled it closed behind him. There weren't any cops down the road to the right that he could see. He ran through the front yard and laid flat against the trunk of an oak tree. Voices drifted from the direction of Morgan's house, but he couldn't understand what they were saying.

A car turned down the road, headed toward Bobby's hiding place. If he didn't move now, he risked them seeing him and notifying the police. He darted into the street and stepped awkwardly on his ankle when he jumped from the curb. Pain radiated up his right leg, meeting the pain flaring down from his lower back. He hobbled the rest of the way across the street and ducked behind a trashcan as the car passed him.

The ambulance driver chirped the sirens as they pulled out of Morgan's driveway and headed past Bobby's hiding spot. The remaining cops were about to fan out again, and Bobby needed to decide if he should go past Morgan's house to get back to the car he'd brought or if he should disappear into the dark side of the street and head the other direction. He needed to act fast.

He hobbled as quickly as possible in the direction of Morgan's house, hiding behind trees as he came to them. The cops spread out, looking again on the opposite side of the street. None had come to his side of the road yet. They all seemed to be focused on the house he'd just left. He ran to the next tree and froze when he heard somebody call out. Adrenaline coursed through his veins until he felt light-headed. No boots pounded the pavement toward his tree, and he relaxed a moment before he took off running. As he rounded the corner, he tried to hold up, but his forward momentum kept him propelled forward, and he ran straight into somebody walking up the street.

The collision sent bolts of pain up his leg as he fell on top of the person. The back of their blonde head hit the concrete, and Bobby stared into their concussed eyes. A small trickle of blood ran from under Ivy Chandler's head and down a crack in the walkway.

"Damn it. I'm sorry, detective. I didn't see you there."

Bobby pushed himself off Ivy as she pulled weakly at his shirt to hold him. He easily pulled away and stood over her.

"You should probably get that looked at. Too bad the ambulance already left with your friend. Seems like a waste now, doesn't it?"

"Sto ...stop," Ivy choked out in a barely audible whisper.

"Sorry, but I really must be going now, detective. Hopefully, we can run into each other again real soon," Bobby said, and started to shuffle down the street.

"Rob ... Rob."

"I can't hear you, detective. I really must go now."

Ivy finally managed to find the strength and screamed at him, "Robert."

Bobby stopped in his tracks.

"What?"

The gun barrel came up from her side, and she fired twice before he knew what was happening. The first bullet splintered a tree branch a foot from Bobby's head, and the second ricocheted down the street.

"Holy shit, you almost blew my fucking head off," Bobby said, and ran down the road. The pain in his ankle was excruciating, but he had to shake it off like his dad used to tell him every time he got hurt. There'd be time to lick his wounds later, after he'd survived the night.

He reached the car and sped off while he looked for the pictures on his phone. He needed to find out why she'd called him Robert.

Chapter Twenty-Eight

Blinding light sliced through her field of vision as a strong hand forced her eyelid open. She tried to snatch away, but another set of hands held her in place.

"Calm down, Ivy. We've got you."

Who was that? She recognized the voice, but the name escaped her. A car sped by and laid on the gas as it turned down the street. A siren went off, and a police car drove after the speeding offender. She tried to move her head and follow the commotion, but they held her firm.

"Don't worry about that car. We've got to get you to the hospital. You hit your head pretty hard."

Car? Carson. Brandon "Johnny" Carson. That was it. She turned to the left. Carson kneeled beside her with his hands on her shoulders. She felt sick and rolled slightly to vomit. Black specks swirled in her vision. She had to get up. The killer was getting away, but she knew who he was now. He'd answered her when she yelled at him. He wouldn't have stopped otherwise.

"Th ... Thanks, but I'm not going. My head is fine. I just need to get up so I can breathe," she said and leaned up so she could touch the back of her head.

White hot pain flamed from the blood-crusted bump on the back of her head, and her vision faded until she thought she was about to pass out. She needed to stand. Everything would be fine if she could just stand for a minute.

"That's not a good idea. Just lie back and let the medic do his job."

"Nah, I'm good. Get me up, or I'm going to get sick on your shoes."

Carson moved his foot but then stood and pulled her up.

"She really needs to get checked out by a doctor. If nothing else, she has a concussion," the medic said.

Ivy stood on shaky legs and wobbled as she took two steps forward and puked in the bushes. Her stomach emptied and threatened to dry heave, but she fought it off. The last thing she needed to do was dry heave. That was worse than puking.

She wiped her mouth on the sleeve of her blazer and stood up straight.

"See. I'm all good."

Carson walked toward her with an outstretched hand.

"Are you sure you shouldn't go to the hospital? He got away. There's nothing else we can do right now."

He almost sounded like he cared. It was weird to see a side of Carson that she never knew existed.

"I'll be good by the time we get there."

Carson turned his concerned face to the paramedic, who only shrugged his shoulders.

"Get where?"

"I know who he is. We need to get to his place in case he goes there first, or we can find something that will tell us where he might be headed," Ivy said and stumbled as she walked toward her car. She looked back over her shoulder, "but you're going to need to drive."

Carson ran ahead of her and opened the passenger side door so she could fall into the seat. She locked eyes with him as she sat and hoped he would take her where they needed to go instead of agreeing and then heading straight for the hospital. Carson ran around the front of the car and didn't break eye contact with her. He didn't trust her right now, and she didn't blame him.

"So where are we going?" he asked as he slid into the driver's seat.

She pulled a file from behind her on the seat and handed it to him.

"Go here."

"Where did you get this?

"Just go, and I'll tell you on the way."

Carson put the car in drive and picked up the radio.

"This is Detective Carson in pursuit of The Suicide Killer suspect. Requesting all available units for backup at The Linen Company Condominiums downtown."

He dropped the radio as unit after unit responded they were en route. Blue lights flashed behind them as most of the police on the scene joined the chase. Ivy closed her eyes from the blinding lights but started talking so he wouldn't think she was trying to go to sleep.

"I got those files from Jonathan Leonard when I went to see him."

"Why did you go see him? I haven't heard about that."

Ivy readjusted in the seat so the lights would stop bouncing off the rearview mirrors and boring directly into her brain.

"I went to tell him to back off. He was pissing the killer off, and I didn't want him or anybody working with him to get hurt because he can't keep his mouth shut."

"Fair enough."

"It was right after he said he had three suspects. I convinced him to let me get a copy of his files. They were far from damning, but he had more than us. Anyway, when the killer ran into me, I called him Robert, and he stopped and answered."

"What did he say?"

"What?"

"What did he say?"

"No. That's what he said. He turned and said, what."

Carson shook his head. He had to be thinking about calling everybody off and going to the hospital now.

"And that makes you think Robert is his name? What made you pick that name of the three?"

"I knew one of them wasn't him because he was almost beat to death, so I guessed between the other two."

"And you think you got lucky and picked the right name?"

"Yes, I do. It wasn't only because he said what. It was the way he said it. It was like a petulant child who didn't like being called out for what he was doing."

Carson laughed.

"So he answered you like you were his mother."

Ivy kept her eyes closed but slid up higher in the seat.

"If that will make you drive to find the suspect, then yes."

"Those must be some phone calls."

"Just drive."

She laid her head back and remembered a member of the RRT had pulled the killer's mask off when they almost had him cuffed. If Robert weren't home, they would need to verify he was the right suspect to pursue. Then she remembered the horrific scene that followed.

"How is Ramsey? Is he going to be okay?"

Carson sighed.

"No. He died on the way to the hospital. That's why we have half the department following us and the other half meeting us there."

Ivy sat quiet again. She never cared much for Ramsey or how he did his job, but she hated that he'd died, and his killer had gotten away when she couldn't stop him or see straight enough to shoot him.

The car came to a screeching halt, facing the curb. Ivy squinted into the sea of flashing blue lights. A few red lights from an ambulance and a fire truck had joined the convoy. A car blocked all front escape routes, and officers fanned out to cover the back.

Ivy and Carson stepped to the curb, and the crash of breaking glass made them look up. A person hurdled at them through the air and smacked the concrete in front of their car. Ivy and Carson both screamed. Ivy kept her hand to her mouth like she was holding more in, and Carson looked around, embarrassed, and pulled at the bottom of his suit coat. The impact sent blood splattering in all directions and left the arms and legs twisted in unnatural positions.

Two paramedics raced to check on the man while Ivy scanned the broken eighth-story window for any movement.

"Ah shit," Carson said and backed away.

One of the medics rolled the man over, and his dislocated jaw ripped the rest of the way from his face. The tongue hung out and grotesquely spasmed. Ivy didn't want to, but she needed to look at the face. She had to confirm what she already knew in her gut. This was Robert Burton, and he was not the killer. But how had the real killer known they would show up here? Her first thought was Leonard. They would need to send somebody to check on him. But first, they had to get up to the apartment.

"We need to get up there before he gets away again."

Both detectives, flanked by too many Crystal Valley police, piled into the Linen Company Condominiums lobby. Carson led one group into the first stairwell, while a cop Ivy couldn't remember led another group to a stairwell in the back. Her head wasn't swimming as severely as it had been when she got up, but she was in no shape to climb any stairs. She hit the elevator button and impatiently tapped her foot until it dinged and the freight door slid open.

Carson's group had already reached the apartment by the time the elevator opened on the eighth floor. She tried to remain hopeful that they had made it up here in time, but the dejected looks on some of the officer's faces told her otherwise. Carson met her at the door.

"Fucker got away again. I don't get it. I don't know how we didn't see him. The door was wide open when we got up here."

Another apartment door opened, and all the cops in the hall trained their guns on the old lady who stepped out. She dropped her coffee cup and slowly raised her hands above her head.

"Please. Don't shoot."

Ivy turned back to Carson.

"These guys have got to settle down before they shoot somebody's grandmother. There's way too much testosterone flying around."

"Hey. Hey guys, let's start knocking on doors to see if anybody heard or saw anything. Hit every floor. I don't care how long it takes."

"That's a great idea. Put them in everybody's face," Ivy said, pushing her way past him.

The apartment was elegantly furnished with dark chocolate brown leather furniture and paintings hanging on the wall. Nothing that Ivy recognized, but they weren't prints. They were authentic pieces. Even if a famous artist didn't paint them, they still made the apartment feel rich. There were no signs of a struggle in the living room or the stark white kitchen. The bedroom was different. A desk chair lay upside down on the white, blood-covered bedspread while blood ran down the side and stained the white shag rug beside the bed.

Officers walked through the apartment, opening doors, and yelling clear, only to follow behind each other and clear the same room. They all knew the killer was brutal. The ones who'd been to the scenes where he'd killed a young woman knew what he was capable of, but this was different. They walked around those scenes with sympathetic, pallid faces, but it changed things when they saw that same brutality unfold in front of them when he killed Ramsey. She had gotten upset with them in the hall, but she understood. They all wanted to catch the person who had been making a fool of them all for months, killing citizens of the city they lived in and taking three of their own out as well.

She walked out of the bedroom and looked out the shattered window. It once had a great view of the city at night, but all she saw were flashing emergency lights, and a group of figures huddled in front of her car. Her head started to swim again, and she stepped back from the window and closed her eyes.

When she opened them again, she focused on a piece of paper on the floor. She slowly bent down and picked up the latest note from The Suicide Killer.

For those wondering why I did it,

I can no longer live with myself. An innocent man branded as a murderer. My past transgressions have been hard enough for me to live with. I don't need all of this pressure.

N

Everything that had happened tonight, and the bastard still wanted to play his fucking game. Ivy started to crumple the paper but stopped herself before she destroyed the evidence and threw it out the window.

"Somebody get me an evidence bag. He left a note."

She sat down at the kitchen table and put her head in her hands. Carson walked up and took the note from her.

"Son of a bitch," was all he said before sliding it into a plastic evidence bag.

"I don't know what we're supposed to do now. He's always one step ahead of us. Even when we catch a break, he finds a way to get by us."

Ivy felt like she was going to cry. She didn't want to but thought it would make her feel better. All the men around her would think she was being emotional. Even the women in uniform would look at her differently. She was about to say screw it and all those who wanted to judge her when her phone rang.

"This's Chandler," she answered through clenched teeth.

"Wooo. Holy shit, detective. That was a close one."

Ivy jumped to her feet, knocking her chair over. Everybody in the room stopped to watch her.

"You bastard. Where are you? I swear to God, I won't miss the next time I see you."

"It's not polite to swear to God."

"Fuck you."

An exaggerated sigh filled the phone receiver with static, and she pulled it away from her ear.

"Now that's not nice. Though I can't say I blame you. I was trying to hit the hood of your car. Almost did. Though you know what almost only counts in."

"Why?"

"Why? That's a loaded question. I mean, it could be in relation to so many things. I wouldn't possibly know where to start. I guess—"

"Shut up. Shut the hell up. I'm tired of dealing with you."

"That's no way to talk to a friend, detective."

"We're not friends," she screamed into the phone and hung up on him.

There was a slight gasp amongst the crowd that had gathered around her. Murmurs circulated between them. They were undoubtedly saying she'd made a mistake by hanging up on him. After he'd killed so many people, there was no need to provoke him any further. And they'd be right if they were dealing with a *normal* killer, whatever that was. The phone rang again. She let it ring enough times for the entire room and the killer to believe she wasn't going to answer.

Then she answered.

"If you hang up on me again, I promise it will be the last time," the killer said in an eerily calm voice.

"Okay," was her only reply. What else could she say? He was the one in charge at the moment. So far, she'd believed that he would harm her, but if she kept pushing him, she would be as expendable of a friend as Greg had been.

"Good. So, how has your night been? Mine has been a bit hectic. As you can imagine. People trying to kill me and all. I'll admit, you almost got me back there at Morgan's house."

Ivy was ready to give up.

"Why did you answer when I called you Robert?"

"Oh, you want to know if ole Robert Burton's death is your fault or not? Well, the short answer is yes. It's true that I beat that pervert Walter Longway half to death, but I hadn't planned on killing Leonard's other two suspects. That is until you called me by one of their names. Then I had to make them a part of the game. But you have to admit, that Longway fucker had it coming. I'm still trying to decide if I feel like going over there and finishing the job."

Now the tears did fall. Ivy had taken a gamble and ended up getting an innocent man killed. She didn't know what put him on Leonard's radar, and she didn't care at this point. He wasn't The Suicide Killer, and that's all that mattered right now.

"Are you crying? There's no crying allowed. You're the one who chose the game to play. I simply obliged you."

"Nobody chose to play this game with you. This is all on you. You're the one who caused all of this pain and death. You can't blame it on somebody else if you're feeling guilty all of a sudden."

The sudden sharp laughter made her cringe and pull the phone from her ear again.

"No guilt here. I don't even have guilty pleasures. I like what I like, and it doesn't matter what other people think about it."

"The law would disagree with you."

"You're right. But a jury of my peers will never judge me. I have no peers. Everyone is beneath me."

"That's the way you see it."

"That's the only way to look at it. I walk around this city, and they prove it to me every day."

This call was going nowhere. He'd already had plenty of time to gloat. Why was he still on the phone?

"What do you want?"

"Why do you think I want something?"

"Because you've already rubbed everything in my face, and you're still talking to me on Robert's phone."

"You're learning, detective. You're also right. There is something I wanted to know. How did you know I would go to Morgan Cramer's house tonight?"

Morgan. With all the excitement, she'd forgotten all about Morgan. She'd made her a target now, too. Ivy put the phone to her shoulder.

"We need to get some bodies back over to Morgan Cramer's house now."

"There's still people there processing the scene," Carson said.

"Then send backup. I don't think there can be too much right now."

She put the phone back to her ear.

"You know I can't tell you my sources," she said.

He sighed into the phone again.

"That's what I was afraid of. She told you about our little code, didn't she? And after I told her I'd never hurt her. That's disheartening. So hard to trust people nowadays, wouldn't you agree?"

"I never said it was her. I don't know about any code."

He was going to know she was lying. She didn't even believe it herself.

"Now you're going to lie to me. Don't worry about Morgan. I told her I would never hurt her and meant it when I said it. But, of course, I might be lying too," he said and hung up the phone.

Ivy moved to the door and down the hall as quickly as she could. Carson caught up with her by the time she'd reached the elevator.

"We've got to get back to Morgan's house. He knows she's the one who told us, and she's in danger."

Chapter Twenty-Nine

Bobby had no intentions of going back to Morgan's house that night, but it would keep the cops busy for a little while, and it'd be a little longer before they found the two cops he killed in the back of the apartment complex while making his escape. There would be hell to pay for anybody caught after killing three cops in one night. He wasn't sure he'd ever be able to return to Morgan's house after everything that had happened. There was no telling how long she'd have surveillance on her. All that said, it didn't mean he couldn't call her. They really should talk. There were some things they needed to get worked out. He pulled up in front of the next suspect's house and pulled out a cell phone he'd found in the car.

"Hello," Morgan answered quietly. She'd obviously been crying. Bobby didn't say anything. "I know it's you, so you might as well start talking."

"I was just trying to get my courage up to speak to you."

"You're afraid of me? That's rich."

Bobby cleared his throat.

"No. I'm not afraid, but you hurt me tonight. Cut me real deep."

"I hope it cut to the bone."

"I don't understand why you're acting like this all of a sudden. I haven't done anything to you. I'm still working on that case for you. In fact, I'm sitting outside the next suspect's house right now. I feel pretty good about this guy."

A heavy shuttering breath filled the phone, and she started crying again.

"I don't want you to find out who did it. This is all my fault. I should have told the police sooner. If I had, all these other people wouldn't have died. I wish you would leave me alone. I can't take any more of this pressure."

Bobby was confused. Out of everybody he talked to, he believed Morgan would be the only one to think of him as a friend one day. Now, it looked like she was the first one to crack.

"You give yourself too much credit."

A loud snot and phlegm-filled snort filled the phone and caused Bobby to pull the phone from his ear.

"What do you mean?"

"You say I think too highly of myself, but none of those people died because you waited to call the police. They all would have died sooner. The results would have been the same. The only difference is that part of the game would have ended earlier than it did."

"You don't know that," she yelled into the phone. "Things could have been different. They could have caught you sooner; before you killed any more women."

Bobby sighed into the phone.

"Am I boring you?"

"To be frank, yes. I called to see what the hell was wrong with you, and you're acting like a sniveling child. It's those cops' fault that they're dead, not yours. I thought you were stronger, but maybe I was wrong about that. It's a good thing you're no longer on the murder beat. You wouldn't be able to stomach it anymore. I'm surprised you made it as long as you did. Look, I gotta go. I have a job to do whether you want me to do it or not. I'll give you all the information I find, and then you can decide what to do with it."

"I can already tell you that I won't be asking you to avenge my sister's death. I'll give it to the police and let them decide what to do with the information. That is, if you can even solve Amanda's murder."

"Sometimes I think you do and say things to try to hurt my feelings. I feel like I'm the only one trying. I'm going to have to seriously reevaluate our relationship when this is all over."

"Ahhh. I don't want to be your fucking friend. I don't want to be anything to you. Leave me alone. I wish they would have killed you tonight."

"You're going to need a magic lamp for that outcome."

Bobby hung up the phone, got out of the car, and placed it under the rear tire. He got back in the car, put it in drive, and let it roll forward enough to crush the phone. The house was dark and, hopefully, empty.

He kicked the crushed cell phone into the sewer, opened the trunk, and pulled out a small black box with twelve antennas attached to the top. The dew-covered grass sparkled in the light from his flashlight. The scent of cut grass floated in the dampening air. It had faded, but a hint remained strong enough for him to pause and inhale deeply.

The cover for the plastic box that contained the connections for the internet to run into the house hung on by one hinge. Bobby pried it the rest of the way off and threw it across the lawn. He wasn't quite sure which line was the internet and which one was the cable, so he cut all the lines.

He ran to the back of the house and beat on the large glass-paneled door. When no dogs came running or started barking inside, he flipped the switch on the cell phone jammer and put his foot through the window. He reached through, twisted the deadbolt lock, and pulled the door open. Before stepping inside, he paused to make sure there was no alarm ringing deeper in the house. When he was finally sure he'd made the correct guess, he walked inside.

Bobby had figured if the house had an alarm, it would most likely be connected to the Internet, so he cut the lines, but he needed the cell jammer because those alarms would use cell towers as a backup. At least the ones he'd seen worked like that, and if this one didn't, he had plenty of wide open space to get out before the responding officers even knew he had been in the house.

The biggest issue was he didn't know exactly what he was looking for or where to look. He made a quick pass on both floors to get a layout of the house. Three bedrooms and two bathrooms that looked like they'd never been used were the only rooms on the second floor. The first floor consisted of the master bedroom and bath, a spare room he used as an office, kitchen and dining room, another bathroom, and an extra-large living room. So much wasted space for somebody who lived alone. Most of the areas were empty and had bare walls. Hubris was a hell of a thing for people to deal with. Bobby was glad he didn't have any defects like that he had to deal with personally.

The only room that looked lived in was the office. Bobby thought that was as good a place to start as any. He walked through the kitchen and searched the cabinets until he found one full of cups. He grabbed a plastic cup with a faded mascot on the side and filled it with water from the refrigerator door. He'd have to remember to take the cup with him and lose it on the way home. Leaving prints or DNA at a scene could get him caught, and he'd be in jail with all the other failed people who made rookie mistakes and ended up behind bars.

The office was on the back of the house and couldn't be seen from the road, but he still fought the urge to turn the overhead light on. Bare pale blue walls seemed to glow in the low light. Bobby walked around the room, looking at the various pictures. He didn't recognize anybody, but they were important enough to display for people to see. He opened and closed all the drawers he saw in the furniture and knocked on the books in the built-in white bookshelves to ensure they were real and not covers for a secret safe. This was boring. There was no excitement. No danger. Nobody to threaten or beat a confession out of.

Bobby walked around the large oak desk, fell into the stuffed chair, and kicked his feet up on the cluttered top. He put his hands behind his head and swung the chair back and forth. Of all the framed pictures in the room, the one without a frame that sat propped up against a baseball trophy on the edge of the desk caught Bobby's attention. He had the matching photo in his file. Amanda Cramer stuck her tongue out, teasing a baseball player covered in dirt and powdered chalk like that found on Amanda's body when they pulled her from the lake.

There had been a part of Bobby that knew who the killer would end up being. He thought of it as a sixth sense, but what he saw now was all the proof he needed. The law might require more, but that was for the cops to figure out if Morgan still didn't want her sister avenged.

Attached in the top corner of the photograph was a horizontal figure eight infinity symbol with a letter M in the middle. Bobby's first reaction was to take the picture and earring straight to Morgan and throw it in her face. She couldn't deny him anymore if he hit her in the face with proof of who her sister's murderer was and that she didn't have any reason to be afraid of him; she'd made a rash decision to involve the cops in their relationship. He doubted she'd see it his way. He decided to take a picture instead and show it to her later.

Either way, he needed to leave. He didn't want any run-ins with the homeowner. For one, he wasn't sure he'd be able to take him on a good night, but there was no way he'd be able to take an athlete like Heath Clement with the night he'd already had.

Bobby grabbed his cup and cell phone jammer and walked back to the car he'd driven. It had been a while since he'd last gotten some sleep, and he'd be crashing soon. As much as he'd like to see Jody when he woke up, he needed to be alone and catch up on sleep so he would be ready for the cops the next time they tried to catch him.

Chapter Thirty

Sunlight fought its way through sagging farmhouse blinds. Bobby sat up, weak and weary. It felt like he hadn't gotten enough sleep, but the sun was heading below the horizon, so it had to be late afternoon. The clock on his phone said 7:47 pm, but he did a double take when he saw the date. He thought he'd slept for seventeen hours, but it was closer to forty-one hours. He had no idea that he was that tired or how he could sleep that long like he'd been wrapped up in a warm cocoon and was finally ready to emerge and finish the last cycle. It also explained the weakness, his incessantly growling stomach, and the burning sensation in his bladder. He needed to eat, but he needed a shower first.

The shower roused his senses, but he still needed half a pot of coffee to feel awake and alive again. There wasn't much left in the refrigerator, so he made a quick sandwich on stale bread with questionable sandwich meat. He'd grab something while he was out. There was so much left to do. When it was all finished, he would need to find another job. He'd never be able to do it, but his first case as a private detective had gone well. He'd had fun solving Amanda Cramer's case. There'd be no way to get a license to do it, but maybe he could be one of those people that only certain people know how to get in contact with, like an assassin, but solved crimes. He shook his head. It sounded too much like the movies. That'd never happen. But it did remind him that his Cramer case wasn't complete yet. He still needed to talk to Morgan and find out what she wanted to do with the information. He'd hoped she'd let him take care of the situation for her, had even thought about doing it anyway, but that could compromise their friendship, and he didn't want to do anything to mess that up even though she had called the cops on him.

Bobby grabbed what was left of his sandwich and headed out the door. He needed to call Morgan to get that over with so he could focus on his next steps. He reached into the back seat and grabbed a burner phone. He drove straight down Hawthorne Springs Road until he felt it was safe enough to call her without causing any more suspicion on himself if they'd happen to be tracing her calls. It took three calls before she finally answered.

"What do you want?"

"That's no way to answer the phone when a friend calls."

Bobby heard a lot of commotion in the background.

"We're not friends, and we never will be."

"I'd think you'd be in a better situation if we were friends as opposed to being enemies, but that's just me."

"What do you want?"

"There's a lot of background noise. I assumed the cops would be watching your house, but are they inside, too? Seems a bit much to me."

"Protecting people from you isn't a bit much."

"If you've paid attention to the news lately, you might have a differing opinion."

"Whatever. They aren't in the house. That's just the TV. But there are a couple outside. Why don't you come say hello to them?"

She was beginning to get her sense of humor back. Bobby was glad about that. It would make it easier to convince her to meet him somewhere else where the cops wouldn't follow her.

"Nah. I don't think those guys riding the clock outside your house would like that too much. It didn't work out for the last ones who tried to ambush me."

"That's not funny."

"No, it's not. But it is business, and they were trying to stop me."

"So that's not your fault, either?"

"I don't see how it can be. I didn't ask them to arrest me. That was ... well, that was you, but I wouldn't dream of blaming you for their deaths. That was on the police department. The two officers who died later that night were their fault, too."

The sudden intake of air paused the conversation.

"You killed two more people after you left? What is wrong with you?"

"With me? I didn't ask them to follow me and surround me in a building where the only way out was through them. That was—"

"The police department's fault, too," she said, interrupting him.

"Exactly. See, you're starting to get it."

"I don't want to get it. I don't want to deal with you anymore."

"Tell you what. I'm sure those cops will follow you if you try to leave, and you don't want me to kill them, so if you think you can give them the slip and meet me somewhere, I'll give you the information I have on Amanda's killer, and then I'll leave you alone."

A low growl emanated from the phone.

"I told you, I don't want you trying to solve her murder anymore. I'll let the cops do it."

"I know what you told me, but I couldn't stop. I had already started. It's like a compulsion I have. I'm no quitter. It was a mystery they couldn't solve, but I did."

"Wh ... what do you mean they couldn't solve it, but you did?"

"I mean what I said. I solved your sister's murder. I know who killed her and have proof."

There was a long pause. Bobby thought she had hung up on him or maybe fainted. He started to say something when Morgan finally spoke.

"Who killed my sister?"

"I'm sure you'd like to know, but I'm not going to give you the information over the phone. I was going to bring it to your house, but you've ruined that, so now, if you want to know who it was, you will need to meet me somewhere private."

Morgan got quiet again, but Bobby could tell she was crying.

"I don't trust you. I never did, but I definitely can't trust you after I tried to set you up."

"I don't know how many times I have to tell you that I'm not going to hurt you, but I mean it. I'm willing to let bygones be bygones. That is, of course, unless you decide to bring a chaperone in blue along with you."

"I want to, but I know they'll follow me when I leave. I can't lose them in my car."

Bobby thought for a minute.

"You don't have to lose them. Drive down to Hiwatt Foods, but go through the gas station parking lot to get there. Park in front of the store, and go straight inside. If they haven't caught up with you, turn left and go all the way to the meat department. Just past the meat counter, you will see two steel double doors. Go through them and make an immediate left. Look to the right when you get to the sink and go out that door. I'll be waiting for you in the back beside the loading dock."

"I don't know if I can do this."

"Sure you can. If they see you, then act like you needed to get something and try to lose them in the aisles. If they don't see you, then you can sneak back into the store and pick up a few things you probably need anyway, and they'll never be the wiser. If you can't get away from them for some reason, we'll figure something else out. This is what you have to do. You want this information, but you're the one who got us into the situation, so you're going to have to do the heavy lifting here."

Morgan breathed heavily into the receiver.

"Okay. I'll do it. When should I leave?"

"Now."

"Now?"

He could hear the surprise and nerves in her voice. If he let her wait any longer, she might lose her nerve or think about it for too long and do something bad for both of them. He was already taking a chance that they hadn't bugged her phone.

"Yes, now works best for me. I have a busy day planned. Plus, it would be better just to do it and get it over with. Don't you think?"

"I guess so. Unless you're going to kill me, then I'd like to hold off on that as long as I can."

Bobby didn't take the bait.

"I'll be waiting for you. I really hope you come alone," Bobby told her and hung up the phone.

He really did hope she came alone. He'd gotten lucky the last time, and the cop who pulled his mask off was the only one who saw him and didn't yell out who he was when he recognized him.

Bobby saw Morgan step from her house as he drove past. The cops sitting in their car weren't moving yet. Maybe she'd be able to get a head start before they followed her.

You know what you need to do.

Bobby jerked the wheel to the right at the sound of her voice. The voice that he once longed to hear but now cringed at the thought of it.

Be careful, honey. We don't need you driving into a ditch and messing up that pretty face.

"Leave me alone."

Bobby gripped the steering wheel tightly until his knuckles blanched.

Every time I leave you alone, you do something stupid and risk getting caught. I can't let you do that again. You know what you need to do. She turned you in. You can't trust her anymore. You never could, but you wouldn't listen to me about that either. You need to kill the bitch as soon as she walks out the door.

"No. I can't do that. Morgan's my friend. It was a misunderstanding with the cops."

Bobby wiped sweat beads from his brow. Emily was the last thing he needed to deal with right now. He had to focus so that he wouldn't get caught.

Did you forget I can read your mind? We are one, Bobby. You can't get rid of me. I'm all you'll ever need if you only allow me to be. Now, get the large knife from under your seat, and slit her fucking throat as soon as she walks out the door.

"I can't do it. I won't do it."

I know you think you can't do it, but you can. Believe me. I would do it for you if I could be there in the flesh. But you can't let her live. She tried to turn you in.

"You said the same thing about Danielle. You just wanted her out of the way."

A blaring horn and flashing lights caught Bobby's attention just in time to swerve back into his lane. He pulled at his hair. The pain did nothing to distract him from her. If she didn't stop, he wasn't going to make it to the grocery store, even if he was going to kill Morgan. A migraine settled in behind his eyes and thumped in rhythm with her voice. His vision blurred, and his Bronco jumped the curb in front of the store. So much for going unnoticed.

You're going to get caught if you don't stop being erratic.

"You're the reason I'm acting this way."

Poor Bobby. It's always somebody else's fault. You are the one who has gotten yourself into all of this.

"Shut up. Shut the fuck up," Bobby screamed at the top of his lungs. He looked around sheepishly, hoping nobody had seen him causing a scene in the front seat.

You don't have much time. She's about to be here with her entourage, and they will kill you. You have to trust me.

Bobby jumped out of the Bronco. He started to close the door but reached back in and grabbed the machete from under his seat. He ran to the back corner of the building and pulled his mask over his face as he watched Morgan run inside the store.

Chapter Thirty-One

It had been too long. She walked in and had changed her mind. It was the only explanation. Bobby thought about walking back around front to see if her car was still in the parking lot, but he didn't want to risk missing her. Emily had stopped talking to him, but he could still feel her presence behind him, out of sight. She used to only show up when he killed, but there had been a few times now that he felt her presence, or she'd shown when he hadn't killed anybody. Those situations would be considered high-stress if he ever felt stressed. She was getting stronger and would need to be dealt with eventually.

The sun beat down like it came from a spiteful, Old Testament God, punishing him for his sins by melting him and letting him die in a filthy back alley. Another dizzy spell hit him, and he held himself up against the trash compactor. He needed to give up and get something to eat. She either wouldn't or couldn't get away from the cops who followed her. He turned to walk back to his Bronco when the back door flung open.

Morgan rushed out and froze when she saw the machete in his hand. She wouldn't take her eyes off it and followed it as he moved.

Do it. Kill her. You have her cornered. There's nowhere for her to go. Cut her head off and put it in the cop car for them to find. Do it, now.

"No. I won't. It's not her fault."

"It's not who's fault?" Morgan asked.

Bobby shook his head.

"Nobody. Don't worry about it. I'm not going to do anything with this," he said, moving it toward her.

Morgan screamed and tried to go back inside the store, but the door locked from the inside once it closed. She beat on the door, laid her head on it, and cried when she'd finally given up.

Bobby threw the machete. It clanged against the trash compactor and hit the ground. Morgan slowly turned to face him.

"I told you it wasn't for you."

"Then why did you have a fucking machete waiting for me?"

"It wasn't for you, but I couldn't be unarmed in case your friends came busting through that door with you, now could I?"

Morgan relaxed a little.

"I guess not," was all she said.

She sniffed and wiped her nose with the back of her hand.

"We need to hurry before they figure out where you are."

Bobby pulled a manilla folder he had stuck against his back in his waistband and handed it to Morgan.

"Here is everything I have. I highly suggest that you don't read it—"

Morgan quickly opened the folder and flipped to the last page. It contained Bobby's notes about why he thought Heath Clement had killed Amanda Cramer, followed by the evidence that he'd found in his house. Morgan's lips quivered as she read. Large tears ran down her face. She covered her mouth with her hand and trembled.

Bobby stood back awkwardly and gave her some space. He wanted to reach out and hug her to him, so she could cry everything out, but that was out of the question. She'd run away and risk causing a scene if he tried to touch her.

"I can't believe it was him this whole time."

Bobby didn't know how to respond. He wasn't sure if the disbelieve was in who it was or that she didn't believe what Bobby was saying.

"I don't know what to say. I followed the evidence and what the other suspects told me. That's what I found in his house. He wasn't even trying to hide it."

"I believe you. It explains a lot. Like why he ghosted me after she died. I still haven't talked to him since the funeral. That bastard killed her and still had the nerve to show up to her funeral."

Morgan made a disgusted shriek and started crying again. She fell to the dirty ground and let the rest of her grief go. Bobby looked around to make sure they weren't drawing any unwanted attention.

Do it. Do it now before somebody hears her and you get caught. Bash her over the head with that rock beside the door if you don't want to use the machete.

Bobby shook his head, hoping Emily would leave him alone.

"This is why I didn't want you to read it until you got home. You're sitting on old rotten vegetables. You still have to go back into the store and make it home without drawing suspicion from the police."

"I ... I can't right now. Just give me a minute. I'll be fine, I promise. You can leave me if you need to."

She's going to get you caught. She's probably stalling until they find you both.

Bobby looked around again. It wouldn't be a bad idea to sneak around the building and leave her in case the cops started looking harder or if they'd called for backup. This place would be crawling with police in a matter of minutes if they thought he was here. You didn't kill three police in one night and get away with it by flaunting where you were.

"I can't leave you. But we can't stay back here too long. You need to pull yourself together enough to sneak back into the store."

Yes, you can leave her. And you should right now...after you kill her.

Morgan stood up, pulled a tissue from her purse, and blew her nose. Bobby wondered if she'd come prepared or always kept tissue in her purse. She walked on wobbly feet to the door and pulled again.

"It locked you out when you let it close. Dry your eyes, and walk back around the store. Hopefully, they aren't out front looking for you or waiting at your car."

Morgan looked back at Bobby. Her eyes were red and full of more tears waiting to fall.

"Thank you for finding out who killed Amanda."

"No problem. But before you go, how do you want to handle him? I'd be more than happy to make him disappear for you and leave all the evidence of what he did so even the cops can find it."

A strange look crossed Morgan's face. He couldn't interpret it, but it looked like a shadow crossed her face. She was thinking about it. He wanted to do this for her, but if she said no, he would let it go until she changed her mind.

"By that, I mean—"

"I know what you mean. It's tempting. Really tempting, but I couldn't live with myself if I agreed to it. I'll try to figure out a way to tell the cops without it looking like I broke into his house."

"Well, if you change your mind, flip on your light, and let me know."

Morgan didn't respond. She put the manilla folder in her purse, hugged her arms around her chest, and slowly walked back to the front of the building. Bobby grabbed his machete and waited at the corner of the building until he thought it was safe to try for his Bronco.

He jumped in the seat and put the AC on full blast as the engine roared to life. The mask peeled from his sticky skin, and he directed the cold air straight at his reddened face. When he was finally ready to move, he looked toward the store, and Morgan emerged with two bags of groceries with her entourage so close they could reach out and grab her if they needed to get her to safety. Bobby wondered what she'd told them. They were looking around like a deer in an open field, but that was most likely because they thought they'd lost her. The parking lot would be full of police cars, and nobody would be able to leave if they hadn't believed her. She would have to tell them why she was actually here.

Bobby decided to give it a few minutes after they'd left the parking lot so it didn't look like he was following them and attract their attention. He pulled out his phone to see the latest post from Jonathan Leonard.

I'm Sorry for the Radio Silence
by Jonathan Leonard

Hello everybody. I hope this finds everyone feeling safer than they ever have in this city. I know I do. It's true, we are still on the hunt for The Suicide Killer, but I have a feeling we will catch up to him sooner rather than later. Now that I know he reads my articles, I don't want to give away too much information about what we have going on, but let's just say he should be looking over his shoulder everywhere he goes. He thinks we don't feel safe, but it is he who should not feel safe anywhere in this city. We will bring him to justice, and it will be because of all the love and support you have shown our group.

The 25% sale has gone better than I ever expected, and I thank you all for that. I hope you all wear your shirts and display your bumper stickers with pride, knowing this is our city, and we aren't going to let any deranged maniac run around like he owns the place. I am truly humbled by the outreach we have received. The sale will continue for a few more days, so be sure to check out the web store before it's too late.

That's all I have for today. I want to thank each and every one of you for the kind letters and greetings I've received while out in the community. I hope you know that we will make this a better place for our children and our children's children. That is our goal, and we will reach it by taking down one sick psychopath at a time. Keep up to date with all of our articles. I have a feeling the next one will be full of great news. Until then, take care of each other.

Bobby slammed the phone down. It was one thing for this lunatic to make grand gestures saying they would catch him, but he was making a mockery of the city and Bobby. Leonard didn't know real fear yet, but he would soon enough. He'd implied their next issue would have big news like they'd caught The Suicide Killer, but they weren't anywhere near catching him. They weren't even in the same realm as Bobby. He'd had enough. Ignoring him would not work. The only way to silence him was to kill him like he'd told Ivy he would have to. It was now time to make good on that promise.

Chapter Thirty-Two

It had been three days since Ivy's run-in with The Suicide Killer. Three days since they almost had him. Her head still hurt from bashing it on the concrete, but the dizzy spells had finally subsided. A chilled hush permeated throughout the Homicide Unit. It was hard not to see the entire sting as a huge failure. The loss of Ramsey had put a lot of angry feelings in check, at least for the last few days. Eventually, there would be consequences unless they could catch the killer and give the mayor and chief a big enough win to let everything go. Everything had been quiet with the killer, too.

They had police sitting on Morgan Cramer's house, but they didn't expect him to show up there again. He was crazy, not stupid. She was more than likely a burned source. However, they still needed to protect her. She had turned the killer in to the police, and there was no way he wouldn't be mad and maybe want some form of revenge. He'd already threatened Jonathan Leonard, and those were only words and bumper stickers. Threatening his freedom and not allowing him to continue his game would be the ultimate sin against him. At least, that's how Ivy thought it would be. She couldn't think like this killer or anybody else that would think of taking a life, for that matter. The only thing that had happened recently was when they had a scare with Morgan yesterday. The patrol unit who'd been assigned to watch her lost her in the grocery store. She was upset and crying when they finally found her. She didn't say what happened, but everybody assumed she realized she was alone and got scared.

Downtown had reassigned those officers, and she had a new unit detail today. One that was more experienced in situations like hers.

Ivy had finished typing up her reports that she'd fallen behind on when her phone rang. She looked down at the illuminated screen, and Brandon Carson's name appeared. It was about damn time. He'd been MIA since they left the condominiums. In truth, he'd been MIA a lot the past few days. She had been doing most of the work, but he would definitely want credit when they caught the killer. He'd be the first one to use it to get a promotion. Ivy swiped a finger across the screen.

"Where are you? York has been asking about you."

"Hello, detective. It seems you have me confused with the previous owner of this phone."

Ivy's stomach dropped. She tried to stand, but her legs betrayed her, and she fell back into her chair.

"Where's Johnny?"

Ivy prayed he'd only stolen his phone the way he had Morgan's, but she had a bad feeling.

"Johnny? His badge said Brandon Cars—oh wait, is Johnny a nickname? It has to be ironic because he didn't say anything funny. His guts made a funny sound when I slit him open, and they spilled to the floor," the killer said, followed by exaggerated laughter. "The way he tried to hold them in was too much. Here's Johnny."

"You sick fuck. Where is he?"

The quiet room was now focused on Ivy. Lieutenant York stepped from her office and walked to Ivy's desk. The look on her face told Ivy she needed to tell her what was happening. She put her hand over the speaker.

"It's the killer. He called from Johnny's phone," was all she needed to say before York was on her phone to have Carson's phone tracked.

"Tell everybody I said hey. I'm sure they'll be joining you when you arrive, but I won't have time to speak to all of them, and the ones I do talk to won't be speaking again."

Ivy stood from her desk, and the group of detectives followed her to the Homicide Unit door.

"So, are you going to tell me where you are or are you going to make us track the phone and find you?"

The killer laughed again.

"I don't guess it really matters at this point. You'll figure it out quickly, either way. Let's just say that I told you he had to die, so I'm making good on my promise."

He had to die? That didn't make sense. The killer had never threatened to kill Carson; even if he had, it wouldn't help her figure out where he was hiding.

"You there, detective? I find it hard to believe that you didn't instantly know who I was talking about. He's the only person threatening me enough that it got under my skin. I could only put up with the mocking for so long. I think I did well to hold off as long as I did."

Leonard. He was at Jonathan Leonard's office. But why would he take Carson there?

"I can hear the gears grinding, and you're probably wondering how Johnny boy got here. Imagine my surprise when I found him here in the midst of one of their super-secret meetings. Scared the shit out of them when the devil they spoke of appeared. You think they would have been prepared, but alas, just another group of posers. Johnny cried the most."

Ivy was in the parking lot before the killer finished. If she could keep him talking, they might be able to get there before he left. Lieutenant York ran up to her car.

"I have the Rapid Response Team on the line. Where do they need to go?"

Ivy hesitated. Those amped-up, gun-loving fools begging for revenge were the last people they needed at the scene. York impatiently waited for her to answer. She couldn't lie.

"Jonathan Leonard's office on Wynnton Road."

York's eyes grew so big that Ivy thought they were about to pop out of her head, and she ran off without saying anything else. York never seemed like the Leonard fan type, but she knew there were a lot of people who were, so the building might have had a lot of possible victims inside. The thought of all the other people he could have hurt propelled Ivy into action again, and she jumped in her car.

"Hello, are you there, detective? You haven't forgotten about me, have you?"

"No, I'm here. How many people have you hurt?"

"Huh, you know what? That's a good question. It seems to have slipped my mind. But if you're just trying to keep me talking, I promise I don't have any intention of leaving until everybody gets here. I do need to go, though. I have some cleaning up to do before

I'm ready for company. Don't worry, detective, I'll make sure we have plenty of time to talk later."

"Wait. What—shit," Ivy yelled and threw her phone into the passenger's seat.

He said he'd be waiting for her, but she didn't want to keep him waiting too long. She floored the accelerator and followed the blue light parade downtown.

Chapter Thirty-Three

The white building looked garish, lit up with the Rapid Response Team flood lights. They kicked on, illuminating the front and side of the building as Ivy stepped from her car. The loud clunk they made startled her, and she instinctively took a step back. It looked like every cop in the city had responded to the call and now stood outside the building with itchy trigger fingers, awaiting their chance to rush the building.

Ivy joined Lieutenant York at her car. She was busy yelling orders into her phone while a helicopter hovered overhead, a massive spotlight sweeping across the front parking lot. A loud explosion erupted, and the front door caved in. The Rapid Response Team filed in two at a time and broke off in different directions. Ivy had to hold herself back. She wanted to be one of the first through the door. She needed to find Carson and make sure he was okay. The killer had said he'd killed him, but she hoped he was lying to distract her from doing her job.

York turned the volume on her radio all the way up and set it on the roof of her car. Other detectives surrounded the vehicle so they could hear everything going on in the building. So far, they hadn't found anything. Disjointed, adrenaline fueled shouts of "clear" broke through the static. They weren't going to find him. He'd already be long gone. He was an arrogant asshole, but even he wouldn't be so full of himself that he'd hang around when he was the most wanted man in the city. Ivy's heart dropped when the voices became fewer.

They were almost finished sweeping the building. Then the real work would begin. Everybody wanted a piece of the killer, especially the RRT. It would be hard enough to keep all the detectives from stepping all over each other, but they didn't need everybody else in there trying to help when they would only end up causing more issues.

Ivy realized she was worried about all this, and nothing had happened yet. She always did that. Most of the time, it didn't happen the way she thought, and she'd be all worked up for nothing. She hoped this was another one of those moments. For all she knew, the killer had never been here at all. A calm, forcefully restrained voice came over the radio and broke Ivy's wandering thoughts.

"Lieutenant, you need to get in here and see this. It's ... it's bad. I don't know—"

York looked up at Ivy. Her face was as pale as she'd ever seen. She nodded quickly and walked toward the building. Without turning, she called out to Ivy.

"You coming? This is still your case, for now."

Ivy tripped over her feet to catch up with York. This was all new to her. She'd assumed York had wanted to be the first one on the scene before she opened it up to everybody else. It never crossed Ivy's mind that York would want her to join her.

"I need you to hold yourself together. No matter what we're about to walk into. I'm sure it's not good with how Campbell sounded on the radio."

"I'll be good. I'm good," Ivy said, trying to reassure herself as much as York.

"You have to be better than good. All these men in here will be watching to see how you handle it. I'm sure you know that already from the other scenes you've worked, but this will be different. This is too big. It doesn't matter that we're on the same side. They'll eat their own," York said in a hushed whisper as they approached the destroyed front door.

Ivy didn't respond, but she didn't need to. The front door had been demolished by an explosive charge. Ivy ducked through the jagged metal edges and high stepped over the charred kick plate. It felt like she was stepping into the mouth of a giant mechanical shark, waiting to swallow her whole. As soon as she stood up straight, the first thing that hit her was the smell. The vomit inducing mixture of blood, shit, and sulfur permeated the air. She felt her lunch coming back up but forced it down again. York turned around and didn't look any better than Ivy felt.

"There's nobody alive in here. I don't know how long they've been like this, but it's been a few hours. The guy who did this is long gone by now," Campbell said, leaning over the arm rail from the second story. "They're all up here in the office."

"They? How many do you have up there?"

"Marv counted eight before he ran out. He's in the toilet puking his guts out. Rookie."

York looked to Ivy as to say, see, I told you. A switch was flipped, and everybody covered their eyes from the blinding light.

"Guess they decided there was no reason to keep the power cut," Campbell said.

Nobody paid attention to Campbell because they were all staring at the wall. All over the stark white paint, hundreds of large Ns had been painted on the walls. At first, Ivy thought it was paint, but the closer she got to the secretary's desk, she realized it was blood. An N covered the computer screen, and blood ran down onto the keyboard and puddled on the warped wood desk top. Ivy noticed that the E, R, O, A, D, L, and N keys were missing from the keyboard.

"Ah, shit. What the fuck?"

Ivy heard York yell from upstairs. When had she gone up there? Ivy had thought York was still in the lobby with her. She turned and ran up the stairs. The stench assaulted her as soon as she stepped onto the landing. She stopped for a second to gather herself and make sure it wouldn't overwhelm her. York stood by the door to Leonard's office with her hand to her mouth, crying. She was done holding it in for the sake of everybody around her. Ivy walked slowly across the landing and gasped when she stepped into the office. Carson's body was on full display.

The killer had propped him against the wall like he was standing guard over the presiding meeting. A knife through his palm held his right arm outstretched, pointing to the ongoing conference. A koozie with red liquid was pinned to the left hand. His face was severely bruised, and his jaw had been broken. Ivy jumped back when she realized she had almost stepped in Carson's intestines that had fallen from his hacked open stomach. The machete lay on the floor beside his foot.

A tear ran down Ivy's face. They hadn't been friends and had barely been decent partners to each other, but she still felt a loss. It always felt strange finding out that somebody she used to know or know of was no longer living, like an emptiness she didn't realize would be left. They hadn't always liked each other, but they were both on the same side, even though it looked like Carson had been moonlighting on another team. That would explain how Leonard seemed to know as much as he did. She'd always suspected he had some cops working with him. Maybe a fresh cop on the street who didn't feel like he was getting as much action as he wanted, but never a detective.

Ivy stepped into the office, and the first person she noticed was the secretary, Bernice. Her throat had been cut. She sat propped against the wall beside the door with a notepad in her lap, taking notes. Ivy leaned over and read the note aloud for everybody.

"In the end, we will win this game and no longer mourn those lost or the loser. The Kool-Aid has been passed out."

"What kind of sick fuck kills a little old lady?" Campbell asked from the hallway. Neither York nor Ivy answered. There wasn't a correct answer. Even if they knew, they'd never understand. The only person that could make sense of this was the deranged person committing the crimes, and then it'd only make sense to them.

"This is officer North. I guess he was helping Leonard with Johnny," York said, pointing at a slouched body sitting in a chair.

North? Where had she heard that name before? They hadn't gone through the academy together. The name would eventually come to her. She tiptoed around red pools on the carpet and worked her way around to the front of the row of chairs. Alex North. She remembered the name as soon as she saw his face. He was the cop that kept checking her out in Meadow Butler's house. Now, he sat as a captive audience of four men and one woman. All had ligature marks around their necks. Everyone in the room wore the slashed-out N logo t-shirts. Alex and one of the other men also wore matching hats. Discarded cups lay at their feet.

How had he managed to kill this many people without anybody knowing about it? Bernice had a slit throat, so he more than likely killed her first when he walked through the door. He took a significant risk. The only way to get away with this was to kill them all in separate locations and bring them here or poison them somehow.

Ivy had been holding off on looking at Leonard. Not that she felt it would upset her. It was more of a waste than anything. He probably could have done some good for the community, but he went about it in the wrong way. She'd warned him, and now she wished he would have listened to her.

A red substance covered the entire surface of his cherry wood desk. She wasn't sure if it was blood, Kool-Aid, or a sick mixture of both. The bookshelves behind the desk had been emptied of most of the books. At first, they seemed like they'd been randomly removed, but the more she looked at it, the more it looked like he'd removed them methodically, creating Ns on either side.

Leonard's body looked the worst. He had been beaten and tortured. It would take an extensive autopsy to find out everything that had been done to that poor man. The only reason she recognized him was his prominence behind the desk and the fedora he had the last time she'd seen him lay in his lap. But it didn't matter what he'd done. He didn't deserve this. His head was taped to the back of his chair with bumper stickers. His entire face was swollen, but it looked like the killer had removed the enlarged skin from around his eyes with a dull knife, so he could see everything that was going on. A gun lay on the floor. It took Ivy a few moments to see the bullet hole through his head. She hoped it was a mercy shot but had a feeling it was done post-mortem as an artistic choice. A bright white notepad that had managed to stay clean through all the carnage, or did he keep it in a bag until he was ready to stage the scene, lay in the middle of the desk.

"They call me a cult of personality, but even my own mother would scream what personality?"

"What the hell does any of this mean?" Campbell asked from the doorway.

"All of his planned kills are suicide tableaus left for us to find."

Campbell blew air through his teeth.

"That's sick. What is this supposed to be? A mass suicide?"

"Yeah. I'd guess Jim Jones. The killer hated Leonard, but not because he wanted to catch him. Everybody wanted him caught. He hated him because of what he stood for and how he manipulated the people around him. He'd be a dangerous politician."

"Careful there, Chandler. Sounds like you might be sympathizing with the guy."

"Hey, fuck you, Campbell. That's my partner staked to the wall over there. I don't need any of your shit. You asked a question, and I answered it. Next time I'll treat you like all the other detectives who can't stand your ass treat you."

Campbell held up his hands in a gesture of supplication and walked away with a smirk on his face. Ivy walked back to the desk when a crash followed by gunfire erupted downstairs.

"He's still here. He went out front. Did anybody see him?" A voice yelled from the lobby.

Ivy and York held each other's stare for a moment, then ran out the door.

Chapter Thirty-Four

Every cop who had been in the lobby had cleared out by the time Ivy and York reached the bottom of the stairs. They both drew their guns and crossed the sticky linoleum floor to the front door.

"I'm going to go out and to the left. You go to the right, and we'll meet up in the parking lot beside the cars. They've probably chased him down the street by now. Hopefully, they'll get him cornered somewhere."

Ivy nodded and blew a stray strand of hair out of her face. York ducked back out the door and took off to the left of the building. Ivy stuck one foot out when movement caught her attention in the back of the building.

"Hey, I think somebody's back here," she yelled out the door and stepped back in.

Dim light fought its way through the tinted glass back door. A shadow moved again, and light flooded into the small hallway as the person ran outside. Ivy was conflicted. She knew she should go to the front and get help, but she didn't want whoever ran out the door to escape. Whoever had seen him said he went out the front door. Nobody would want to follow her to the back and risk missing their chance to catch the killer. She didn't have a radio, so she fished her cell phone out of her jacket pocket and searched for York's number as she moved down the hallway.

York's phone went to voicemail two times before she gave up and stepped outside. The back parking lot was much smaller than the front. There was enough room for three cars and the trash dumpster. She cut across the pavement, and something clanged against the dumpster.

"This is the Crystal Valley Police Department. Come out with your hands up."

No response or movement came from the dumpster. Ivy clicked on a flashlight and walked toward the dumpster.

"Come out from behind there. I know you're there."

She continued slowly and jumped around the side of the dumpster with her gun held out in front of her.

There was nobody there.

"Damn it, Ivy. Don't freak yourself out."

Ivy walked to the edge of the parking lot and stared at the line of trees behind the building. He could be out there right now, watching her, and she wouldn't know. A dry susurrus of wind weaved its way through the copse of trees separating the building from the neighborhood behind it.

A branch bent down, and through the light, Ivy saw a figure entering the tree line.

"He's over here," Ivy yelled, but she doubted anybody could hear her. She tried her phone again, but it wouldn't work. She pulled the phone from her ear, saying no service on her screen.

She ran to the edge of the trees and turned around, hoping she could see anybody to call out to before she ducked into the darkness. She didn't want to go into the woods alone. All her training told her no, but this could be the last chance they had at catching the killer, and she didn't have time to wait. Whoever it was that entered the woods before her hadn't gotten far. She could still make them out in the dim light. She stomped her foot and pushed under a low-hanging branch.

They lumbered along at a steady pace, leading her further away from the building and the safety of the group. Every instinct she had screamed at her to turn and go the other way, but she couldn't let him get away again. He had caused too much pain for this city and would continue if she didn't try to stop him. And he looked like he might be injured by the way he moved. She pointed the gun at her target and ran to catch up with him. She didn't care how loud she was being. Hopefully, somebody else would hear them and come help.

The shape moved behind a tree. Ivy swung out wide from the trunk, so he couldn't leap out at her, but when she made the turn, he wasn't there. The hairs on the back of her neck stood on end as she swept the area, only seeing empty woods. She lowered her gun, disgusted with herself. How could she have lost him when he was right in front of her?

Ivy stomped through the underbrush toward the tree. She glanced back the way she'd come, but no backup had followed her into the forest. Pine needles fell from above and landed in her hair. She looked up, hoping he hadn't somehow climbed the tree.

Nothing but empty branches hung above her. A branch snapped behind her, and she turned to see trees. Another branch broke to her left, and she followed the sound to another dead end. Soon, the forest was alive with noise surrounding her. She didn't know what direction to look and spun in a circle. Fear had already gripped her but was now taking control, and her body locked up. She couldn't move. Her hand began shaking uncontrollably, and she closed her eyes. A dizzy spell overcame her, and she ran forward to keep from falling on her face.

When she stopped and opened her eyes, Ivy stood fifteen feet from the suspect. Her arm twitched, and she raised her gun and yelled.

"Freeze. Crystal Valley Police. Don't move, or I'll shoot."

The shape stopped in its tracks but didn't turn around. He moved awkwardly, like he was having trouble walking. Maybe one of the other cops had shot him before he disappeared. It was weird that he hadn't said anything yet. There usually was no way to shut the guy up, but now she had him at gunpoint, and he didn't have anything to say. It was eerily quiet. Ivy didn't like this at all. She wouldn't be able to get him to walk out of the woods in front of her. There's no way he would do that. He'd want to be close to her. She would have to cuff him.

"Lace your fingers behind your head and get on your knees."

He didn't move.

"Come on. As much as I like to shoot you right now, it would be a lot easier if you'd just do what I tell you to do. Now, hands behind your head and get on the ground."

This time he moved, but it was subtle. Almost imperceptible, like he was trying to get an angle on her so he could see her. She held her gun higher so he could see it.

"Get on the fucking ground right now or—"

He turned on her faster than she had anticipated. The gun in his hand went off. Flame burst from the barrel. She hadn't even noticed she was holding her breath until she realized she hadn't been shot. He moved again, and she pulled the trigger three times.

All three bullets hit their target, and he fell to the ground behind a tree. Ivy expelled a yelp and ran to the man lying still on the ground.

She kicked the gun away from his hand. Blood poured from under the ski mask where one of the bullets had hit his throat. Ivy reached down and slowly removed his mask. The man coughed, and blood flew from his mouth. She didn't recognize the face and looked down at his chest. Something was wrong. He was wearing Kevlar.

Ivy's hand went to her mouth, and she stood up quickly. Her head swam with the sudden movement and implications, and she stumbled back and fell against the tree.

The first blow to the back of the head knocked her to the ground.

"So nice of you to join me, detective. I've been waiting for this moment," she heard the killer say before taking another sharp blow to the head.

Everything went black.

Chapter Thirty-Five

Did the light above her head flicker, or was she fading in and out of consciousness? Ivy's head lolled around from her chest to rest against the back of a wooden chair. She tried to move but couldn't. Where was she? The last thing she remembered was chasing the killer through the woods and shooting ... shooting another cop. She suddenly felt sick and tried to turn her head to vomit. It wasn't the lights. It was her head. Nothing came up, no matter how hard she tried to puke. Where was she, and why couldn't she move? She tried to move her arms and legs and looked down to see them tied to a chair. Fear rushed through her body, and a sudden clarity hit her. She was sitting in a dark cinderblock room with a washer and dryer against the far wall. A small rectangle window just above the detergent shelf let in minimal natural light. So it was daytime now. A dark masked shape manifested from the shadows to her left from behind a cord full of drying clothes.

"Oh good, you're awake. I was beginning to worry about you. That second hit was pretty hard. Thought I might have scrambled your brains with that one. Sorry about that."

She fought to recognize the voice, but fear turned to panic when she realized whose voice it was and who now had her tied up in a basement she'd never seen before. She tried to speak, but her mouth was dry. Her tongue was fat and stuck to her mouth.

"Maybe I did scramble something up there, huh? Let's try some water before we go jumping to any conclusions."

She tried to fight him off, but he was too strong. He held her head still in a firm headlock and poured water on her dry and cracked lips until she finally parted them and drank. She kept telling herself it wasn't poisoned as she drank deeply. Why would he go through all of this just to poison her water when she woke up?

"Slow down before you get sick."

She pulled her head away from the cup, and water poured down her blouse.

"Where am I?"

Her voice was dry and raspy like her tonsils had been removed with sandpaper.

"You're at the end. You had your chance, and you blew it. You lost the game."

"This isn't a game," she croaked out and sat up straight in defiance that she could scarcely pull off.

This couldn't be the end. If he thought it was the end of the game, there was no reason for him to keep her alive. A defiant tear ran down her flooded eyes.

"There, there. That's no reason to cry. You can't win them all."

She sniffed and looked him in the eye.

"So ... so what are you going to do with me?" she asked, not wanting to know the answer. She tried to close her legs, but each chair leg held them apart. She felt vulnerable and pulled against the knots in the rope.

"I don't think you're going to get out of those, but be my guest and try. All you're going to do is hurt yourself."

"It can't be any worse than what you're going to do to me," she said through gritted teeth.

Another laugh. She could go the rest of her life and never hear him laugh again. Maniacal with no feeling like he was laughing because that's when he thought he should laugh. That's how all the TV villains laughed.

"I'm not completely sure what I'm going to do to you. You've been a good friend. I'd really hate to kill you."

"You won't get away with this. They'll find you."

"See, that's what I like about you. So defiant, even in an unwinnable situation. I hate to say it, but the game was stacked against you from the beginning. But you cops are all the same, aren't you? I really thought you might be different."

"I don't know what you mean."

"You're all so damn predictable. You always do the same thing. Is that all they train you to do at the academy? Keep going and firing until the target is neutralized. What if the target is smarter than you and goes off script?"

He walked behind her and started to massage her shoulders. His touch revolted her, and she tried to shrug him off, but he squeezed harder until she quit fighting him.

"I guess that's supposed to be learned from experience in the field. Doesn't really do any good in a town where nothing like me happens. Though, I'd like to think there wouldn't be any place prepared for me. Anyway, I didn't expect you to kill that officer. He had his vest on. Who knew you would go for the throat? That was off script. No center mass for you. Unless you're just that bad a shot."

Ivy hung her head low. He took it as a sign to move lower on her shoulders, but she was too exhausted to keep fighting.

"I don't understand."

"Understand what?"

"Any of this. How can you kill people the way you do? What about the people they loved and the people who loved them? Don't you have anybody you love?"

"Everybody I love is dead."

"What about Morgan?"

He froze and backed off, letting his hands leave her shoulders. She'd stung him with that one. There was a connection there that she'd never understand. Morgan probably wouldn't ever understand it either or want it.

"Morgan and I have a complicated relationship. But I can love anybody if I want to. Love is a construct we've created mostly because we don't want to be alone. We can love anybody. The true test and proof are with the ones we mourn once they're gone. How many people have you loved in your life, but you would never mourn their death? Sure, you'd feel bad about their passing, but you wouldn't truly mourn them. True love, true glory is in the mourning."

She tried to push his words out of her head. The last thing she needed was to have him in her mind. He put his hands back on her shoulders, and she recoiled at his touch. There was a small laugh, lost in the shadows behind her.

"I could fall in love with you if I wanted to. You're certainly attractive enough. Have a great personality. I don't particularly care for your profession, but love is give and take, am I right?"

"I wouldn't want your love," she said, trying to pull away from his touch.

"You don't know that. I bet if we met, and you didn't know who I was or what I'd done, you could fall in love with me if you wanted to. You'd have to open yourself to the idea and want to love somebody first."

He walked back around in front of her and stared until she felt gross and uncomfortable. He looked at his watch and pulled a knife from a sheath he had on the back of his belt. Ivy pushed back into the chair as far as she could.

"We don't have too much time left. I sent a text from your phone telling Don Murphy our exact location, so I'm sure the calvary will be here soon enough."

"No. You can't do that. You've taken too much from that man. You can't let him find me," Ivy screamed.

She no longer tried to hold back the tears. They streamed freely down her face. The killer walked up to her and put the blade in her face.

"How about we make a deal?"

"No. Go to hell."

She fought against the ropes that held her, but they didn't budge, only cut deeper into her exposed skin.

"You don't negotiate with terrorists? How about I'll promise to take mercy on your friend, Don? How does that sound?"

Ivy continued to fight. He waved the blade in front of her face, traced it down her arm, and rested it on her thigh. Her eyes lit up, and a new wave of fear and anger overcame her. She rocked back in the chair, and it flipped over. She barely held her head up before it crashed against the concrete floor.

"Jeez. What the hell's gotten into you? Calm down so I can sit you back up."

"Fuck you."

She rocked back and forth on the floor, and he started laughing.

"You look like a turtle on its back. Hold on."

He flipped her chair upright faster than she had anticipated. Her head swam, and she had to get her bearing again. Black and green globules flowed through her vision. She felt sick again.

"Now, I really need to hurry. Let's make a deal. I promise I'll leave you and all your friends alone when they get here, but you have to promise that you will not try to catch me. Ever."

She couldn't agree with those terms. There was no way she could just stop doing her job. If she didn't do it, somebody else would take the case. And what if she agreed but worked the case anyway? He'd kill her as soon as he found out. He'd kill her if he even thought she was still working the case.

"Fuck you."

"Is that going to be your only response? Promise me you won't actively try to find me after I walk out of here today, and I'll let everybody that shows up live. If you don't, I'm going to kill you, wait for them to find your corpse, and kill them all."

She made eye contact and stared into his cold pupils.

"I know what you're thinking. We really could be a power couple. My detective skills are pretty good, too. But if you agree and then break your promise, I will kill Don, the rest of Greg Burns' family, and every cop I see between them and you. Then I'll kill you. How does that sound?"

Sirens came through an open window she hadn't noticed. They were still a way off.

"There they are. You better decide before I decide for you, and I don't think you'll like that decision."

She didn't know what to do. Everything inside of her screamed to say no and hoped they were able to take him out first. Her words would be empty either way, but it would still hurt to say them.

"Well, I guess—"

"Okay," she said, cutting him off.

"Okay, what?"

"Okay. I agree. If you let us live, I won't chase after you."

"Promise?"

"I promise."

"Cross your heart," he said and drew an X over his heart.

"Cross my heart, and I hope you die."

"Guess I'll have to take your word for it, but we have to seal it in blood. It'll also leave you with a little reminder of our pact," he said.

He quickly grabbed her thigh. The sudden movement caught her off guard, and she screamed. She tried to flip back over to waste more time, but he held her fast. With more dexterity than she anticipated, he pinched the pant's fabric and sliced them with the knife. He slid the blade down to her knee. Using both hands, he ripped the fabric from knee to hip.

"Here's a little something to remember me by," he said, sticking the blade into her skin high on her inner thigh.

White pain flared through her body, and she fought to stay awake. He slid the knife down her thigh, peeling the soft skin back as he carved a deep N, marking his territory.

She'd never felt pain so intense in her life. Stars and green blobs floated through her vision. A hand slapped her hard across the face.

"Stay with me, Ivy. You can't pass out before they get here. You might bleed out."

He pulled a shirt from the drying laundry and stuck it in her left hand. The cord fell to the ground when he cut it from her wrist. It tingled as the blood flowed back into her fingers. He pulled her hand and pushed it onto her thigh. Another lightning bolt of pain shot through her body.

"Keep pressure on it, and you'll be fine. It looks like it's time for me to go. I had fun, but I really hope you keep our deal. I'd hate to be forced to kill you. I did have one last question, though. Did you really believe you could save Michelle from me?" He asked her and was gone.

The basement door slammed behind him before his words registered in her fatigued and overloaded brain. This had to be Michelle's house. He'd brought her back to the one place they'd been able to stop him.

Squad cars flew up the driveway and parked beside the opened window. Ivy tried to yell to them, but her throat was raw, and more blood gushed from her thigh from the exertion.

Heavy boots thudded across the floor above her head. They made a circle and ran to the back of the house before turning around. Ivy looked above her head and followed the movement. It was only one person. Was he still in the house? Hopefully, they would have him cornered.

A squeaky door opened and slammed, followed by a loud burst that Ivy thought was a door breach round. Broken, twisted metal fell to the floor as they kicked the door in. She yelled to the ceiling.

"He's in the back of the house. Hurry and get him," she screamed as loud as she could, feeling her vocal cords fray.

Boots thumped through the front rooms. She traced all their movements and thought she heard them yelling clear. They were getting closer to the kitchen and the basement door.

Ivy let out a loud sigh. She gave up. The killer got away again, and he wouldn't stop killing. She felt sorry for herself and everybody in the city she'd let down when she heard everybody upstairs yelling.

"Police. Get down. Don't move."

She heard Don Murphy's voice clearly above them all until something happened, and they all started screaming like a raging cacophony of adrenaline and testosterone.

She heard one cop yell, "Stop resisting!" before one gunshot rang out, followed by a barrage of bullets as everybody in the house emptied their clips into the suspect.

Chapter Thirty-Six

It felt like an eternity before her ears stopped ringing, and she could hear heavy boots plodding down the basement stairs. Tears flooded her eyes when Don Murphy's face came through the dark stairwell. She couldn't hold back any of her emotions, and she broke down as he cut the ropes from her right hand and ankles.

"We got him, Ivy. We got the son of a bitch. It's finally over," was the first thing he said.

She fell against his chest. He put his arms around her and wept. She put one arm around him and continued to apply pressure to her thigh. The big man shuttered in her arms as she held him tight. She cried harder when she thought about what he'd been through and what it meant to him to be over finally. He could finally mourn properly for Mary and Greg. They stood like that until the paramedics found their way downstairs and asked her to sit down so they could care for her wound.

She started to sit in the seat she'd just been freed from but changed her mind and sat on a bench against the back wall even though she had to walk a little further and cause it to bleed more.

Don helped her up the stairs after the paramedics had finished. They took the stairs one at a time. When they'd finally made it to the top, they were greeted by Lieutenant York and all the other police officers who were on duty in the city.

Ivy saw Mark Harper standing beside the couch and hobbled over. She ignored him and his stares as she looked down at the body of Michelle Parker. The Suicide Killer took one last life before they could stop him for good.

The stench of death filled the house. It was a scent Ivy had been around too much lately. She'd promised the paramedic that she'd ride in the ambulance to the hospital to be checked out for a severe concussion and to have her leg looked at. She didn't want to go, but Don said he'd follow behind and give her a ride home, so she couldn't back out now.

She put her weight on anything she could grab as she worked her way to the back family room. Surrounded by a large group of police, lying in a pool of blood, was The Suicide Killer. They'd already ripped his mask from his head and stood talking amongst themselves. A few said he looked familiar, but they didn't know where from. They were all full of shit. There would be a lot of stories going through the police department for a while, but most of them would be fish stories.

The officers parted to let her through. The subject instantly changed from the killer to whispers about her. She stood at the edge of blood. She didn't recognize him. There wasn't enough of his face left to make any kind of guess at who he'd been. She looked down at the man who had caused so much pain and grief for an entire city and the loved ones left behind to mourn. Healing doesn't begin where mourning ends. Mourning never really ends; it only evolves. Though she doubted anybody would mourn The Suicide Killer.

Chapter Thirty-Seven

The shovel pierced the compacted ground. Rain showers from earlier in the day made the topsoil easy to dig, but the dirt below would be slow moving. The Eleven O'clock News broadcast poured in through a phone speaker.

"The Suicide Killer is dead, and Crystal Valley can sleep a little sounder tonight ..."

A backhoe sat in a shed on the back of the property. It would be a lot easier to figure out how to use it instead of staying out here all night digging six feet deep.

"Seven brave men and women from local law enforcement will receive official commendations for their work on bringing the elusive serial killer to justice and saving one of their own in the process ..."

So many questions were left unanswered that nobody in the media would ask. Only one reporter left in the city would be skeptical enough to ask those questions, but she was busy trying to decide what to do with the information about her sister's killer.

"Thirty-seven-year-old Lee Thomas Westin's reign of terror ended in a hail of gunfire at a house in Wagner Estates. His body has been sent to the state crime lab for an autopsy. At this time, all that is known about the man is he was a transient from Florida who had been living in the area for the past year."

They'll all be celebrated, and the dead will be mourned. Evidence will be gathered, but it will be okay if it doesn't all quite fit. They'll want this to be closed, and in the past, as soon as possible.

They got their man. He was in the house. The lead detective in the case confirmed that the body was wearing the same clothes in the basement, including the tear in the left knee. He also has a healed cut from his wrist to his elbow. Not a scar, but it could have been hard for the eyewitness to tell when staring down the man who'd just killed his girlfriend. Case closed.

But would it be closed for her? Did she believe they got the right guy? Does she have a gut feeling that she can't explain that he's still alive every time she looks down at that cut that will no doubt leave a scar for her to remember everything she'd been through and possibly mourn who she thought she was at one time?

He'd let them have their glory. Let them revel in it, believing they'd gotten him. Some of them might even lament his being gone because they'd have to return to their normal, mundane lives. What would they do now that the existential threat to the city and their way of life was finally gone? Sure, it bothered him they gave somebody else the credit he deserved. Recognition that he'd fought so hard for. But he'd let it go for now. For as long as he could, anyway, until it scratched and prodded at the back of his throat like a nicotine craving that couldn't be satiated.

Bobby could hold out for longer than they'd think he'd be able to. They might even forget about him, but he'd be back one day, and they'll never see him coming until it's too late. In the meantime, he'd have his hands full digging Emily up. The only way he'd be rid of her for good would be to take her to another place far away.

He'd dig her up tonight and drive her somewhere else tomorrow. It'd already been a long day, and Jody would be waiting for him to get home.

Acknowledgments

This book almost didn't happen. The story wasn't there. My initial concept for The Suicide Killer was to have a sequel or two or three or whatever I ended up with, but I had no idea how I had planned to get to that point. Eventually, I decide I didn't want to do a sequel and moved on. Readers had been asking about a sequel since the initial release and I'd like to believe it's because of my writing and intriguing characters, but I'm sure it was because of the ending. And I'm okay with that, mostly. People don't like to hear that's the only way the story could end.

After Dark Water Sacrifice came out, I started a different novel, but stopped after about eight thousand words. Bobby started talking to me and he had ideas, so I switched gears and followed him, but we got lost in the pandemic and went our separate ways. Again, I moved on and started another story that is also still sitting unfinished on my hard drive.

I was at a standstill with my writing. I wouldn't call it writer's block, as I could have written something if I'd tried. It was more like writer's anxiety to live up to the first one. There's a temptation to go overboard and make everything bigger, but I resisted that feeling and just let the story tell itself. If you're still reading to this point, you'll have to let me know how I did. I'm sure I'll hear about this ending too, but it really is the only way it can end.

I'd like to thank everybody who has picked up one of my books, especially those who have stuck around and picked up a second book. This is for everybody who wanted the sequel. I hope you were prepared this time.

Thank you to Nicole Mancha-Mercado who edited Mourning Glory and was awesome to work with. Everybody in need of an editor should contact her. Just check with me so I can get my next book to her first. Any mistakes you believe you've found are my own, and wouldn't have been there if I'd listened to her.

I'd also like to thank Kealan Patrick Burke with Elderlemon Design for dealing with me and creating a fantastic cover. And for having the kind of dedication to his craft, that left The Suicide Killer's N symbol a part of his house.

Finally, I thank my family and friends who have supported me since the last two acknowledgement pages. And Tina and Greenlee, who I could dedicate every book I write and every breath I take.

About the Author

Zach Lamb is a fictionist who creates thriller, horror, and dark fiction stories. He is the author of The Suicide Killer and Dark Water Sacrifice. Zach has an MFA in creative writing from Southern New Hampshire University. He lives with his wife and kids in the nonfictional town of Ellerslie, Georgia, named after the fictional character Captain Ellerslie from the Waverly Novels.